THE COMPLETE CASES
OF THE PRINCE OF THIEVES

THE COMPLETE CASES OF THE

PRINCE OF THIEVES ™

T.T. FLYNN

ILLUSTRATIONS BY
JOHN FLEMING GOULD

POPULAR PUBLICATIONS • 2023

TABLE OF CONTENTS

THE HOUSE OF VANISHING MEN

THERE IT STOOD—GRIM MONUMENT TO GAMBLED FORTUNES LOST—A HORROR DEN OF SPINNING WHEELS. AND THERE, TO COLLECT A MURDER I O U, WENT JERRY PRINCE. FOR THAT PLACE OF DISAPPEARING DOLLARS HAD BECOME A HOUSE OF VANISHING MEN.

CHAPTER ONE
PRINCE OF THIEVES

IT WAS a nasty night. Sharp sleet pelted out of a black, opaque sky, driving before the chill northwest wind like tiny cold needles which froze where they fell. Street lights glittered softly on icy pavements and sidewalks. Driving was none too safe, except with chains. But the rear wheels of Jerry Prince's car had them.

He drew up to the curb, cut his ignition, turned off his lights and stepped out.

The sleet had started falling less than an hour before. Not one car in twenty which rolled carefully through the streets had chains as yet. The fact that Jerry Prince's car had them was proof of the care he gave to small details.

He dropped the ignition key in his overcoat pocket. It was a single key, obviating the danger of becoming confused with other keys; easy to find and slip into the ignition lock.

That, too, was another little detail which would not have occurred to most men.

The fact that he did not lock the door of the speedy black coupé was a third. The chance that it might be stolen was outweighed by the fact that he might find it necessary to dive behind the wheel and leave instantly.

For the ways Jerry Prince walked were not the ways of most people. The rules by which he lived were not the rules of everyday life.

COAT COLLAR turned up, hat pulled low over his forehead, Jerry walked back north to the next corner

into the teeth of the wind. He turned right, striding briskly. By the illuminated dial of his thin wrist watch it was ten thirty-five. There were few lights in the houses about him. Solid, substantial houses they were, the majority surrounded by sizeable plots of ground, some hedged,

"Drop it!" he barked from
the anteroom door.

some fenced, some merely having smooth lawn sweeping to the sidewalk edge. It was not a neighborhood replete with flamboyant display of wealth. Nevertheless, half an eye could see that anyone who occupied one of these homes was financially independent.

Jerry whistled softly through his teeth and paid little attention to his surroundings. He proceeded like one heading toward a definite goal. When he was less than fifty yards from the next corner a burly patrolman, swathed in a big overcoat, suddenly appeared in the zone of light ahead, and unlocked the metal door of a call box.

Jerry frowned at the sight—but the tune he was whistling did not vary a note, his brisk stride did not hesitate. As he came up the patrolman stared at him curiously. Jerry lifted a gloved hand in greeting.

"Good evening, officer. Rotten night, isn't it?"

The patrolman smiled ruefully, nodding agreement. "An' 'twill be worse, I'm thinkin'," he replied.

"I hope not," Jerry chuckled over his shoulder. He turned south again at that corner, resuming his whistling. He had a feeling that the patrolman was watching him, but didn't turn to see. He had, by all appearances, dismissed the incident from his mind.

But as he walked now, Jerry keenly scanned the houses on his side of the street, checking the lighted windows. One house near the center of the long block got all his attention from the moment he spotted it.

That house had been dark when he had driven past a few minutes before. It was still dark, save for a dim light in the front hall, and a thread of yellow below a window at the back. That would be a servant's room. Without slackening his pace, Jerry turned in at the gate and walked briskly to the big two-story brick house.

The slight crunch of sleet under his shoes was lost in the grinding crack and creak of tree limbs overhead, and the rustling patter of sleet. Jerry stopped at the edge of the porch steps, stooped for an instant to each shoe. He might have been removing overshoes—but he wasn't. When he straightened up, each of his slim oxfords bore a felt oversole, held in place by narrow straps over the toes and ankles.

His steps were noiseless as he walked to the front door now, slipped a small key into the lock carefully.

Jerry turned that key. The slight click of the lock could not have been heard five feet away in the quiet interior. The door opened, closed—and Jerry was in the front hall, immovable, listening....

The dim quiet of the interior was not disturbed by a sound. Jerry drew a small flashlight from his coat and walked noiselessly up the stairs, into the darkness of the second floor.

DEEP CARPETS covered the floor. The bedrooms upstairs were luxuriously furnished. The darting beam of the small flash picked out good paintings, fine etchings on the walls.

Working methodically back from the front of the house, Jerry's gloved hand opened the door of the fifth room— and as the light speared briefly into it, he drew a slight breath of satisfaction, moved inside, closed the door behind him.

It was a man's bedroom, large, comfortable, almost indecently luxurious. A huge tiled bath adjoined. Cupboard doors lined one of the walls, three of them set with full-length mirrors, hinged to swing out and afford a full view.

The most striking thing in the room, as the silver pencil of light roved quickly about, was the number of feminine pictures in sight. In hand-polished wood, leather and silver frames, they smiled from every side. Each picture was a different woman, every one of them young and stunning.

Jerry paused long enough to scan the lot, recognizing several of the faces. He smiled wryly, shrugged, began a swift, careful search of the room, taking care to replace each object exactly as he found it.

A small writing desk against one wall contained nothing that interested him. He searched for secret panels and drawers in it, and finding none examined the walls, looking behind the pictures hanging there. Finally he turned to the row of doors.

Behind them were stacks of built in drawers, commodious cedar-lined cupboards filled with wearing apparel of every kind. Suits, coats, overcoats, racks of shoes, an assortment of canes, golf bags and sticks were there. Hats, caps, and even a pipe-clayed solar topee, looking strangely out of place in the small compartment where it rested.

From that mammoth assortment of wearing apparel a man might dress to perfection for every occasion and climate. The neat orderliness bespoke the close attention of a trained valet.

But again Jerry Prince's interest was perfunctory. He looked along the floor, behind the suits at the cedar-paneled walls, rather than at them or in the pockets. The valet would have seen that all the pockets were empty.

As he searched, Jerry glanced at his wrist watch. Eleven forty-six now. He stepped clear to the back of one of the cedar-lined cupboards. It was brightly illuminated, for opening the door turned on an overhead light automatically. He risked the light streaming out into the bedroom, for the window curtains were tightly drawn.

That little detail saved him from complete surprise.

He was still at the back of the cupboard when he heard a muffled cough out in the hall. Jerry's deliberate movement vanished as he whipped around and sprang for the cupboard door, to snatch it shut and blank the light which streamed out into the room.

He was not quick enough. As his hand grasped the knob, the hall door opened, framing a powerfully built figure in black, carrying an automatic. Each had a light behind him. Each saw the other at the same instant. And the powerful figure in the doorway leaped into the room, gun in one hand, his other hand slapping the switch beside the door and flooding the room with light.

Jerry's own flat automatic was barely halfway out of his overcoat pocket when the other rasped: "Don't move! I'll let you have it!"

JERRY FROZE, raising his empty hands instantly. And he could have sworn that when the light came on overhead and the other saw him clearly, a spasm of surprise crossed his face. The surprise was still there as the man took a step toward him, eyeing him narrowly.

"You might," Jerry suggested steadily, "take my gun and let me put my hands down. It's an effort to keep them up this way very long."

"You carried them into the house," the other retorted. "Hold them up until I tell you to drop them."

He wore sober and correct attire which looked strangely out of place on his powerful shoulders. Jerry studied the broad flat face, the narrowed eyes under bushy black brows, the almost prognathous chin and strong, thick-lipped mouth. Here was a man much larger and heavier than himself; whose build suggested a truck driver, but whose manner, speech and attire were vastly different.

"Who are you?" Jerry inquired. The fellow wore slippers, obviously belonged in the house.

"I am Mr. Grenville's valet, Carl. Who are you? What are you doing here in Mr. Grenville's bedroom?"

"Valet?" said Jerry thoughtfully—and did not try to keep a grim smile of amusement from his lips at thought of this big fellow fussing around with shirts and socks and pressing iron.

For the hand that held the automatic on him was huge and muscular, backed with a mat of coarse black hairs. And it was steady, too. For all his dainty profession, Grenville's valet did not lack physical fortitude. Jerry's smile was read correctly—and resented.

"Valet, I said!" the big fellow snapped. "Come on—who are you? What are you doing in this house?"

Jerry shrugged. "To be quite frank, I strolled in to look around."

"A crook, eh?"

"I have been alluded to in that manner," Jerry admitted with a smile. "Would you mind taking my gun, so I can lower my arms?"

"Turn around. I'll frisk—I'll search you."

Jerry did so, still smiling slightly. The automatic was jerked from his overcoat pocket. A big hand ran over his person expertly, feeling first under his arms where shoulder holsters might be worn. He asked over his shoulder: "How did you know I was up here?"

"Who said I knew you was here?" Jerry noted those slight lapses from careful diction, becoming more frequent as they talked.

"You must have known it," he commented. "Unless you have a habit of walking around the house with a gun in your hand."

"Huh! Smart guy, aren't you? Well, I'm a little smarter, mister. I knew somebody was up here, and since Mr. Grenville hadn't come back, it had to be somebody who didn't have any business inside. All right—pull 'em down."

Jerry faced around, said curiously: "I repeat—just how did you know I was up here? You didn't see me come in."

The thick-lipped mouth of the valet broke into a grin this time. "I was in the kitchen, and happened to look at the electric-light meter," he said with relish. "The meter wheel was turning at a certain speed—and suddenly it speeded up a little. It meant another light had gone on somewhere. Lights don't switch on by themselves. I looked for the reason."

Jerry chuckled. "Pretty keen observation and deduction. Good thing most people aren't so bright. Meters should be kept down in the cellar."

A scowl creased the valet's forehead. "What are you trying to make out of this, a picnic? I suppose you know I'm going to call the police and turn you in. Say, you're a pretty smart worker at that. It'd be hard to tell you from one of Mr. Grenville's friends."

"I might be a friend," Jerry suggested with a slight smile, but his gaze was thoughtful as it went to the telephone on a small mahogany stand by the bed.

"You're too late with that story, mister. Friends ring the bell when they come to the door, and they don't prowl the house with a gun in their pocket."

"But sometimes they come with guns?" Jerry suggested.

"Huh? What do you mean by that?"

"Nothing. If you're going to call the police, hurry up. We're not getting anywhere standing here."

And that puzzled the big valet. He stared at Jerry for a moment, as if trying to read his face, then shook his head and muttered, "You're a cool one," and moved toward the telephone, lowering his automatic. An unarmed man was no menace.

JERRY PRINCE'S right arm, down at his side, flicked slightly. It would have taken a keen eye to have caught the glint of metal sliding down out of his coat sleeve into the fingers tensed for it.

One moment a wiry young man was standing there helplessly, with a queer smile on his lips. The next his hand was raised, and the light was glinting on the dull blue barrel of a very small, snubnosed automatic.

Jerry's voice lashed the quiet. "Drop it!"

The valet caught the lift of Jerry's arm and turned with a snarl, whipping up his big automatic. To his credit he showed no fear, though he must have seen the tiny weapon in time to pause. Perhaps it looked too insignificant.

Jerry dodged aside. The toylike weapon in his hand spat an instant before the valet's automatic roared. Glass crashed. The big fellow ripped out a furious oath as the automatic flew from his hand and bounced on the rug.

Ringing silence descended on the room, heavy with the biting odor of burnt powder. A wraith of plaster drifted down from the wall near the door and powered the nap of the dark rug. One of the big wall mirrors had a jagged radius of cracks around a single hole. A tiny hole had appeared in the edge of Jerry Prince's left coat sleeve.

The valet fished out a handkerchief and mopped at a crimson trickle welling over his fingers. His broad flat face was white, staring, almost ludicrous with surprise and dismay.

Jerry glanced at his coat sleeve, moved his arm experimentally. "Pretty close," he remarked coolly. "You're a neat shot, my friend." He stepped closer. The snap came back in his voice. "Who else is in the house? Quick! And make it the truth if you value your health!"

"N-no one," the big fellow stammered. "The maid and cook go home at night."

"Sure about that?"

"That's straight."

Jerry relaxed slightly. "I believe it is. Is that hand hurt bad? Let's see it."

A glance showed lacerations in the flesh. The fingers were numb and useless. But the bullet which had driven the big automatic to the floor had evidently glanced off and struck the mirror. The chief damage was shock to the hand and arm.

"You'll be all right," Jerry decided. "Now then, I haven't any more time to waste. Should have hunted you up in the first place. Where in this room does Grenville keep his private valuables?"

The valet wound the gory handkerchief tightly around his hand and glared at Jerry sullenly. "I don't know," he denied. "I don't think he keeps any valuables around. They'd be in a safe-deposit box at his bank."

"Don't lie to me!" Jerry rapped. "He's got a private cache in this bedroom. You couldn't be his valet and not know where it is."

"I don't know anything about Mr. Grenville's private affairs," the man insisted balefully. "If you think there's anything worth stealing in here, look for it. I can't stop you now."

The door had been left open when the valet rushed into the room. Now a voice said suavely in the doorway behind Jerry: "Perhaps I can be of service. Drop that gun, whoever you are."

CHAPTER TWO
THE MAN IN THE
DOORWAY

JERRY HESITATED a moment, and then tossed the little automatic on the bed, faced around with a rueful smile on his lips. "Surprises seem to be in order, tonight," he declared. "You're back a trifle earlier than usual, aren't you, Grenville?"

The man who leaned nonchalantly against the side of the doorway, in dark hat and chesterfield overcoat, was tall, fit, handsome. His face had a debonair leanness, his slender mustache was carefully trimmed, smart. In his left hand he held carelessly a pair of light tan gloves. Beneath the silk muffler that had been loosened around his neck, a wing collar and evening tie showed. He was handsome enough to be an actor.

In his right hand he gripped a nickeled revolver. Thirty-eight caliber, by the looks of it. His knuckles stood out bloodless from the tension of his grip on the gun.

Grenville's lean face had a pale, drawn look. But he was perfectly self-possessed, though puzzled. "How do you know my name?" he questioned. "I've never seen you before." And he cocked his head slightly and studied Jerry. "There is something familiar about you," he decided suddenly.

Carl, the valet, broke in harshly: "He's a crook, Mr. Grenville. I caught him going through your room here.

He had a gun, and I took it away from him. I was just going to telephone the police when he pulled that little gun and shot the automatic out of my hand. He must have had it up his sleeve. I frisked him, but didn't look there. Damn him! I don't know whether he's broken my hand or not." Carl waved the big, blood-stained paw in the air and glared at Jerry.

Grenville showed even white teeth in an amused smile. "That's one on you, Carl. Sorry about the hand—but look in their sleeves next time. He's evidently clever, to have one in reserve like that. Better search him again. I don't care to be messed up like you are. Next time he might not shoot at a hand."

"You bet I'll go over him right this time!" Carl promised through his teeth.

Jerry shook his head. "You won't find anything. I'm not a walking arsenal."

But Carl searched him with his good hand just the same, roughly, thoroughly, completely.

And while he was doing that, Grenville studied Jerry, with a half frown, as if trying to probe his memory. "Blast it, I've seen you before, somewhere," he said finally. "I don't go wrong on faces that way. Where was it? Who are you? And what brings you in my house this way? I believe I heard you trying to force Carl to produce my valuables."

"You did," Jerry agreed. "That makes it plain, doesn't it? Burglar caught in act. And I'm sorry to disappoint you. We haven't met before."

"I didn't say we'd met," Grenville corrected. "But I've seen you somewhere. I'll get it presently. You don't look like a common burglar."

"I'm not a common one. Perish the thought."

While he was carrying on that polite interchange Jerry's mind was working fast. He was not as cheerful inside as he appeared. He was caught—cold, a thing which had not happened in a long time. For this was not the first house Jerry Prince had entered, not the first time he had put himself outside the pale of the law.

On the evidence Grenville and his man could give a court, there was no doubt what the verdict would be. Guilty! Prison! So Jerry thought fast behind his veneer of careless humor. And he watched Grenville and the valet warily, without seeming to do so.

The window was closed and locked. No chance of getting out that way. The only other exit was into the hall and downstairs. Both Grenville and his valet were armed. And Grenville was not the sort to give credence to a glib story. Jerry didn't even think of begging. The truth would only make matters worse. The role of ordinary burglar was the best he could do.

"Dammit—you might belong to one of my clubs," Grenville commented.

"I might," Jerry smiled. "What are they?"

"Want me to call the cops, Mr. Grenville?" Carl suggested, moving toward the telephone.

IT LOOKED like the end. And it was characteristic of Jerry Prince that he did not waste time in futile regret. "Tell them to send a comfortable car," he requested.

"No!" said Grenville sharply. "Don't call the police!"

Jerry glanced at him in surprise.

The valet stopped short by the telephone. His nostrils flared as he dragged a heavy breath. "You aren't going to let this fellow go, Mr. Grenville, after what he did? Why, he might have killed me. Or you too, if you had been in here."

"I think not," said Grenville. "Not if you hadn't tried to shoot him first. He doesn't look like a killer to me—or a very desperate character. I'm sure there's an explanation, even if he does have felt deadeners on his shoes."

Carl looked baffled. "But that's foolish, Mr. Grenville," he protested. "Let the cops handle him. They'll get at the truth mighty quick. He broke into the house, didn't he? He tried to rob you, didn't he?"

"That will do, Carl." Grenville's voice was crisp. He jerked his head to the hall. "Go downstairs and do what you can for that hand. If it needs a doctor, I'll talk to you about it later. I'll settle with this chap. Oh, yes, leave your gun up here."

Carl drew a deep breath and his face turned red. He started to speak, thought better of it. With irritated reluctance he threw his gun on the bed and left the room, Jerry's bigger automatic still in his pocket.

Grenville stood in the doorway until his man was downstairs. Then he stepped into the room, closing the door behind him. He walked over to the bed in silence and picked up the two weapons, slipping them into his overcoat pocket. His face was still pale and haggard, but there was a grim smile under his mustache as he sat down on the edge of the bed and regarded Jerry.

"I'll speak plainly, my friend," he said coolly. "You're in a bad spot. Even if it's a first offence, you'll get years in prison for this. Am I not right?"

"You are," Jerry conceded. "Unless a bit of luck shows up."

"Luck won't do you any good before a jury—with the evidence against you."

Jerry waited silently. Grenville seemed to have something on his mind, behind his apparently pointless words. "You're not a common thief, as I said before. A bit down on your luck, I suppose?"

"I certainly am now," Jerry admitted.

He was wondering if he could get to Grenville before the fellow could use his gun. He decided there was little chance of it. Grenville was alert, watchful. And a quick thinker.

Grenville's next words drove the thought out of his mind. "I'm going to give you a chance to go free," Grenville told him calmly, and watched closely for the reaction.

"Why?" asked Jerry slowly.

Grenville laughed. "I see you are suspicious. Quite right. I have an ax to grind, too. You do me a favor, and I'll do you the same. Fair enough?"

"Seems so. What can I do for you?"

"I was gambling tonight," Grenville told him—and stopped short. "I've got it!" he snapped. "I remember where I've seen you! At Fiaschetti's South Bay place. You were across the roulette table from me four—no, five nights ago. You were playing red straight through."

"Correct—and a very good memory. Perhaps I'm respectable after all."

Grenville frowned, shrugged. "It doesn't matter. You broke in here. I can get a line on you there, or rather the police can, if you double-cross me. Here's my proposition. I was in a poker game tonight with some acquaintances. I lost more than I could afford to. There was no limit and the play was heavy. I gave my I O U for twenty-eight thousand dollars before I walked out. I can't take it up—and I don't intend to if I can find a way out. You seem to be the answer.

"My I O U was put in a billfold, and will be there until morning. If you got into this house so easily, you can get into that chap's house as well. Go there, get his billfold with my I O U, return it to me, and we'll forget what you've done here. You can keep any cash you find. And I'll add a thousand dollars on top of it."

Grenville made the proposition unblushingly.

SLEET PATTED thinly against the window panes while Jerry digested the offer. Grenville lounged easily on the bed edge, revolver ready across his knee, other hand nervously slapping the yellow gloves against his legs. *Slap—slap—slap—slap...* Grenville's face was expressionless as he watched, waited....

"I know a crook when I hear one," said Jerry. "Greetings, brother." His voice had a bite to it.

Grenville did not take offense. "Make up your mind," he ordered. The soft rhythm of his slapping gloves did not miss a beat.

"Suppose I do it—and get caught?"

Grenville shrugged carelessly. "That's up to you. I'd suggest you don't get caught. Even if you have to use a gun."

"I haven't any gun."

"I'll give you this revolver and two bullets."

"You make me feel honest."

"You can't get involved any worse than you are now," Grenville said without emotion. "If you're caught, I'll say nothing about your being here."

"Your valet?"

"Carl won't talk." The gloves stopped slapping. Grenville's lips pressed tightly together. His face grew cold, dispassionate. Something queer there to make that change. Jerry wondered about the combination. Carl was no gentleman's gentleman; valeting was not his profession. How explain a potential bruiser like him serving a chap like Grenville?

"What makes you think I would return?" Jerry questioned.

Grenville showed amusement. "Do I look like a fool? I wouldn't let you go, unless I were certain you'd be back. You'll leave your fingerprints around the room. It may be a bit obvious—but the police won't look too closely into it if they're called. They'll be glad enough to nab the one who broke in here."

He was right, Jerry thought wryly. The alternative was to commit another crime for this welsher—this crooked welsher.

But Grenville did not seem disturbed by the idea. His face hardened as if he read Jerry's thoughts. "It might be necessary to have an accident here," he bit out. "Resistance on your part… the necessity to shoot on mine. Regrettable—but justified by the circumstances. Carl's testimony would clear me."

And Grenville showed his hand there. He was hard as nails, despite his debonair respectability.

Jerry nodded shortly. "Right. I'll do it. Where is this house? How much do you know about the chap's habits?"

"First," said Grenville as he got lightly to his feet, and pocketed his gloves, "we'll take care of your fingerprints. Move over there by the wall and keep your back to me for a moment. We'll have no more tricks."

Jerry did that without expression.

Grenville opened a drawer in a big hardwood dresser against the wall. After a moment he said: "All right. Smear this over your fingers."

He had removed the cap from a tube of cold cream, crushed out several inches of the cream, as a man might do who pressed it accidentally in the dark. Grenville stepped back watchfully while Jerry put his fingers against the white greasy mess. Following Grenville's directions he left good sets of prints on the front of the dresser drawers, on the polished metal of a small trench mirror, the white enamel on the inner side of the bathroom door, and on two of the big mirrors against the wall.

"That should be enough," Grenville approved.

As Jerry wiped his fingers with a handkerchief, Grenville produced his valet's automatic. He broke the revolver, removed the cartridges from the chamber, then tossed revolver and two cartridges over on the bed, pocketing the rest.

"You can load that when you get out of the house," he said. "Now, the man you're going after is a Mr. Lawrence Richey. His wife and daughter are in Florida. You will find him alone in his house at Sixteen Seventeen Haggerman Drive. He is at home by now, and should be asleep. His billfold will undoubtedly be in his clothes, or near him. Mask if you care to. Hold that revolver on him if you have to. But get his wallet. Have you an automobile?"

"I have," Jerry said shortly.

Grenville did not seem to mind his mood. He drew out a thin platinum watch on a slender chain and slid a glance at it.

"Eleven ten now." He had cheered up, in contrast to the pale, distraught air that had marked his manner when he first appeared in the doorway. "Let's see—the streets are icy. You'll have to drive slow. It should take you about twenty or twenty-five minutes to get to Richey's house. Not long to get in. About the same time to come back here. I'll wait for you. If you bring back my I O U we'll erase these fingerprints and close the matter. By the way, how did you get in my house so easily?"

"Forget it," said Jerry. "I might want to do it again."

Grenville smiled thinly. "I hope you have better luck next time." There was an enigmatic quality about the remark.

CHAPTER THREE
MURDER I O U

IT DID not take Jerry twenty-five minutes to get to his destination. The tire chains let him drive fast. He rolled through the sixteen-hundred block on Haggerman Drive, swung quickly through the immediate neighborhood and then parked on the next street over, as he had done at Grenville's. Before leaving the car he opened a small compartment in the right door and took out a flat leather packet.

Sleet was still driving before a chill wind as he walked to his goal. The neighborhood lay near the business section, one of the old, thickly built up parts of town, fast losing caste. On such valuable land the houses had been built close to the sidewalks, with very little land around them. Dingy, massive old brownstone and granite homes, most of them three stories high, still haughtily resisting the advance of modern commercialism, and doomed inevitably.

The house was easy to find, a three-story structure of dark granite blocks, a narrow strip of lawn, mostly bank, and a driveway leading under a stone-pillared canopy at the side of the house. Similar houses on either side pressed in closely. Not a light showed.

The boulevard curb lamps pushed a vague glow to the front porch. Every few moments an automobile rolled past, tires crunching the sleet. Pedestrians were not infrequent. The neighborhood was probably well patrolled by the police.

Jerry turned into the driveway, leaning forward against the slippery footing.

A screened door led into the side of the house at the canopy. It was locked inside. Working quickly, without a light, Jerry opened the flat leather folder he had taken from the door compartment of his car. It yielded a small keen knife. The blade ran through the screen wire with a grating sound. Reaching through, Jerry unsnapped the catch and confronted the door.

It was locked. One tiny flash of a small light, held close to the old-fashioned keyhole, revealed the rounded end of the key inside. He took a pair of slender, long-nosed steel pliers from the case, gripped the end of the key, turned sharply.

The door opened when he tried it.

Inside the air was warm, heavy from lack of ventilation, tainted with the odor of strong cigars. Jerry slipped on the felt soles. He went up two steps, along a hall, the felt pushing noiselessly into heavy carpets. He found himself at the back of a big main hall. Doors opened off. A great circular staircase swept up to the second floor.

The walls of the hall were paneled in dark wood, gave back the dull patina of age to his flash. The ceilings were high. The furniture in the hall was massive, old-fashioned. And the graceful curved rise of the great staircase was eloquent of the handwork of a former age. The house fairly shouted long-established, conservative wealth.

Mindful of his surprise at Grenville's, Jerry moved softly, listened much. The house was like a tomb. Then—something moving upstairs!

Jerry dragged the revolver from his pocket and slid in to the side of the staircase. For ghostlike, creepy, a low cry of horror floated down from the darkness overhead.

NOTHING FOLLOWED that low, choked, terror-stricken cry which cut so abruptly through the stillness. It seemed to Jerry, crouching tensely by the stairs with his revolver ready, that long minutes passed before any other sound followed. It was probably seconds.

Then hurried, stumbling steps moved up on the second floor. Queer choked sounds accompanied them. A ceiling light burst into radiance at the head of the stairs. Footsteps patted swiftly.

Looking up, Jerry saw her—a woman descending the wide staircase. A woman in a fur-collared coat and small pert hat running recklessly, heedlessly down. It was a miracle she did not fall in that panic-stricken flight. For flight it was.

Jerry stepped out to meet her.

At sight of him standing there in the shadows at the foot of the stairs she gave one involuntary scream, muted instantly by a quick hand clapped to her lips. She tried to stop, stumbled, reeled down the last three steps in helpless confusion.

Jerry's arm saved her from a hard fall. "It's all right," he soothed as he set her on her feet and slipped the revolver in his pocket. "I'm harmless. What's wrong?"

She was slender, light, no weight at all in his arms. The brown fur collar of her coat framed a small firm face that mirrored emotions like a fluid surface. Fright, dismay, horror passed over it swiftly as she stepped back from him; back until her shoulders touched the time-darkened wall paneling.

Her red lips were parted. Her eyes, large, brown, with soft even lashes under the curved arch of narrow eyebrows, were wide and fixed as she stared at him. The blood had receded from her cheeks, leaving the shaded rouge in vivid relief. Her breast rose and fell to quick short breathing. He could see the mad throbbing of a vein in her white neck.

The soft slender fingers of one hand came up. She glanced at them, shuddered, buried them quickly in the brown fur collar. Tears swam in her eyes, from grief, fright or shock.

Jerry moved back a step also, smiling reassuringly. Unless he were mistaken, she was very near hysteria. "You'd better tell me what is the matter," he suggested.

"Who—who are you?" she gasped.

She was young, not more then twenty or twenty-one. And very lovely in her agitation and fear, in her distrust of him. Grenville had said Lawrence Richey's wife and daughter were in Florida. Had he been mistaken? Was this the daughter?

While he pondered that, Jerry listened for other sounds. Any sleeping man should have been awakened by the disturbance. But there was no sign of Richey.

"Who are you?" the girl questioned again. Her panic was giving way to a measure of self-control. She seemed to know he did not belong in the house.

"I'm a friend of Mr. Richey's," Jerry told her. "Are you his daughter?"

"Why—yes," she said abruptly. "Yes, I'm his daughter. How did you know? And—and there's a dead man upstairs! I walked into the room and stumbled over his body in the dark!" She shuddered, said shakenly: "It was terrible. I touched his face! There's blood on my hand! I think I lost my head for a moment. And—finding you down here made it worse."

Jerry was almost as startled as she had been. He spoke sharply. "A dead man? Who is it?"

She had pulled a silk handkerchief from a pocket, was rubbing a crimson stain off her right hand. She shook her head, said uncertainly: "I don't know. It was dark. I d-didn't stop to see. I wanted to get out of the house—get help."

SHE WAS pathetic, helpless, so open to grief that Jerry felt a rush of pity for her. Apparently she had not as yet stopped to think that the dead man might be her father. Just a kid scared out of her wits.

"I thought you were down in Florida with your mother," he said. "Is your mother with you?"

She dabbed at the moisture in her eyes. "Mother is still in Florida. We had a quarrel and—and I caught the first train north. I just got here from the station."

"Where is your father?"

"He'll be here shortly. I—I wish he were here now!" A thought struck her. "What are you doing here, when he's out?"

"Waiting for him," Jerry said gently. "Has it occurred to you, Miss Richey, that the man upstairs might be—your father?"

"No! It couldn't be! I telephoned him from the station, and he said he had to go out for a little while, but would get back as soon as he could. I—I must get a policeman. I can't stay in the house alone."

Jerry touched her elbow hastily, as she turned toward the door. "You're not alone. I'll telephone the police. First, let's see who this man is."

"I don't want to go up there again," she cried vehemently.

If he left her down there, she was apt to call the police. "Just step up in the hall," Jerry coaxed. "You don't have to look. It will only take a moment."

She looked at him queerly, twisting her handkerchief nervously between her fingers. Then she nodded. They went up the stairs together. She pointed to an open door near the front of the hall. "In there," she said faintly.

The room was dark. Jerry, with the aid of his flash, found the light switch inside the door. And a low whistle escaped him as the light went on and he looked about the room.

It was evidently a library; the walls were lined with books. And in the middle of the floor a huddled figure lay motionless. There was blood. A faint odor of burnt powder still lingered in the air. The man, about fifty, had been shot. It was not a pleasant sight.

But that wasn't what had brought the whistle of amazement to Jerry's lips. Scattered on the rug at one side of the body was a small fortune in jewelry. Platinum rings and bracelets set with diamonds lay on the rug, winking and glittering in the light. Two pearl necklaces writhed like milky snakes. Several large square-cut emeralds lay green and dull, and a ruby glowed deep red. Blood red!

At the wall nearby a narrow section of the bookcase had been pulled out on concealed hinges. In the wall behind it the door of a safe stood open. An empty safe, now, Jerry's light disclosed.

On the floor to the right a morocco-leather jewel case from which the treasure had spilled, rested on its side, top open. Several feet away a thirty-eight caliber revolver lay on the rug.

Jerry picked it up with a gloved hand, and held the muzzle to his nose. It had been fired recently. He broke it, found two cartridges had been used.

The dead body on the floor had been shot twice in the head. Either wound would have been fatal.

Tossing the gun on the floor where he found it, Jerry scanned the scene with wrinkled brow. He didn't know what to make of it. It looked like suicide—but the first of those two wounds would have stopped an ordinary man. Why the second?

Yet robbery seemed to be ruled out—for any motive for robbery lay there on the rug, untouched. His glance went back to the gun with its two empty cartridges.

The girl had said her father had gone out for a short while. Jerry stooped, touched the dead man's cheek. It was already cooling. Death had come at least an hour back.

It hadn't taken her an hour to come from the station. The father must have been in the house with the dead man when she telephoned. Why did he leave the house so hurriedly, with his jewels scattered about this way? The police should have been here long ago.

He thought of Grenville, who had just come from the poker game in which Richey had been heavy winner. That game could hardly have broken up much more than an hour past.

THE MYSTERY grew deeper the more one pondered it. Jerry swung to the door, outside of which he had left the girl. "Will you take just one look, Miss Richey, and tell me whether this is your father or not?" he asked, and his voice sounded loud, startling in the thick silence.

She did not answer him.

He stepped to the door, saying: Miss Richey...."

But when he looked into the wide hallway where he had left her, she was not there.

"Miss Richey!" Jerry called. His voice rolled hollowly through the empty halls; and the silence that followed was suddenly ominous, threatening. The girl was not upstairs. Fear might have sent her down to the telephone, or out in the street for an officer. Hard to tell what a woman near hysteria would do. But it was queer she had left without a word.

Jerry ran lightly down the stairs, looking for her. The lower hall was still dark. He stepped to the front door and tried the knob. The old-fashioned bolt was shot, the key was gone.

The girl had left the house.

Jerry parted the curtains covering the small leaded panes set high in the heavy door. Out in the street sleet still fell. The curb lights glinted yellow against the bright sheen of ice overlying everything.

The girl was not out in front of the house either. She would hardly have hurried out and locked the door behind her; unless—

Jerry snapped a gloved finger. Had she suspected him after all? Humored him until she could lock him in the house and go for help?

There was no answer to that either in the dull quiet which swathed the interior of the house. The close, stuffy atmosphere pressed warmly about him. His damp overcoat steamed rankly of wet wool. The hatband on his forehead was clammy against his flesh. Jerry dragged off a glove, pushed the hat back, found he was perspiring. Found he was nervous, jumpy too. He had come to find a sleeping man—and he had found a dead one. He had been promised an empty house—and he had found a girl.

Queer about that girl!

Things had happened so fast since he first heard her cry of horror that he had given the facts little thought. Suppose a daughter had come home, walked in the house, expecting her father? She would have turned on the hall light; she would have had light upstairs.

There had been no light up there where she had been!

She had walked into a room she should have known well, and passed by the light switch inside the door, to stumble over the dead man. A girl who lived in this house would have turned the light on first.

Jerry's eye roved quickly about the hall. No luggage in sight either. A taxi driver would have carried it in. He hadn't seen any upstairs. She would hardly have come clear from Florida without a bag.

"Something tells me," said Jerry under his breath, "that an idiot has been running around here."

The slight crunch of leather soles on the sleet outside snapped his hand to the window curtains again. He raised one corner slightly—and froze tensely. Easing up the front steps onto the porch was the form of a patrolman, limned against the street glow. Overcoated to bulkiness, he was sliding toward the door, making as little noise as possible. An intruder any place in the house but right by the door would never have known he was there.

And while Jerry looked a second man in plainclothes followed.

The dull glint of drawn revolvers flicked in their hands.

Jerry lowered the corner of the curtain carefully—and slipped with quick steps to the back of the hall, swearing at himself for delaying so long. He should have gotten out of the house the instant he found there was a dead man in there. It looked as if the girl had found help. By the way those two walked, they knew there was trouble in the house, someone inside.

A cold draft struck his face as he turned into the hall leading to the side door. That door was solid, no panes. Jerry's hand stopped at the knob. He listened.

Outside, the screen creaked softly as it was pulled out.

This door was watched too!

JERRY LOCKED the door instantly. The knob was turned hard as he slipped back along the hall. It looked like a perfect trap. He recalled the cold draft. Somewhere a door or window was open. He found it, followed it as the door was rattled hard behind him, and outside a voice called excitedly.

The draft led him back through a hall to the rear of the house, into a dark kitchen. Through curtained windows, whose shades were drawn only halfway down, he could make out the distant gleam of a street light over on the next street, where his car was parked.

There was a back porch. Heavy steps shuffled out there. The house was surrounded. Jerry had Grenville's revolver in his hand now. Two cartridges. Not much with a whole squad of police out there. If he shot, and was caught, they'd slap a charge of murder against him without bothering much how that fellow upstairs had died. He didn't want to shoot anyway. His quarrel this evening was not with the police.

While that flashed through his mind he was groping through the blackness, trying to run down the cold draft. No chance to use a light either. It would be seen from the back porch.

His hand struck an open door. His sliding foot found a step. He went down into the cellar with the cold air still pouring past his face. And as he went, glass shattered in the front of the house.

Hard cement floored the cellar. Jagged little blotches of flame glared at him through the draft holes in a furnace door. The crackle and whisper of fire, the slow roil of boiling water was damped out by the heavy tramp of feet overhead.

A muffled voice, harsh, rasping despite the intervening floor, said: "You boys search through the back! He's in here!"

And Jerry padded ghostlike over hard cement to a pale grayish blotch at the edge of the Stygian blackness. Padded to a partly open door through which the icy draft was pushing. The spit of sleet met his ears, the full blast of the night struck him. His foot found the bottom step of a short flight leading up into the back yard, in the shelter of the back porch.

They had overlooked this little areaway to the cellar. Somebody was up there on the porch—but not in the yard. The porch floor creaked as the lurking copper moved.

The porch was screened. There was a high board fence at the side of the yard. Jerry was almost to it when a powerful flashlight swept the back of the house, picked him out dimly, swerved over, nailed him in full relief against the fence.

A shout rang out. "There he is! Hey, you—stop!"

A running stride brought Jerry to the fence. His hands caught the top and catapulted his body over.

On the back porch a gun thundered an angry fusillade. Bullets crashed through the damp fence boards as Jerry hit the ground on the other side and threw himself toward the back of the yard.

One flash of his light showed the way to the back fence, the gate. It was locked. He rolled over it, crossed the alley, leaping a third fence there. And behind him was shouting confusion as the chase took form.

He skirted a house and came to the street. Fifty yards down, his car was standing as he had left it. He dragged open the door a minute later, slipped behind the wheel, stamped on the starter, and rocked away from the curb in low gear with the first spitting spin of the motor.

CHAPTER FOUR
THE MISSING MIRROR

JERRY PRINCE was a mad and puzzled young man as he stirred a cup of black coffee at an all-night lunchroom downtown. But none of it showed on his face as he scanned the first edition of a morning paper he had purchased outside.

That face was worth looking at. It had the leanness of perfect condition, to the point where skin and muscle molded finely from temple to jaw. Here was a man whose body and mind were healthy, whose nerves were iron, whose control was perfect.

His movements were deft, quick, easy. Latent in him was that flexible mobility which makes a man at ease and part of any surroundings. And yet, if one looked close, it was not hard to imagine him entirely aloof, alone, poised always for action. He had that look now as he sat on the lunch-counter stool—the air of a hawk searching out the point and moment to spring.

Less than half an hour had passed since he had raced out of the neighborhood where Lawrence Richey lived. The tire chains had justified themselves in that first mad dash. If there had been pursuit by a police car, it had been quickly left behind on the slippery pavements.

A man in a dark overcoat and hat had been pilloried for a moment against the fence by that glaring police beam.

Jerry Prince now wore a tan topcoat, tan gloves, a brown hat. Grenville's revolver, the felt sneakers, the leather folder of tools were cached safely. The men on the back porch had not seen his face. But it had been a close shave. And since then Jerry had had time to think.

That girl could never have called the squad which had surrounded the house. Too many of them. Part had been plain-clothesmen from the nearest precinct, or headquarters. She had left the house by that back cellar door. There had been no draft blowing in the hall when he first passed through it.

There was mystery over it all—and meanwhile his fingerprints were still at Grenville's. There was no safety until he saw them removed. Grenville was waiting for him....

Jerry drained the cup, took his check, stood up. And as he turned to the cash register up front, the door opened and a big man with overcoat collar turned up around his neck stepped into the restaurant. Jerry grinned a greeting and swore to himself.

"Sergeant Smith, as I live," he hailed. "Out late tonight, aren't you, Sergeant?"

Smith, sergeant in the headquarters squad, was a large man, in both height and breadth. He moved inside with a curious flat-footed lumbering motion, as a man would do whose arches had been punished by years of pavement pounding.

He closed the door carefully and turned down the collar of his coat. Smith had been a big, muscular man to start with. Flesh now padded him to the point of corpulence, bulging his middle, running down the vast area of his cheeks into frost-reddened jowls.

He pulled off his sag-brimmed hat, that had once been gray and now had aged to a tint no color chart could match. He slapped it against a great fat hand, and then looked up with almost childlike surprise on his huge pinkish face.

"Why, if it ain't Jerry Prince! Ain't this a happy meeting? Just when I was lonesome for someone to talk to."

Smith lumbered past the cash register and dropped heavily on the first stool. He looked at his damp hat pensively, swung around heavily and laid it on the counter, and unbuttoned the front of his heavy overcoat.

Jerry put his check and a nickel beside the cash register and beamed. "Sorry, Sergeant. It's late. I'm headed for home and bed. Not used to late hours like this."

Smith's great pink face was solemn. His little eyes, sunk deep in folds of flesh, were woeful. He crossed one rubbered shoe over the other and heaved a lugubrious sigh. "Me neither, Jerry. It's a pretty pass when a man that's finally got off night pavements, has to run out in weather like this. My rheumatism'll come back sure as sin. Bad for a young fellow like you, too, Jerry."

Smith's little eyes ran over Jerry reflectively. He waved a massive hand to the stool at his side. "Sit down and talk a few minutes. I'm all unsettled having to run around this way after midnight."

JERRY HOPED his face was bland. Inside he was far from it. Smith, for all his fat clumsiness, his artless innocence, was about the keenest man at headquarters. There was no fat in his brain. He could stalk a victim with disarming befuddlement, and pounce like a fox when he was ready.

"I never ran out on a friend yet," Jerry chuckled. "To tell the truth, I was lonesome myself." Jerry sat down on the stool, proffered Smith a cigarette, and when it was refused lighted one himself. "What brings you out tonight?" he questioned casually.

Smith rubbed the top of his head, where a bald area gleamed pink and shiny. Vague resentment tinged his voice. "Business, of course. What else would keep me out this late? I suppose you've been working too?"

Jerry laughed. "I never work, Sergeant. Lucky investments, you know. I just got restless and went out for a ride."

"Someday," said Sergeant Smith confidentially, "I'm going to get you to explain those investments, Jerry. I'd like to take a long vacation, too. Was you riding around all evening?"

"No," said Jerry deliberately. "I started about ten, I guess."

"And you've been riding around ever since then?"

"More or less. Nice night for that. Storm all around and the car cozy and warm. It rouses the primeval in me."

"Shucks, a nice young fellow like you couldn't have any primeval in him. It takes a hairy chest. Nice coat you've got there, Jerry. Same color underneath?"

"Same." Jerry flipped open the coat. "And I've got hair on my chest. Want to see it?"

Smith nodded at the coat. "I'll get me one like it, next time. I take to browns. By the way, Jerry, you wouldn't be having a gun on you I could borrow, would you?"

Jerry's eyebrows lifted. "A gun? Why, Sergeant! I never carry dangerous weapons—although I did take out a permit once."

Smith rubbed the palm of his hand up across his nose and nodded sympathetically. "I know about that permit. Judge Casson recommended it, didn't he? The judge they ran out of office. You wouldn't hold out on an old friend, would you, Jerry? Maybe I'd better frisk you, just for fun."

"Sure," said Jerry agreeably. "Just for fun, Sergeant. You're so playful. But what put guns in your mind?"

Smith's little eyes mourned at him. "I was just talking," he sighed. "Sure, I knew you wouldn't tell me anything but the truth. I'm lookin' for a bad egg, Jerry. There was a fellow killed tonight. Shot down in cold blood in his upstairs library, and they've turned out everybody to look for him."

"Why Sergeant," Jerry said, shocked. "Tell me about it. Who did it?"

Smith big face was expressionless, but his answer was reproachful. "Would I be running around this way, risking my death of cold if I knew who did it? Of course he left some clues, and we'll know by tomorrow. But we're trying to pick him up right away. You see, a couple of the boys saw him run out of the house. Got their light on him, only he went over a fence before they could drop him. Did you happen to be over by Thirty-ninth and Cleveland about three quarters of an hour ago?"

"Sorry, Sergeant. I was not. If I had been there when your man got away, I'd have helped hunt him."

"I know you would, Jerry. I just know you would. Only it wasn't around Thirty-ninth and Cleveland. And the man was just about your build. The boys might have shot you by mistake. Funny thing about this killing. Fellow by the name of Lawrence Richey got it. Good citizen. Big real-estate man, I understand. Headquarters got a telephone call that someone had been seen sneaking into his house.

"The dope was straight. The fellow was in there—but he got away. And upstairs the boys found Richey dead, with a slather of jewelry lying around on the floor. It kind of looked like suicide at first, but the medical examiner says he never would have lived to fire a second shot. And there's no powder marks around the wounds. He was knocked off, for something besides that jewelry on the floor. Headquarters is curious about little things like that."

Smith dropped a huge hand on the damp crown of his old hat and regarded it mournfully. "That's why I got to run around this hour of the night," he said heavily. "Got any ideas that will help me, Jerry?"

"No," said Jerry regretfully. "But if I see a man my build with a dark overcoat, I'll turn in the word." He got up.

Smith heaved himself upright heavily and clapped the damp hat on his head. "You don't mind if I look around your car, Jerry? I still could use that gun."

"Not at all, Sergeant."

Smith tramped out to the curb and leisurely poked through the car using a flashlight. He found nothing, said philosophically: "I didn't think you'd have one. Going straight home, Jerry?"

"I don't know."

"Well, see you soon, Jerry."

The elephantine figure of Sergeant Smith was standing at the curb like a great fat overcoated Buddha as Jerry drove off. Standing there unmindful of the whipping sleet, watching inscrutably.

JERRY PRINCE was not worried—but he was thoughtful as he drove off through the night. He took a tortuous course for some minutes to make certain no machine was trailing him. Apparently none was.

When he was certain of that he reached under the dashboard and snapped a concealed switch. Not two minutes later the low even voice of a police radio announcer droned its formula of calling all cars. Then—

"All cars are requested to check the movements of black Chrysler coupé, number Forty-three—six-eleven... black Chrysler coupé number Forty-three—six-eleven. Name of driver, Jerry Prince... black Chrysler Forty-three—six-eleven... do not arrest... check movements... last seen turning east from Seventh and Main...."

So the inscrutable hand of Sergeant Smith reached out through the night, out through the wind and sleet, laying down a city-wide net. Smith was not certain of anything. But behind the bewildered pinkness of his fat face some bit of suspicion had stirred, and he had acted as soon as Jerry was out of sight.

The muscles set in hard ridges along Jerry's jaw. The net was tightening, the mystery growing deeper. Uppermost in his mind at the moment was Smith's statement that head-quarters had been notified that Richey's house had been entered. Had some neighbor seen him? Not likely. There had been no pedestrian in the block when he turned into the driveway.

Checkering over the city, like hounds questing for a scent, the squad cars were looking for him. Jerry drove straight for a certain all-night garage not far distant, left his car with the attendant, walked a quarter of a mile to another garage, and a few minutes later was driving through the night in a sleek blue sedan. Week in and week out that car sat in the garage for just such needs as this.

A short time later he stopped before Grenville's residence. There would be no sleep tonight while his finger-prints were still scattered over Grenville's bedroom.

Lights were burning in the house. He entered as before, using the key.

The front door clicked softly as he closed it, but that was all. No one challenged his entrance. The living room to the right of the hall had been lighted since Jerry left. Grenville was not in there. Carl, the valet, was not in evidence either.

A secret compartment in the blue sedan had yielded another automatic. With it in his hand Jerry went upstairs. One experience in this house had made him wary. He was grim, his eyes narrowed, Grenville had a lot of explaining to do.

Grenville's bedroom door was closed. Jerry shoved it open, stepped in. An empty room greeted him. The light was still burning, the window shades drawn as they had been—but there was no Grenville.

Jerry moved to one side of the doorway where he had solid wall at his back.

These silent houses were getting on his nerves. He felt the slow tingling crawl of tension up his spine, into the roots of his hair.

Water dripped slowly through a leaking tap in the bathroom. Since entering the front door he had heard no other sound. He carefully closed the door beside him and stepped to the bathroom. The light was on in there also. One look—one stride—and he was inside.

Crimson-stained water had been splashed over the gleaming white porcelain of the washbowl. A towel lay across the edge of the bathtub, and it was streaked with red stains.

No second look was needed. That was blood!

Carl, the valet, had gone downstairs with his wounded hand. It was not likely he had come up again, and used this bathroom hurriedly.

JERRY STEPPED back into the bedroom. The big mirrors against the wall reflected his cautious movements. His face was set as his glance roved carefully about.

And then suddenly he saw it—a small, sinuous trickle of blood thrusting out from under one of the cupboard doors!

It was a silent, sinister sight, ominous in its implication. What had happened in this richly furnished bedroom since he had walked out and left Grenville alone? Smiling lips, arch eyes, beautiful faces watched him from the gallery of pictures scattered around the room. They knew—those beautiful women in the pictures. They had seen but could never tell. Jerry stepped to the cupboard door, opened it.

And the next instant he leaped back, suppressing an exclamation. For as the light went on in the cupboard, the crumpled body of Carl, the valet, sagged out toward him, sprawling woodenly on the floor, pallid face staring sightlessly at the ceiling.

Carl was dead.

He had been shot in the back. The thick lips were drawn away from uneven teeth in a snarling smile, as if in death he defied the fate which had overtaken him.

The fetid odor of powder fumes drifted out of the brightly lighted space where racks of clothes hung trim and neat. And the cedar paneling at the back had been slid half open.

Jerry stepped quickly over the body to that panel. A shove sent it rolling easily all the way over. In the space behind, a sizable office safe stood.

The door of the safe was ajar. A double handful of papers was scattered on the floor. With his gloved left hand, Jerry pulled the safe door open. The compartments were practically empty. This was the thing for which he had been looking when he first entered the house.

He sorted quickly through the littered papers on the floor, and those inside the safe. Envelopes, letters, receipted bills, some old snapshots of Grenville on a sea beach in a bathing suit, posing with various women, all young, pretty. Women and Grenville seemed to go together. There was nothing in the lot which interested Jerry. He left the mess there and stepped back over the body.

Hardly two minutes had passed since he had entered the room. His fingerprints were exactly as he had been forced to leave them, shouting their invitation to any detective. Jerry drew out a small bottle of alcohol, moistened one end of his handkerchief and swiftly began to remove the prints.

The little metal trench mirror was missing. It was not in the dresser drawers.

He scrubbed the prints off the bathroom door, looked in there for the mirror, and then began a quick search of the bedroom. A worried frown crinkled his forehead. That small, steel mirror carried a perfect set of his fingerprints. Jerry got down on his knees and looked under the dresser.

The mirror was not there. But an automatic pistol lay on the floor against the baseboard. His own automatic, that had been taken by the valet. A smear of blood reddened the end of the barrel.

Jerry began to swear softly to himself as he carried the gun into the bathroom and wiped the smear of blood from the blued steel. His gun—his fingerprints.

It was a perfect plant. He searched again for the mirror, without success. It was apparently not in the room.

Baffled, disturbed, apprehensive, Jerry left that house of mystery and death.

CHAPTER FIVE
EX-MOUTHPIECE

MARVIN J. BROADHURST, junior partner of the eminent law firm of Miles, Stearman, Gottlieb and Broadhurst, was a man whose height was slightly less than the average. His body was already growing pudgy and round from much desk work, and his eyes behind their pince nez were sharp, shrewd, keen.

There had been a time in the recent past—a time which Marvin Broadhurst hoped would quickly be forgotten and buried—when his name was better known around the grimy criminal and magistrate courts than anywhere else in the city. A time when his clients were usually not listed in the telephone directory, although they often made the front pages of the newspapers. In those days consultations with clients had more often than not been held under the watchful eyes of a turnkey.

But Marvin Broadhurst had been too clever for that sort of thing. He had realized he might attain a dubious reputation as a successful attorney for the criminal class, with its attendant emolument of fat fees from the big shots. But he would never get to the pinnacle of dignity and position which is the lot of a leader of the bar. So he had put the past behind him, and in due time had attained a junior partnership in a firm that would hardly have known what to do with a criminal case if it were brought to the door by one of their wealthy clients.

And this was exactly what had happened. And when the matter had hastily been referred to Mr. Broadhurst by the other partners, with the adjuration that there must be no publicity or failure, Marvin Broadhurst had been tempted and had fallen. He had dipped back into the past for ways and means.

That had been some days before, and it was either mental telepathy or an uneasy conscience that flashed the matter into his mind when the insistent ringing of his apartment doorbell awoke him in the middle of the night.

His wife called petulantly from the next room: "What is it, Marvin? Who is ringing that bell?"

"I'll see," Marvin told her hastily. "Go back to sleep, dear." And thereupon he set his glasses on his nose, belted a bathrobe around his pudgy frame and padded to the door.

At sight of his visitor, Marvin Broadhurst glowered. "What is it?" he asked impatiently, and a trifle uneasily.

Jerry Prince stepped in, turning down the collar of his tan coat and stripping the gloves from his hands. He eyed Marvin appraisingly. "You're getting fat," he said briefly. "You look like a kewpie who's been poured into that bathrobe."

Marvin ignored the comment with as much dignity as he could muster with hair tousled, bathrobe cord cutting into his rounded middle and loose slippers flopping on his naked feet.

"What brings you here at this hour of the night?" he asked nervously.

"Plenty," Jerry said briefly.

"What do you mean? Is anything wrong?"

Jerry grinned, and pushed his hat up on his forehead. "Nothing much, Marvie, old man. Just murder."

"*Shhhh!* My God—not so loud! Wh-what? Murder? You didn't shoot anyone, did you?" And in Marvin Broadhurst's hoarse whisper horror struggled with fear. Blood rushed into his round cheeks and his eyes popped behind his glasses.

"Grenville's valet is dead."

MARVIN BROADHURST clutched the back of the nearest chair for support. The blood left his face as quickly as it had come, leaving it chalky. "Did anyone see you?" he questioned thickly. "God—what a mess! I should have had better sense than to try it! Are the police after you? You want money, I suppose. How much—I—I'll—"

"Hold your horses," Jerry cut him off. "Here's what happened." And he gave Marvin a terse account of his movements since entering Grenville's house.

A suspicious look came gradually into his listener's eye. "Are you sure you aren't covering up on me?" he demanded at the end. "You didn't get the stuff out of the safe and kill the valet doing it?"

Jerry lost his smile then. "Still back in the police court, aren't you? Ready to double-cross and looking for a double-cross. Don't say things like that to me. I don't like it, even from you."

Marvin Broadhurst winced. "Sorry," he mumbled. "Well, what do you want? What are you going to do? It—it looks bad. I thought you would have no trouble."

"It is bad," Jerry agreed. "With those fingerprints of mine out, I'm not safe. Somebody has tried to frame me for murder. At this chap Richey's house, I missed it by an eyelash. And if I hadn't gone back to Grenville's, that charge would have popped up against me too. Double murder. I wouldn't have had a chance to beat it—not even with your help, Marvin."

"I don't take criminal cases any more."

"Ah—but you would have taken this one, Marvin. Something tells me you would. Now listen. I didn't come here to cry trouble on your shoulder. I came here to warn you, and to see if you know anything about this chap Richey. Hell's popping, and I am on the hot end. Sergeant Smith is wondering whether I know anything about Richey's death. He rather suspects I do.

"Sometimes that man can smell things clear across town. A set of my fingerprints are wandering about. God knows where they'll light. I don't know why Richey was killed, or why Grenville's valet was shot with my gun and the safe looted. Until I do know, and find out who did it, I'm not safe. Did you get anyone else to tackle this thing?"

"No," said Marvin Broadhurst. "And I don't know anything about this man Richey. Never heard of him."

"You have now," said Jerry laconically. "And you'd better get your clothes on. I'm in a hurry."

Marvin Broadhurst stared through his pince nez as if wondering whether his visitor had suddenly lost his mind. "I'm going back to bed," he stated tartly. "I'll see you in the morning."

"You're going out with me," Jerry retorted calmly. "Did you think I woke you up to chat? You're my alibi, Marvin, old son. And you may as well dress and like it."

"You're crazy!"

"And you're insane if you don't do it," Jerry insisted calmly. "We may both need alibis before this is over. Hurry up. I have work to do."

JERRY PRINCE was a man the underworld and the law did not know—a rare thing. They might guess about him—and they did; but no one was ever certain the guesses were right. He was an enigma. Aloof, alone, he moved through circles the ordinary citizen never touched, and in many they did. He had at various times been classed as a master forger, an expert cracksman, a skilful con artist, and an international jewel thief.

But those were all wild guesses.

Jerry always had plenty of money; he lived well, he listened much and said little. He had an uncanny knack of being around when there was trouble. No man ever teamed up with him, or got his whole confidence. Marvin Broadhurst, tonight, had come as near to it as any person—and that only because his own fortunes were deeply involved.

Broadhurst was an angry and disturbed man as the blue sedan slipped through the streets. He huddled in his corner of the front seat, overcoat collar turned up around his ears. "I won't hear the last of this for months!" he burst out. "My wife knew my going out this way was damn queer! She had plenty to say."

"I heard her," Jerry chuckled. "In fact, I think everyone else in the building heard her. I hope you asserted yourself."

Marvin Broadhurst sighed deeply and let the matter pass. "Where are we going?" he demanded.

"To a gambling joint."

"What! I won't be seen in such a place! The partners of my firm cannot afford to—our reputation—"

"Will be nicked all to bits, if this business does not turn out right," Jerry cut him off calmly. "It was your idea, my friend. I agreed to help you out, for old times' sake. But that did not include putting my neck in a noose. My collar feels tight already."

"So help me—if I ever get out of this without a scandal, I'll never try to save a client a dollar again!" Marvin Broadhurst groaned. "I worked hard to get a partnership in a decent law firm, and now I've probably lost it, and my reputation as well."

"Try my recipe. Don't have a reputation," Jerry advised cheerfully. "It's good for the appetite and sleep. By the way, don't forget that I picked you up about three quarters of an hour before I actually did."

"Perjury!" said Marvin Broadhurst bitterly.

"You should know. You used it in the criminal courts."

Marvin Broadhurst winced and sank lower into his greatcoat. He was an unhappy man, and showed it.

THE CHARTER of the South Bay Club, as registered in the state records, set forth its serious purpose as a fraternal and social center. Sitto Fiaschetti, the permanent president and owner, saw that the social and fraternal aims were carried out handsomely. One dollar covered the initiation fees and dues for one year. The little pink membership card stated all that clearly, in black type on the back. One dollar—and the South Bay Club opened its doors widely and gladly.

Inside, every element and stratum of society mingled in fraternal freedom, in social equality. Well-dressed bootleggers shot craps across the table from debutantes in the social register. Gunmen in evening clothes played at the roulette tables beside prominent business men whose money was no better than theirs. And if the pretty young wife, smiling at the traveling salesman who cast a glance of admiration at her, was reprimanded by her dancing partner who perhaps had never met her husband, the by-laws of the club had nothing to say about it. In short the sky was the limit inside the great rambling frame house nestling among the South Bay shore pine woods.

The only rigid rule was that no roughness was allowed, and no crooked raids on the guests. One daring pickpocket had been taken out into the pines and almost beaten to death by Sitto Fiaschetti's strong-arm men when a stolen wallet was quickly traced to him. The money of the club members was reserved for the club itself. And Sitto Fiaschetti did prefer that everyone be out by daybreak.

It was no secret that the law more or less winked at the place. The reason—most of the underworld sooner or later appeared there. And many of the patrons were politically potent.

The blue sedan rolled swiftly along the sandy shore road along which scrub pines became pillars of sleet-covered glory in the headlight glare. It rounded a curve, and the flood-lighted property of the South Bay Club spangled the night ahead. Marvin Broadhurst stirred to life, took one look, and groaned: "The place is packed!"

And all the comfort he got was: "The more the merrier. Buck up. Try to look as if you are getting some pleasure out of it."

"Hah! Pleasure!"

Leaving their machine in the brilliantly lit parking area at one side of the building, Jerry led the way briskly to the massive entrance door, which wise ones knew was lined with sheet steel. There was no porch. One was either in or out, and the light over the door was not dim.

Mad music within beat defiance to the weather as a pair of eyes inspected them through a small aperture. The door was opened immediately.

The doorkeeper, a chunky, swart-faced young man, had a broad smile on his face. "Good evening, Mr. Broadhurst," he greeted with the warm familiarity of old acquaintance. "Haven't seen you since I was bailiff in Judge Stenger's court. You don't come here often."

Marvin Broadhurst's sour grunt might have meant anything.

"Where is Fiaschetti, Mike?" Jerry questioned casually as he stripped off his gloves.

Mike shrugged. "I don't know, Mr. Prince. Might find him in his office. He's usually there about this time of night. Shall I ring for him?"

Mike's finger made a tentative reach toward one of several almost invisible buttons set in the wall beside him.

"No," Jerry refused. "I'll look him up."

And when he and his companion reached the checkroom a few steps further along the wide entrance hall, Jerry said: "Keep your coat on, Broadhurst, We'll only be here long enough to ask Fiaschetti a few questions and let the crowd see us."

To the right of the big hall was an immense dining-and-dance floor, under a high beamed ceiling. An orchestra was playing enthusiastically. A sprinkling of couples were on the dance floor. The tables were empty.

DIRECTLY AHEAD was another big room, wide, long, low-ceilinged. This was the heart of the South Bay Club. A long mahogany bar ran across one end, with a scattering of tables before it. It was well patronized even at this hour of the night. Some of the men and women wore dinner clothes; some did not. And, surprisingly, there was little evidence of drunkenness.

Most of the big room, however, was taken up by tables, each under its own battery of lights, each with its crowd of spectators and players. Craps, chuckaluck, blackjack, roulette, stud poker and upright wheels—all were there. And the droning cries of the house men, the steady murmur of players and spectators filled the vast room with a restless murmuring hum, electric with tension.

"Have a drink," Jerry invited.

"No," Marvin Broadhurst refused ungraciously.

Jerry stood in the doorway and swept the room with a glance, then turned to the left to a flight of steps. "Come up," he said, "and meet Fiaschetti. You know him, don't you?"

Marvin Broadhurst did not reply, but he followed.

The upper floor of the building was smaller in area than the one below. The rooms were smaller, the ceilings lower. Some were private dining or gaming rooms. Two formed the office of Sitto Fiaschetti.

Once past the entrance door downstairs, no further attention had been paid to their movements. But up here, beside Fiaschetti's office door, a poker-faced young man tilted a chair against the wall and eyed them appraisingly.

"Looking for someone?" he questioned evenly.

"Fiaschetti."

"He's in there—but he's busy."

"Not too busy to see me, I hope," said Jerry politely. "No—sit still. I'll announce myself."

"Hey!" said the young man as the front legs of his chair hit the floor hard and he came to his feet. "None of that! I got orders." His eyes had narrowed, an underlying note of cold warning had come into his voice.

Jerry stopped with a hand on the door knob. "My friend," he said gently, "don't try that on me. I've seen better gorillas than you make mistakes before."

And leaving the other staring uncertainly, Jerry walked into a small anteroom, circled by leather-covered benches against the wall. He crossed to a door opposite, opened it without knocking and stepped through. And a slight smile came to his lips as the chunky figure behind the big flat-topped desk across the room sprang up with ill-concealed irritation.

"Who the devil let you in?" Fiaschetti burst out; and then caught himself. "Oh, hello, Prince. I didn't notice who it was. I'm busy right now. Will you wait outside? I told that mug at the door not to let anyone in."

Fiaschetti wore a dinner coat and an immaculately tied tie. His shoulders were square, solid; his face was thick, deep, with heavy ridging black eyebrows and a close-trimmed black mustache under a strong high-bridged nose. Long black hair was roached back perfectly. A magnificent diamond flashed on a finger as he waved his apology.

But Jerry hardly saw the moving hand, the flashing diamond. His eyes were riveted on the woman who sat beside Fiaschetti's desk.

She had not looked around when he came in. Her eyes did not lift from the rug she was studying as Fiaschetti spoke his name. She did not need to. He had seen that trim little felt hat before, that fur-collared coat, now thrown open to the heat of the room.

"Who's your friend, Fiaschetti?" he inquired slowly.

She turned then. He had made no mistake. There sat the girl who had posed as the daughter of Lawrence Richey.

CHAPTER SIX
THE LADY LIES

MARVIN BROADHURST had stopped just inside the doorway. His mouth sagged, he stared incomprehensively as the girl left her chair with a startled gasp, shrinking back a step, staring mutely at Jerry Prince.

"You!" she got out faintly.

"Me," Jerry agreed with a thin smile. "This is an unexpected pleasure. I see we are both friends of Fiaschetti. Introduce us, Sitto."

The famous flashing smile of Sitto Fiaschetti was not in evidence at this moment. His brilliant black eyes shifted from the girl to Jerry, and back to her again. Swift suspicion brought his thick eyebrows down. All attempts at cordiality vanished. He clipped out bruskly to her: "You know this man?"

"Just a speaking acquaintance," Jerry murmured.

He was staring at her, wondering what she was doing here with Sitto Fiaschetti. He had thought her gone for good. She could—and she would!—answer some of the questions that had been pounding in his mind; clear away some of the mystery cloaking that close shave at Lawrence Richey's.

And at the same time he was aware that she was the one person who was most dangerous to him. She could implicate him in the Richey murder. Sergeant Smith would give a lot for her knowledge.

His presence had obviously upset her. But once more her self-control returned quickly. In this light she looked older, but no whit less pretty. He found it hard to believe that the smile which quickly curved her lips was not spontaneous, real.

"We met yesterday, in a restaurant!" she told Fiaschetti lightly. "I knocked my pocketbook to the floor, and tipped over my coffee cup while trying to pick it up. This gentleman was kind enough to come to the rescue with a napkin."

Was there a mute appeal in the swift look she threw at him? A desperately veiled shaft of fear? If there was, Sitto Fiaschetti did not catch it. The suspicion cleared from his swart face. His hands, which had gripped the edge of his desk as he leaned tensely forward, relaxed. He chuckled.

"I thought from the way you looked at him, he was bad medicine. His name is Prince. And if there's any more than that to tell, he'll have to hand it to you. I don't know it. This is Miss Barbara Todd."

"This is my lucky night," Jerry told her; and forced her to shake hands.

Her fingers were icy cold. She could not control the color in her cheeks either. They were still pale. And her lips seemed stiff as she said: "How do you do, Mr. Prince?"

Jerry was looking at her, past her, as she spoke. And his eye caught the furtive movement of a door in the wall behind her. Someone was standing behind that door listening to what was said! Someone who did not care to be discovered!

"Pardon me a moment," he murmured, and stepped past her to the door. But quick as he was, whoever was on the other side was quicker. He heard the soft click of a bolt as his hand went to the knob.

"Say—what's the matter?" Fiaschetti burst out angrily, starting from behind the desk and abandoning his pose of cordiality. "Why'd you run over to the door like that?"

"I was just wondering whether anyone was behind it, Sitto. I always look behind doors before I talk. It's a healthy habit."

"Well, there's no one behind my doors!" Fiaschetti burst out. "That's my bedroom and private bath in there!" He paused, and then winked. "At least no one you got any interest in."

"Ah. Sorry, Sitto."

"Who's this with you?" Fiaschetti queried bluntly, turning to the anteroom door where Jerry's companion stood.

"Mr. Marvin Broadhurst, a friend of mine. Perhaps you know him already, Fiaschetti?"

"Never met Mr. Broadhurst," Fiaschetti disclaimed with a flashing smile. "But say—ain't you the lawyer who got Tony Rohan off with a suspended sentence about four years ago?"

Marvin Broadhurst nodded glumly. "I don't take criminal cases any more," he said shortly.

"Thank God, I don't have much law business. Sit down, Miss Todd. I'll be with you in a minute." And Fiaschetti moved toward the door.

JERRY TOOK the hint, followed Fiaschetti into the outer office. The young guard was there, surly now. "These guys busted in past me, chief."

"Glad to see them any time," Fiaschetti told him. "Go on back in the hall, Slim."

Sitto Fiaschetti shut the inner door to his office, and turned, washing his hands together. Gold teeth still gleamed in his broad smile, but his eyes were not quite so pleasant. Evidently some bit of suspicion still lingered.

"Who is that girl?" Jerry asked bluntly.

Fiaschetti's smile barely shaded a leer. "You like her, eh? Well, she's just a girl. One of the customers, fixing up her credit."

"That all you know about her?"

"As the Holy Virgin is my witness," Fiaschetti swore, lifting his eyes piously.

And Jerry knew that he lied. "I'm looking for a friend, Sitto. A chap named Grenville," he said.

Fiaschetti was a crack stud-poker player. He proved it now as his face remained blank. Only his eyes narrowed slightly—very slightly. "Grenville?" he repeated. "Who is he? Do I know him?"

"One of your customers, Sitto. I've seen you talking to him."

Fiaschetti wrinkled his heavy brow and shrugged volubly. One hand came up and caressed the end of his black mustache as he smiled apologetically. "So many people I talk to," he confessed. "They say, 'Good evening, Mr. Fiaschetti,' and I say, 'Good evening, my friend.' But if you ask me their names I don't know. What does your friend look like?"

"Like a gentleman," Jerry sighed. "But looks are deceiving, Sitto. He isn't a gentleman."

"Hah!" said Fiaschetti. "Then you know him well?"

"We've met," Jerry conceded drily.

"But if you know him so, why come to me? At this time of night? Is something wrong?"

Fiaschetti was just a trifle too eager. He was lying, covering up. But Jerry let it pass.

"Just killing a little time," he replied casually. "Thought maybe he'd been in. Sorry to have bothered you, Sitto. 'Night. Give my regards to Miss Todd."

Fiaschetti kissed the square tips of his thick fingers dramatically. "Romance!" he breathed—and his teeth were flashing as they left.

DOWNSTAIRS MARVIN BROAD-HURST demanded tartly: "Do we go home now? Every minute I'm away will make my wife that much worse."

"What?" Jerry said absently. "Oh, your wife? Forget her!"

His mind had been on other things. The girl by Fiaschetti's desk. What was she doing there? What was her business with Sitto Fiaschetti? Why had she tried to cover up their meeting? Why that mute, fleeting fear on her face?

And who had been listening behind that door?

One thing certain—he did not trust Barbara Todd. Her childlike face her panicky fear had fooled him once. He knew now she could think straightly, swiftly, certainly. Jerry glanced at the stairs. She would be coming down them shortly. But—would she?

He said abruptly: "Let's go outside."

But in the car Jerry merely sat behind the wheel. Marvin Broadhurst said impatiently: "Well, let's get going."

"Sit still," said Jerry.

He was staring out over the lighted parking area. No watchman was braving the cold. Three times parties went hilariously to their cars, backed out, and roared away along the shore road. Barbara Todd was not among them.

Jerry suddenly sat forward, peering through the front glass. A dark shadow was slipping around the rear corner of the building. That was she, Barbara Todd, coat collar turned up around her face, small feet picking a swift way over the icy ground.

Jerry watched her get into a small coupé. "Wait here," he said, and went quickly over to it.

The grinding whir of the starter stopped abruptly as Barbara Todd looked out the window and saw him by her car. She sat still as Jerry opened the door and got in beside her.

He came to the point at once. "All right, let's have the story."

"I don't know what you mean," she said in a still, small voice that reminded him of a child, badly frightened and upset.

This time Jerry was not impressed. "My compliments on the way you handled me at Richey's house," he said shortly. "What were you doing there? And what's your business with Sitto Fiaschetti?"

"I—I was talking to him about a check. I lost at roulette."

"Bosh!" said Jerry flatly. "Did you shoot Lawrence Richey?"

"No. I—I—"

"Exactly. Think fast, sister. And drop the baby-doll air. You were smart enough to lose me and get the police."

Her manner changed abruptly, amazingly. Voice, manner, and the girl herself seemed to grow older, more experienced. "I did not get any police," she denied calmly. "This is the first I've heard of them."

"You're hearing it now?"

"Were you caught?"

"Obviously not."

She put small gloved hands on top of the steering wheel, gripping it tight, staring out at the flood-lighted parking area about them. "I don't know who killed Lawrence Richey," she said slowly. "I had only been in that house a few minutes. I stepped into that dark room and stumbled over him. It frightened me. I was at the foot of the stairs before I knew what I was doing. And—you were there."

"And you," said Jerry grimly, "handled me smoothly."

A corner of her mouth quirked reminiscently. She looked at him squarely and without attempting to evade the issue, said calmly: "I did not know who you were. I had no business in that house. I might have been charged with the murder. You called me Richey's daughter—and I played up to it until I could get away."

"What were you doing there?"

"That," she said calmly, "is none of your business. And you won't find out because you dare not go to the police. Mr. Fiaschetti told me about you."

"What?"

"You live outside the law. The police will be glad to get anything on you."

ANTAGONISM THRUST an invisible barrier between them. Her chin was haughty, her manner imperious her eyes scornful. "You are a thief," she went on coldly, distinctly, bitingly. "A housebreaker, a dangerous character. If I did my duty as a citizen, I would turn you over to the police."

Jerry chuckled. "All right. Go ahead."

"I may," she threatened.

And in the silence that followed a step crunched outside. The bulky overcoated figure of Sergeant Smith loomed by the door.

"Damn!" said Jerry under his breath. Smith was the last man in the world he wanted to see at the moment.

Sergeant Smith opened the door and said apologetically: "Did I hear someone say they wanted the police? Oh—hello, Jerry. My goodness, this is a surprise. I thought you were home in bed asleep."

Barbara Todd kept quiet.

Jerry said cordially: "I hope your rheumatism is killing you, Sergeant. Are you following me tonight?" And back of that Jerry was wondering how long Smith had been lurking by the car. How much he had heard.

The sergeant's big pinkish face was innocent, placid. His voice was almost apologetic. "Following you, Jerry? How could I be when I thought you was home in bed? I was jealous of you snoozing under the covers. I got orders to come out here with a couple of men and look Sitto's place over. You're in a new car, aren't you, Jerry?"

"I have moods," said Jerry blandly. "The same car bores me sometimes."

"It must be them investments," Sergeant Smith marveled. "You got company, I see. Here he is now."

And there was Marvin Broadhurst, accompanied by a central office man, furiously silent, uneasy.

Sergeant Smith peered under the flopping brim of his old hat. "Why, bless my soul! It's Mr. Broadhurst! Marvin Broadhurst! I haven't seen you for—let's see—over a year, ain't it? I didn't know you knew Jerry Prince."

"I don't, very well," Marvin Broadhurst muttered.

"Tut-tut," Sergeant Smith chided. "You don't run around in the middle of the night like this with men you don't know very well, do you?"

Jerry answered for Broadhurst before that unhappy man said the wrong thing. "Business, Sergeant. I was getting some legal advice."

"About those investments?" Sergeant Smith inquired brightly.

"I was asking Mr. Broadhurst what I could do if nosy detectives from headquarters kept following and bothering an innocent man."

Sergeant Smith took off a glove and rubbed a cold ear vigorously. "Shucks, that's easy. The innocent man ought to go right home and go to bed. Ain't nobody would stand around outside tonight, bothering him. Who's the lady, Jerry? You ain't very polite."

Again Barbara Todd surprised him. Calmly, coldly, she said to Sergeant Smith: "Miss Barbara Todd is my name. This car belongs to me. There is no liquor in it. Is there anything else?"

Sergeant Smith drew on his glove again slowly. "Can't think of a thing," he admitted meekly. "Do you know Jerry very well?"

"Very well," said Miss Barbara Todd distinctly.

SERGEANT SMITH peered in at her again, his round moonlike face mournful, apologetic. "Sorry to have bothered you, miss," he said humbly. "Come on, boys. I guess we better look in Fiaschetti's place, an' then get back to town." And he plodded heavily across the ice-coated ground with the two detectives following him.

Barbara Todd waited until they were out of earshot. "Who are they looking for?" she asked sharply.

"The man who killed Lawrence Richey."

"Do they—suspect you?"

"It seems so," Jerry said whimsically.

And Marvin Broadhurst, by the open door broke in with suppressed anger in his voice. "You see? I knew something like this would happen! You've involved me! I'll find myself on the front pages next!"

"If you land in a cell, your wife can't get to you," Jerry comforted. "How long was Smith standing beside the car here?"

"Only a minute. They must have been waiting nearby. They didn't drive up. I thought I was under arrest when that dick came to my car."

"One of Sergeant Smith's playful little tricks. Miss Todd, isn't there another exit from Fiaschetti's office?"

"Yes," she agreed coolly, "but you won't find it."

"You've talked a lot," said Jerry. "I'm tired of it. Get out and show me that exit." His hand closed over her gloved wrist, drew it toward him, twisting despite her resistance.

"Oh—you hurt!"

Jerry eased a bit. His face was hard, cold. His whole manner had changed.

"You unspeakable brute!"

"Do you show me?" he asked evenly.

"I'll scream!"

"Scream—and I'll slap it down your throat!" Jerry said calmly. "A woman gets a break from me as long as she rates it. You don't any more. My neck is in danger. I value it more than I do that pretty red mouth of yours."

"Watch—watch what you're doing," Marvin Broadhurst warned uneasily behind him.

"Shut up!" said Jerry, without taking his eyes from the girl.

She was breathing fast; her face was flaming. Now her eyes dropped before his. Her surrender was as abrupt as had been her defiance. "I"ll show you. Let go of my wrist."

Jerry released her. "And no tricks," he warned.

She did not answer. Neither did she make a disturbance as she got out and followed, regarding him silently. Her manner seemed puzzled.

"What do I do?" Marvin Broadhurst asked across the hood.

"Drive my car down the road and come back in half an hour."

Marvin Broadhurst went with obvious relief. Jerry steered his companion toward the back of the big frame building. They passed out of the glare of the parking space. Sleet crunched softly beneath their shoes. His companion looked at him again in the same puzzled manner.

"Why do you want to go this way?" she asked.

"Do you know Grenville?" Jerry countered.

The startled look she gave betrayed her. She did. But she said: "No."

Lies! Everywhere he turned— But Jerry let her negative statement go unchallenged.

The blacker shadows at the rear of the house reached around them. Inside the orchestra was playing an exotic rumba. The small windows along the side of the building were heavily curtained. No porch. They turned the back corner of the house.

A crouching figure jumped to Jerry's side and a gun snapped hard into the small of his back.

"All right! Raise 'em!" a low voice snarled.

CHAPTER SEVEN
SUB-CELLAR SET-UP

JERRY STOPPED, lifted his hands. By the reflected light from the front he recognized one of Fiaschetti's strong-arm men, a burly, square-faced mug.

Barbara Todd stopped too. She showed no surprise, Jerry noted. She had known someone was back here. She had tricked him again, trapped him. Her words confirmed it. "A Sergeant Smith and two detectives went in the front a few moments ago," she warned calmly.

"Yeah. I saw 'em go. What're they after?"

"I don't know."

"Where you taking this guy?"

"He insisted that I show him the way we came out."

"He did? I'll take care of that."

"What are you going to do with him?"

"Never mind about that, kid."

"I forgot something I wanted to tell Sitto," she decided. "I'll go back."

"Suit yourself. But scram out of here."

Barbara seemed about to say something else, then changed her mind and walked swiftly along the shadowy back of the building. But she did not go in.

The trees had been cleared away behind the main building. Scattered in that area were a coal-and-wood shed, a large garage, and a long, low storehouse. Barbara Todd turned toward them.

Jerry's interest flared. Where was she going?

The gun prodded him. "Don't stand gawkin'! Keep your mitts up an' walk straight ahead."

Straight ahead carried them along the back of the building and on to the trees beyond. As they went Jerry noticed that Barbara Todd had entered one of the buildings. An electric light flared briefly through door cracks, and then went out.

His captor stayed just behind his shoulder, prodding him with the gun. They left the cleared ground, the vast rambling pile of the club building, and pushed through scrub pine and undergrowth.

There was no path. Jerry was no fool. This was trouble.

He blundered over a fallen tree trunk and almost sprawled flat. The gun jabbed him viciously as he recovered balance.

"Watch your step!" his captor rasped.

"Listen!" said Jerry over his shoulder. "Did Fiaschetti order this?"

"D'you think I'm out in weather like this for the fun of it?"

"Does Fiaschetti want me bumped off?" Jerry asked casually.

"Naw! We're takin' a little walk for our health. Swing to the left toward the beach."

Jerry had the humor to smile grimly. The hunter had been hunted. No need to wonder what awaited him at the beach. There was a boathouse in front of the club, fast motorboats moored inside. Sitto Fiaschetti would never make a move like this unless he meant business.

And that meant—death.

Jerry stumbled again—where there was no log—sprawling forward into pitch blackness. But this time he lurched up to the side, his left arm striking where the gun would be groping for him.

His elbow hit a forearm—and drove it aside. A startled oath spat out.

JERRY PIVOTED, hooking a fist from the hip in a smashing blow that had all his weight behind it. Driving to the spot that oath had come from. And lips, teeth and nose pulped and crumpled under his knuckles. The shock of it went clear to his shoulder.

A dull thud followed as his target struck the ground; and flame etched momentarily the trees around them as the ear-shattering roar of a shot hammered out. It missed. Jerry dodged aside, dove behind that yellow burst of flame.

His full weight struck a head and chest. His wrist struck a clenched hand and gun waving in the air. He grabbed the gun barrel, shoving it away. Pivoting catlike on the body underneath, he got both hands on the gun.

With a savage wrench he tore it from the hand.

A desperate heave rolled him off. Fingers clawed for his eyes. Jerry palmed the gun flat in his hand and struck. He felt the dull crunch of steel against flesh and bone—and limp weight sagged against him.

Panting, he found his small flashlight and surveyed the damage. His right fist was bleeding. Fiaschetti's man would never look the same around the mouth. But he was not dead. Jerry left him there and turned back.

No one seemed to have heard the shot. He was alone in the night as he ran back to the building where he had last seen Barbara Todd.

The door she had used opened readily for him. Inside it was dark, quiet, cold. It was the garage. His light showed three expensive cars and a truck. But no Barbara Todd. No explanation as to why she had come to this cold, deserted building after declaring her intention of seeing Sitto Fiaschetti again.

It was built of frame, like the huge main building. The roof sloped up to a peak. The floor was cement. There was no upper story, no cellar. A long tool bench ran along the back wall.

"You were too smart to come in here for nothing, sister," Jerry said to himself. "I don't get it—but there's an answer."

Yard by yard he quickly covered the interior of the garage. The cement floor was a solid slab without a break. There was no side or back exit from the building. No windows either, he noticed suddenly.

A big metal can stood at the end of the repair bench. Jerry lifted the lid and glanced inside. Old metal car parts, oily rags, crumpled papers filled it almost to the top. But something about that big metal receptacle struck a false note. Jerry stared at its gleaming bulk with a frown.

Suddenly he got it. The gleaming metal itself.

The work bench was dirty, dusty, but the can itself was surprisingly clean. Even the top, where dust would settle in a few days, was clean. It was not a new can either. The inside was oil-streaked, dirty. The debris had lain there for months by the looks of it.

The back had not been neglected either. He started to pull the can out to make certain. And it would not move. His strongest effort failed to budge it.

Jerry looked at the floor. A soft whistle escaped his lips. There were two dark spots there by the can. Fresh spots, dark red in color. Blood! And it had not been there long either.

A STEEL vise was clamped on the end of the bench. And it too was clean and free from dust. A sudden idea struck Jerry. He looked under the bench. Back of the thick corner leg, where it was almost invisible, a thin steel rod ran down into a bunch of dirty waste on the floor. Lifting the waste, he found a small slot in the cement, and the steel rod ran on down through the slot.

He turned the vise handle. It worked smoothly, silently on well-greased threads. And as it turned, the immovable metal waste can began to tip back away from the bench.

An extra high ratio of leverage had been used, for not many turns had to be made before the can was tipped back far enough to uncover a round hole in the floor, big enough to admit a human body.

His flash showed it to be a concrete-lined shaft with iron rungs set in the side. Ten feet or so down the circular shaft widened into an underground room.

It was dark down there.

Jerry hesitated only a moment. He had come unarmed, but in his pocket now was the gun he had taken from Fiaschetti's man. He had no idea what was down there. Barbara Todd evidently had come this way. He climbed down into the shaft.

At the bottom a light steel ladder let him down to a cement floor. He found himself standing in a small bare room about six feet square and as many high. And several more drops of blood were on the cement floor by the bottom of the ladder. Floors, walls and ceiling were cement. Straight ahead of him a narrow tunnel, head high, went for half a dozen paces and curved out of sight.

At his right, projecting from the wall, was what seemed to be the end of another vise. Its use was almost obvious. Jerry turned the handle. A slight creak overhead followed. The beam of his light flashing up the shaft showed the waste can descending again on the ingenious lever arrangement.

This then was why Barbara Todd had turned away from the house. And if her other actions were not enough to damn her, the fact that she knew about this was proof that she was far more intimate with Fiaschetti and the secrets of the South Bay Club than she had admitted. But the blood....

Past the curve, the tunnel straightened out again. It was lined with cement, dark with dampness. Here it was below the water level of the bay. The porus sandy soil all around was probably saturated with water.

Light bulbs were set at intervals in the ceiling, but they were dark.

He had gone some fifty yards when he came to a door blocking the passage. Not wood, easily broken, but of stout steel, studded with rivets. It had a handle that turned easily and noiselessly to his touch. The door went open and Jerry stepped over a steel sill into a huge cavern.

That was the first impression he got, and then he saw it was a room at least forty feet long by fifteen wide. It too was lined with cement. Shaded lights hung from the ceiling. A long wooden table stood in the middle of the floor. Chairs were scattered about. Half a dozen cots with bedclothes were against the walls. The air was warm, comfortable, dry, despite the damp concrete. And there was no one in it.

His flash showed other doors opening out of the room. He went to the nearest. It too was steel with a barred slit at top and bottom. It was locked. Jerry dropped to his knees and flashed the light through the bottom, slit.

A small room beyond had a rug on the floor, a desk against the wall, two chairs that he could see, and the end of a filing case. An office in there.

The next door he tried was unlocked. It gave into a small room resembling a ship's cabin, with a double-decked berth against the wall. Another door led into a small kitchen having an electric plate, shelves loaded with canned goods, and a sink with water faucets.

THREE STEEL doors were set into the wall at the end of the room. Strong bolts on the outside secured them. Jerry slid a bolt back—and looked into a prison cell. There was no other name for the bare, cement-lined cubicle with its wooden cot. The second one was filled with sacks, cases, cans of liquors. He passed up the third room. But as he turned away from it, a low gasping groan rooted him to the spot.

Another groan followed, then a muffled oath. The faint rasp of shoe leather on cement drew him to that third door.

He slid the bolt, opened it, flashed the light in. And with stunned surprised exclaimed: "What are you doing in here?"

Marvin Broadhurst, pale, disheveled, swayed unsteadily on his feet, blinked at the light. "Who—who is it?" he mumbled.

"Prince."

Broadhurst's tie was awry. His hat was gone, his hair mussed, his overcoat soiled. A red trail of blood came down out of his hair and ended over an eye. He was wild-eyed, fearful. But when he discovered who it was, Broadhurst became almost apoplectic. He staggered to the door, supporting himself by a hand against the wall. He shook a clenched fist.

"Damn you! You're behind this!" he blazed thickly.

"Hold your horses! Don't make so much noise!" Jerry ordered crisply. "What do you mean I'm behind this? How did you get down here? What happened?"

"You know what happened!"

"I don't."

"Then what are you doing here?"

"I just discovered this little paradise."

Marvin Broadhurst passed a hand over his forehead dazedly. "Where are we?" he questioned uncertainly.

"Underground. Beneath the club building. I thought you drove my car away."

"Take that light out of my eyes!" Broadhurst requested irritably. "I did try to drive away. But when I turned into the road, beyond the light, someone jumped on the running board, opened the door, and put a gun in my face. I was forced to stop. There was somebody else behind him; I couldn't see who. The next thing I knew I was struck over the head. I came to a few minutes ago in here. Dammit, this is like a prison!"

"Just as good as one," Jerry admitted.

Marvin Broadhurst gulped: "What kind of a place is it, anyway?"

"I'd call it," said Jerry, "the lower South Bay Club. Sitto Fiaschetti has the answer to the rest. And I'm on my way to get it."

"I'll be murdered yet!"

"There's a good chance of it," Jerry comforted. "Sorry I haven't an extra gun for you. We may need it."

"I don't want a gun! I want to get out of here!"

"You'll stick with me now and like it, Marvie, old son. You had your chance to leave. If you're caught outside now, they'll know something's wrong. I've got work to do before that happens."

"What are you going to do?"

"God knows," Jerry sighed. "Stick close and find out."

Jerry looked for the way up. And found it without trouble, beyond the door opposite the one through which he had entered. Another steel door with well-oiled hinges, opening inward. Metal dogs fringed it. It bore a close resemblance to a tight bulkhead on a ship or submarine. And the door through which he had entered was the same.

A NARROW passage led off to the right. At its end still another door barred his way. Past it an almost vertical flight of steps went up.

Up—up... And music, life, noise became audible, stronger....

That flight of steps terminated in a small cell-like landing. A tiny shaft of light drove through an aperture by his face. Looking through, Jerry saw the gambling room spread out before him. More of the patrons had left since he had last seen it, but enough remained so the room was by no means deserted.

Examining the wall he found a sliding panel with a small finger hole to work it. At his shoulder Marvin Broadhurst whispered hoarsely: "This—this is dangerous!"

"Quiet!" Jerry warned.

And he left the panel for a second flight of steps that went on up. Another landing at the top; another peephole. And through it, over the top of a filing case, was Fiaschetti's private office.

Fiaschetti was at his desk, to the left, talking. His voice was thick with suppressed rage. "So those lousy dicks are still down there, are they? Go back an' keep an eye on 'em, Slim! That fat slob, Sergeant Smith, has got something on his mind!"

And Slim, the gunman from the outer door, said doubtfully: "He's just pokin' around down there like he don't know what to do with himself."

"I know that guy, I tell you! He don't stick around like that for nothing! Wait—who's that coming?"

Jerry could see part of the anteroom door. It opened. A chunky, powerful, broad-faced man stamped in. He wore an overcoat, a hat pulled well forward, and was dabbing at his mouth with a bloody handkerchief.

Fiaschetti snapped: "What are you doing here so quick, Tony? You haven't had time to get him out in the bay yet. What's the matter with your face?"

Tony mumbled thickly from his bruised, broken mouth: "He got away."

"What!" Fiaschetti's leap to his feet was audible.

"It was black out there in the trees. I couldn't see. He fell over something, an' before I could get my rod on him again he was up and cracked me in the mouth. I tried to let him have it, but it was so dark I couldn't see 'im. My foot slipped on the ice an—an' I cracked my head on a tree. I just come out of it, almost froze to death. He took my rod an' lammed."

Fiaschetti loosed a string of epithets. "Hell to pay now!" he bit out. "Slim, you just come up from downstairs. You sure that guy ain't got to Sergeant Smith or any of his men?"

"Sure," said Slim flatly. "I been watching them. We got his car. He can't be very far away."

"Go down and tell Mike not to let him in the door. Tony, take a couple of the boys and look for him. Here's a rod. Burn him if you find him."

The two men left the room hurriedly. Fiaschetti was swearing in a monotone as the door closed behind them. His desk chair creaked as he sat down again.

Jerry felt like swearing himself. For now there was no doubt as to what was in Fiaschetti's brain.... Murder!

This panel would not slide. Jerry pushed. It swung open easily and Jerry ducked through the low opening into the room.

CHAPTER EIGHT
TORRENTS OF TERROR

FIASCHETTI, SITTING behind the desk, lunged to his feet as Jerry came through. He made a grab for a desk drawer—then froze, fingers on the desk edge when he saw Jerry's gun—and Jerry's face.

"Hello, Sitto," Jerry greeted casually. "Nasty weather to be sending those men out to look for me."

Fiaschetti moistened his lips, said nothing. His eyes were beady black coals. The shadow of uneasy fear rushed over his face.

"Sit down," said Jerry. "Keep your hands on top of the desk. Broadhurst, come out of there. Nice little place you have down there underground, Sitto."

Fiaschetti sank back in his chair slowly, placed both hands on his desk blotter. He said nothing. His eyes wandered, came back to the gun as Jerry half sat on the front of the desk.

"What's it all about, Sitto?"

The gun was resting across Jerry's thigh, pointed unwaveringly at Fiaschetti's chest. No threat was in Jerry's voice. His face was blank. And yet Sitto Fiaschetti, meeting his eyes, shivered. For in them once more was that wild air of lean, deadly aloofness, like a hawk about to spring and destroy.

Broadhurst, who had sidled fearfully into the room, caught some inkling of the silent threat in the air.

Sitto Fiaschetti stirred uneasily in his chair. His eyes slid again to the door. The rays of the ceiling light sparked from the big diamond on his finger in lancets of fire as the hand tensed, half clenched. A shiny film of moisture appeared on the pallor that had come to his face.

"I—I don't get you," Fiaschetti said.

"Of course not," Jerry agreed. "I didn't think you would, Sitto. But I can bring back things. Think hard now."

"I thought you had gone home," Fiaschetti muttered.

"Was that where Tony was taking me? Home! I wonder if I misjudged him."

Fiaschetti grasped at that straw, however slim it was. "Sure!" he nodded hastily. "You got things wrong. There's a mistake somewhere, Jerry! I—I don't know what happened—but we can settle it. Put that gun up. It might go off."

"You're right—it might. And don't call me Jerry. Prince is the name to your kind. I'm here to settle, Sitto. In full."

And suddenly Sitto Fiaschetti, of the flashing smile and voluble hospitality, dinner-coated, suave, threatening when he need be, was no longer all that. He was just a cheap, chunky, flashy fellow, too well dressed, who shrank in his desk chair like a trapped animal; who stared apprehensively at the expressionless young man before him, who tried to fawn, placate, reassure all in one breath.

"Sure, Mr. Prince! Anything you say! I'll go the limit with you."

"So I noticed," Jerry said drily. He leaned forward, held Fiaschetti with his glance. "You lied to me when I caught you with that girl, Sitto. You started gunning for me as soon as I got out of the room here. She lied to me outside. You sent that cheap gun to put me out of the way."

"No!" Fiaschetti denied, his black mustache twitching.

"Out in the lake for me, Sitto, wasn't it? Down on the bottom in the mud probably, with a weight to keep me there. Home—to the crabs and fishes. I wonder how many more you've sent out there, Sitto."

Fiaschetti's voice shook. The moisture was beading his face. A drop rolled down to his collar, but he kept his hands on the purple desk blotter. "I don't know what you're talking about!" he declared hoarsely.

Jerry slid off the desk edge, reached Fiaschetti's side in one swift, swooping motion. His left hand slapped to Fiaschetti's thick neck. And though the hand looked slight, and the body under the neck heavy, Sitto Fiaschetti came out of the chair as if driven by a spring. And not of his own volition. His heels hardly had time to touch the floor before he was dragged out from behind the desk like a dinner-coated dummy. His head snapped one way, his body the other as the steel fingers digging into his neck shook him ruthlessly, savagely.

A final jerk, a kick against one of his ankles, and Fiaschetti sprawled on the floor.

And at that instant the anteroom door opened and Barbara Todd entered.

SHE STOPPED short, red lips parting soundlessly. Fiaschetti was pushing himself to an upright position on the rug. His hair was awry, tie crooked, cheeks flushed with rage and fear.

"Shut that door and come over here," Jerry clipped out to her.

She reached back and closed the door without taking her eyes off the three of them. And she said a strange thing. "So you've come back?"

"Yes. It's a surprise, isn't it? I suppose they don't often come back."

A little frown put lines between her eyes. "What do you mean? At this hour of the night when they go home, they usually stay. Haven't you had enough?"

Jerry laughed mirthlessly. "Home! I see you and Fiaschetti both talk the same language. And you're right. I have had enough. All cards are coming on the table now. Sit down in that chair."

"No."

Jerry caught her arm and sat her down abruptly. She was up again an instant later, cheeks flaming, voice shaking. "You insufferable cad! Don't touch me again. I'll—I'll—"

Jerry slammed her back in the chair with a sweep of his arm. "You slippery little hellcat!" he said without great animosity. "Save your breath. Twice tonight is enough to go wrong on you."

She stayed in the chair this time, her eyes large, round, startled. Then appealed to Fiaschetti. "Can't you do something?"

"Shut up!" Fiaschetti snarled.

"She might as well," Jerry agreed. "You can't use her for murder bait any more, Fiaschetti."

"What do you mean?" she demanded hotly.

"I mean," said Jerry curtly, "that I've never seen a baby-faced moll who could put a man on the spot as smoothly as you did out back a while ago. You didn't take an extra breath when you saw me headed for the bottom of the bay."

"Oh!" She bit her lip, looked once at Fiaschetti, said nothing more.

"Broadhurst," Jerry directed, "take this girl down to that little hell hole underground. I'll follow with Fiaschetti, as soon as I look around the office and his rooms. We'll get to the bottom of this Grenville business—and everything else connected with it."

"Y-yes," Marvin Broadhurst stuttered in a queer choked voice.

It was so queer that Jerry glanced over his shoulder to see why. Marvin Broadhurst was standing stiff, still before the opening in the wall. Over one shoulder the dark snout of an automatic poked threateningly. Just behind, Grenville was standing with a sneering smile on his thin face.

"Drop it!" Grenville barked and moved over to where his back was to the anteroom door, still covering Broadhurst, using him as a shield.

Jerry slowly opened his fingers and let his gun fall to the rug.

Grenville's words abruptly changed everything. Sitto Fiaschetti, unleashed from fear, bounded to his feet. He was suddenly exploding with rage. "Pour it into him!" he shrilled. "Let the dirty rat have it!"

He pounced on the gun Jerry had dropped, leaped in close and brought his square-tipped fingers against Jerry's face with a smack that rang through the room. "This time you won't make it!" he promised with livid hate. "I'll do the job myself! Here! Now!"

Fiaschetti raised the gun.

Grenville shoved Marvin Broadhurst reeling and jumped forward. "None of that!" he blazed. "You fool! The police are downstairs! You'll make a mess of everything!

Damn an idiot like you anyway! Keep your head! I never know what you're going to do!"

AND STRANGELY enough, Fiaschetti heeded. But his rage did not lessen. Another chop of his hairy hand sent Jerry sprawling toward the chair where Barbara Todd sat. And Grenville did not mind that. It brought a smile to his thin lips.

He raised a hand, smoothed his small dark mustache. "So you're going to get to the bottom of this Grenville business?" he mocked.

Jerry shrugged. "I intended to. Why aren't you at home, Grenville?"

"Business," Grenville sneered.

"Here?"

"Yes. With Fiaschetti."

"Your valet is dead," Jerry said casually. "Your safe is cleaned out. Know who did it, Grenville?"

It was Fiaschetti who rapped out: "What? Carl dead?"

"Very dead. Shot from behind. I left him with Grenville a short while before. What happened, Grenville?"

"I don't know anything about it."

Surprisingly Fiaschetti's face had been swept by a momentary spasm of grief. His voice choked as he challenged Jerry. "How d'you know it?"

Jerry had not missed those visible marks of concern. And he wondered about them. His glance was thoughtful as he explained. "I went to see Grenville. I'd been talking to him a short while before. I don't think Grenville thought I was coming back. He wasn't at home when I got there. In his bedroom I found his valet—dead. And I've been looking for him since, to see who did it."

"Damn you! Don't suggest I did it!" Grenville cried furiously. "The gun that shot him can't be traced to me!"

"Right,—" Jerry agreed. "But—how do you know that, Grenville? Just what gun did shoot him?"

Grenville's face paled. He looked at Fiaschetti, who was staring at him silently. He quieted suddenly. "I don't know," he said. "The police will have to settle that. Perhaps there will be fingerprints."

"Perhaps," said Jerry. "By the way, what became of that little steel trench mirror that had a set of my fingerprints on it? It left your room about the time your man was murdered."

"I don't know what you're talking about," Grenville flared. "Fiaschetti, let's get them below, have this thing out."

"Sure," Fiaschetti agreed. "We'll have time down there. The cops are liable to come in here any minute."

Sitto Fiaschetti's thick, deep face was blank. No emotion of any kind showed on it. He did not look at Grenville as he spoke to him.

Grenville bit his lip, snapped at Barbara Todd: "You come down too!"

Barbara Todd was on her feet now, her coat wrapped around her slender figure. "You're going to get rid of them, aren't you?" she asked indifferently.

"Never mind about that."

A smile curved her red lips. A taunting smile, as she swayed over near Jerry. "It looks," she said sweetly, "as if you're going to learn manners after all, my friend. Too bad you didn't get some sense before it was too late. You spoke about the mud on the bottom of the bay. I'll think about you down in it when I'm having my breakfast."

Jerry winced.

Grenville laughed. "You're a cool one, girlie. Maybe I've been overlooking something in you. We'll get together when this is over."

Fiaschetti said impatiently: "Let's get below." He caught Broadhurst's arm.

A groan burst from the pudgy lawyer. "I haven't anything to do with this," he wailed.

Fiaschetti shoved him toward the opening in the wall, followed after.

Barbara Todd stepped in front of Jerry and snapped slender fingers in his face.

"Next time you meet a lady, treat her like one," she said—and her other hand came out of the front of her coat, and pressed something in his fingers.

BARBARA TODD had given him a gun; a small pearl-handled revolver that could almost be concealed in a hand. She'd done it so discreetly with her body concealing the move, that Grenville was unaware of it.

She said clearly as she turned away: "Luck to you, my friend."

"He'll need it," Grenville said.

"He's got it," said Jerry, and snapped the little gun up.

Grenville was caught off guard. His surprise, dismay, fear, would have been ludicrous any other time. He dodged instinctively and began to shoot. The room thundered and shook to the crashing reverberations of the big automatic.

A smashing blow against the side knocked Jerry back a step as he shot the first time. The light went out in a shower of glass fragments. Twice more, orange stabs of flame licked out—and suddenly there was silence.

Through ringing ears Jerry heard the metal side of the filing case crackle as something drove against it. And he

THE HOUSE OF VANISHING MEN 85

dared not shoot. Barbara Todd had been standing near there when the light went out. He groped for the little flashlight.

And her voice reached him, shaky, frightened. "Are you hurt?"

His side ached. He could feel blood soaking into his underwear. He seemed able to move well enough though.

"I'm all right," he told her and turned his flash on the file case. Grenville was gone. The dark opening in the wall gaped at him. Jerry plunged through it only a matter of seconds after Grenville had disappeared.

As he started down the steps he heard the hammer of feet below. His light just outlined Grenville's shadowy figure turning at the landing, going on down.

Jerry paused an instant at the panel and looked through the peephole. The shots had been heard in there right enough. The music had stopped. The players were gathered in startled little groups, some of them hurrying from the room. Sergeant Smith and his men were not visible. All that in a look—and Jerry pounded on down the stairs.

He had found out to his own satisfaction who had killed Carl, the valet. Grenville himself!

And already he was certain who had killed Lawrence Richey. But he had no proof of either.

He reached the bottom, plunged along the narrow passage. Grenville had not locked the first steel door. Jerry burst through. His light just showed Grenville dodging through the bulkhead door into the big underground room.

The light showed more too. Marvin Broadhurst was crouching fearfully against the wall, his eyes rolling with fright. He shrank back as Jerry burst by him. And not until Jerry tried the bulkhead door and found it secured within did Marvin Broadhurst seem to recognize who he was.

"What happened up there?" Broadhurst babbled. "Is anyone killed?"

"Not yet!" Jerry threw out at him.

"Let's get out of here then! We'll both be arrested! Have you got a gun? Who was that who ran— My God—what's that?"

The startled fright in Broadhurst's voice held Jerry still for a moment. A low rumbling growl, a sullen rush of water reached his ears. And the light showed a gray frothing torrent of water pouring out of a series of grated openings along the floor. Half a dozen streams bursting out with such force that they splashed back from the opposite wall.

In a matter of seconds the water was many inches deep around their feet.

CHAPTER NINE
HOUSE OF
VANISHING MEN

IN THAT moment Jerry realized why the door into the big room was built like a bulkhead—so it could be fastened tight against a wall of water. He thrust a finger into the flood rolling about his shoes. It was icy cold. He put the wet finger to his mouth. The water was brackish.

He remembered that they were below the bay level. This narrow passage was connected to the bay itself. No more perfect protection could be devised. In a few minutes the passage would be full, and that watertight door safe against attack from police or anyone else. Safe even from discovery, if the water rose before the first door at the end of the passage were discovered.

Marvin Broadhurst had floundered to the door. And his wail of fright rang hollowly above the rush of incoming water. "This door is closed! We're trapped!"

It had opened in, seemingly freely. Jerry had not closed it. But when he got there he found that Broadhurst was right. The door was tightly shut. They were trapped.

Jerry jerked at the handle—but the steel door did not move. He flashed the light over it, found something he had overlooked before. A steel arm curved back into the concrete wall; a movable arm, evidently fixed to close the door when the water was turned on, or when a lever or button was pressed somewhere else.

The ceiling was not far above their heads. The bay shore sloped up some from the bay edge. Gravity was carrying this water.

"There may be some space left near the ceiling when the water stops coming in," Jerry suggested. "It's a chance, anyway."

The water was halfway to their knees already, chill with ice and greedy death. There didn't seem to be anything more to do but wait.

And the thought that Grenville and Sitto Fiaschetti were free to get away was bitter. Out that other passage, into the waiting cars in the garage, and everything would be clear before them. Perhaps there were other exits also.

A sudden hammering of fists against the door jerked him around to it. He heard voices on the other side. He hammered back without much hope. No help could get through that door before the passage was flooded.

And then, abruptly, the door swung in against him. The bright beam of a powerful flashlight shot through.

And as water slopped and rushed over the sill into the dry space beyond, the startled voice of Sergeant Smith exclaimed: "What the devil's this? Water! The place is flooded!"

Jerry had never been so glad to hear a voice before.

Marvin Broadhurst staggered through, careened off Sergeant Smith and brought up in the arms of a detective. Barbara Todd was standing behind them, on the steps.

"Anyone else in there?" Sergeant Smith questioned.

"No," said Jerry.

"Great snakes, you look like a drowned duck! Lucky thing that girl knew this lever in the wall would open the door. What are you doing in all that water, Jerry? Where's that other fellow she told me about?"

"He's escaping! Follow me! Maybe we've got time to head him off! Back to the garage!"

"I've sent a man back there. She told me to. I guess nobody'll be coming through that water. Let's go."

JERRY USED the panel into the gambling room this time. And as he ran for the front entrance in sopping feet, the well-dressed patrons fell back, staring at him, calling to know what was the matter.

The doorman had vanished from his post. Jerry plunged out into the night, back through the floodlighted parking space toward the garage.

He gave thought to his injured side as he ran. It seemed to be a raking furrow across a rib—not bad.

The garage doors were still closed but the garage was lighted. He found a broad-shouldered detective standing by the tool bench. The waste can was in place on the floor.

"Has that can moved?" Jerry panted.

"Nope." The detective stared at him. Sergeant Smith came lumbering in, his big face beet-red, his vast middle shaking as he breathed heavily. "This night'll be the death of me!" he exploded. "Nothing, Kelly? Huh! I wonder if that girl was spoofing us."

Jerry twirled the vise handle and the waste can tipped back. Sergeant Smith's eyes popped as he saw the hole down through the floor.

"Glory nation! Where does it lead to?"

"Back under the house," said Jerry. "There are two men down there—Fiaschetti and a chap named Grenville."

"Who's Grenville?"

"A smart blackmailer and kidnaper; specialty, foolish women," said Jerry. "Broadhurst has a wealthy client who's put herself in his power. He's been trying to wangle the thing without bringing her name into it—or paying Grenville's price. He—er—engaged me to see what I could do about getting the evidence back."

Sergeant Smith mopped his face with a blue-bordered handkerchief and blinked. "Blackmailer, heh? I want to meet him. Was you in on that shooting upstairs?"

"Yes. They held me up."

"Huh! What for?"

"You'll have to ask them," Jerry countered. "Afraid Marvin and I were dangerous, I suppose." He was watching the hole intently as he spoke. So far there was no sign of anyone coming out.

Barbara Todd hurried into the garage. Her face fell when she saw they had had no success. "There's something funny here!" Sergeant Smith grunted. "Why didn't you go on to town in your car, Jerry?"

"How do you know I didn't?"

"Because I phoned in an' had a radio patrol watch the end of the road. Another fellow come bustin' out in your car. But I didn't think you'd get in a shootin' scrape. You told me you didn't have a gun."

"I didn't—then."

"I gave him a little gun of mine when I saw he was helpless and would probably be killed if something wasn't done," Barbara Todd said calmly.

"Kilt, miss?"

"Yes. Grenville meant to. It was plain what they were up to. And I think Grenville suspected me also."

"*Hmmm.* You? What could he suspect you of?"

"Of not being what he thought I was," Barbara Todd said calmly. "And as a matter of fact, I wasn't. Grenville blackmailed my sister a year ago, and she killed herself. I was in California. She wrote me a letter before she took poison, telling me why she was doing it. I came back here to settle with Grenville. She met him here at his club."

"His club, miss?"

"Yes," Barbara Todd said calmly. "His club. Grenville owns this place."

"What!" Sergeant Smith ejaculated.

And Jerry was no less surprised. No whisper of that had ever gotten out.

BARBARA TODD said coolly: "Fiaschetti was only a hired man, with a cut of the profits. This place was a mask for a blackmailing and kidnaping ring that paid far more than the club.

"I found that out after I convinced him I was a crook, and got him to put me on the payroll. They didn't know I was learning so much. Fiaschetti introduced Grenville to the right women here at the club—and Grenville did the rest. Their kidnaped victims were brought blindfolded down under the ground here and held.

"They made so much money out of it that Fiaschetti grew jealous. They often quarreled. Fiaschetti wanted to stop it, and merely run the club. But Grenville had some hold on him. I don't know what. I do know Fiaschetti's brother was forced to serve as Grenville's valet. I've heard them quarreling about that also. I think Fiaschetti and his brother were plotting to make some move against Grenville. You can find out when you get them."

Carl, the valet, Fiaschetti's brother!

That explained a great many things—and particularly the look of grief on Fiaschetti's face when he heard the man had been shot in the back.

Sergeant Smith shook his head. "This is a pickle. Here I go out on one case, get damp feet, rile my rheumatism, an' then run into a thing like this. An' it don't look like those fellers are coming out of there. Sure this is the only way they got to get out?"

"It's the only way I know," Barbara Todd said. And then she tensed. "Wait! I wonder if there isn't another way! They have a boathouse out there on the bay front. I've seen boats come into it, and no one walked up from the boathouse. But they were in the building after while. There may be a passage out to it."

"I wish you'd thought of that before," Sergeant Smith reproached. "Kelly, run out to that boathouse. I'll watch this hole."

"I'll go too," Jerry decided, and as he went out, Barbara Todd went along.

"So Grenville's valet was Fiaschetti's brother," Jerry said to her. The detective was ahead and could not hear them.

"Yes."

"I'd hate to be Grenville, down there alone with Fiaschetti," Jerry mused. "I think Fiaschetti suspects him."

"So do I," Barbara confessed.

"Where does Lawrence Richey come in? I think Grenville killed him."

"I'm sure of it," Barbara assented. "Grenville was blackmailing Richey, over some indiscretion of his daughter. When I found out he had a hold on Richey, I went to the man, laid my cards on the table, and asked for evidence. Richey was reluctant to give it. The girl is engaged and scandal would ruin it.

"But Richey told me Grenville was coming to see him tonight for money. He suggested that I be there in hiding to hear what was said. He gave me a key and said to slip in the back way as Grenville insisted they be alone. When I got there, I found Richey dead. Grenville must have come early."

"Doesn't make it hard to guess what happened," Jerry mused. "They quarreled. Perhaps Richey drew a gun. He was shot. Grenville took the money and left the jewels. He was either frightened or afraid they could be traced to him. And then he sent me there on a cock-and-bull errand and telephoned the police to surround the house. He gave me the gun he had been carrying. The one he shot Richey with, undoubtedly. If the police had found me in there, without an excuse, with the gun in my pocket that killed Richey, I wouldn't have had a chance."

Barbara Todd caught his arm. "What's that?"

The bay was just ahead of them; the dim bulk of the boathouse vaguely visible in the reflected light from the parking space. Kelly, the detective, had begun to run. His flashlight bathed the boathouse.

At the same moment the deep-throated roar of a motor broke on the night. A speedy motorboat was shooting out of the shelter into the bay.

Kelly began to shoot as he reached the front of the boathouse, firing steadily, carefully, while his powerful flash held on the boat.

Jerry, sprinting up, saw a dark figure crouched over the steering wheel of the motorboat.

AND THEN, without warning, an unbelievable and ghastly thing happened. A tongue of flame licked up from the middle of the boat, where the motor was. In the space of seconds, it lengthened, rose in a towering mushroom of livid fire, engulfing the whole middle of the boat.

For long seconds the craft raced ahead, a speeding torch.

They saw the man at the wheel clamber out on the bow, shielding his head with an arm. And the red light that beat over him was so intense that he was easily recognizable.

Sitto Fiaschetti rode with the fire.

Kelly said with awe: "I hit his gas tank!"

And then it happened—a terrific cataclysm of livid flame, sheeting high into the air. The boat disintegrated as the shock of the explosion thundered out.

And as suddenly as it had happened it was over.

"God!" said Kelly heavily. "He never lived through that!" Nor did he. Men from headquarters picked his blasted body out of the water later on.

But before that happened, before Fiaschetti's employees were rounded up for questioning, Jerry led Sergeant Smith and his men down into the garage shaft and along the tunnel. Grenville was yet unaccounted for.

They went cautiously, with drawn guns, expecting the door to be barred against them. It was not.

And they found Grenville in the little office off the big room. He was dead. He had been shot three times—in the back.

On the desk was a briefcase stuffed with letters and papers. The safe was open, empty of money, but rich in other evidence of interest to the police.

It was Jerry who picked up a small steel trench mirror from the rug by Grenville's body and handed it to Sergeant Smith.

"You should've used a handkerchief," Sergeant Smith reproved mildly. "That's part of the evidence. If I hadn't seen you handle it, an' your prints had been found on it, somebody might have accused you of murder."

Sergeant Smith tossed the mirror on the desk. "He must have been superstitious," he commented. "Carrying an unbreakable mirror for luck. But it didn't help him this time. He'd better have left it home."

Jerry smiled wryly. "I think," he said softly, "that you're right for once, Sergeant."

RED DOLLARS

STAINED WITH BLOOD THEY
WERE, THOSE CRIMSON-
SPATTERED BANK NOTES.
AND TO JERRY PRINCE—
PRINCE OF THIEVES—THEY
PRICE-MARKED A MURDER
TRAIL. DANGER DOLLARS
THAT COULD BUY DEATH,
AND DEATH ALONE, IN
THE HORROR MARTS OF
CRIMELAND.

CHAPTER ONE
RED BEARD

JERRY PRINCE wore a red rose in the lapel of his coat as he walked through the revolving doorway of the Hotel Royale. It was after nine in the evening. The brightly lighted lobby was still well filled. Jerry looked about sharply, taking in everything to the smallest detail. He noticed particularly the inconspicuously dressed, bulky-shouldered man loitering by the cigar counter.

That was Sam Winston, the house detective. Jerry knew all about Sam Winston—but Winston did not know him.

Out of the corner of his eye Jerry saw Winston glance indolently in his direction. But Jerry Prince's unhurried stroll toward the elevator bank did not deviate in the slightest. His face did not change its slightly bored expression. He knew what Sam Winston saw—a tall, athletic, carefully dressed young man who might have belonged to one of the best families of the city—not Jerry Prince, Prince of thieves.

JERRY SALUTED himself genially in a mirror, entered an elevator, and in company with several other passengers, he was shot skyward.

"Nine," Jerry murmured to the elevator boy.

At the ninth floor he was the only one to get out. He turned to the right along the deeply carpeted corridor.

There was no hesitation in his progress after he picked up the trend of the room numbers. 911—913—915.... Whistling softly between his teeth Jerry turned to the left at the cross corridor. There it was—939!

Jerry cast one swift look about. The corridor was deserted except for himself. The red globe above the fire-escape door at the end of the corridor glowed ahead of him. His knock on the door of Room 939 was almost gentle. There was no answer. Jerry rapped again.

This time he heard a slight stir inside. Soft steps came to the door, and halted. A voice inside demanded gruffly: "Who is it? What do you want?"

"Bellboy, sir," Jerry said politely.

"What is it? I didn't ring."

"Telegram, sir, marked 'Urgent.' The clerk thought it had better be brought up at once."

"Slip it under the door."

Jerry Prince smiled to himself in the dimly lit corridor. "Sorry, sir," he refused. "You'll have to sign for it."

The muttered comment inside the door was not pleasant. But after a moment the lock clicked. The door opened inward, revealing a bushy, red-bearded face, a pair of shoulders clad in blue silk pajamas. The man gave Jerry one startled look and then exclaimed accusingly through his beard: "You're not the bellboy." The door started to close hurriedly.

Jerry stopped it with his foot. His manner changed abruptly to curtness. "Open up!" he ordered. "I'm coming in."

But the blue-clad shoulder remained against the door. An explosive frightened note entered the man's voice. "What do you mean? I'll call the management and have you arrested! Get out! I'll ring for help!"

Jerry Prince's smile was hard, brittle, unworried. "You won't do it, Stanley," he said briefly. "Open up if you know what's good for you."

STANLEY WAS not the name written on the hotel register by the occupant of this room. Yet the name worked as if magic had been uttered. A startled gasp came through the bushy red beard; a gasp that had every element of fear and apprehension in it. "What do you mean, sir?"

"I mean Stanley," said Jerry Prince firmly. "P.O. Stanley. Do you open up or do I have to take steps?"

"Hey, you! Halt!" a voice shouted.

Slowly, unwillingly, the other stepped back. Jerry pushed the door open and entered, closing it behind him.

"That's sensible," he said amiably. "I knew you wouldn't want the door forced."

P.O. Stanley had stepped back against the wall as if he needed support. Inside the blue silk pajamas he was short, sagging, corpulent. His hands were soft and puffy. His eyes above the red beard were puffy also with dark circles under them. His red hair was thinning on top. Little red tufts stuck out of his ears. His nose hooked out of the red tangle like the curved beak of a fat vulture.

That was what Stanley reminded him of, Jerry Prince thought, with a faint feeling of disgust. A vulture gone fat and gross from excessive feeding on the carcasses of helpless victims. Only now the vulture was more like jelly. His puffy hands shook. His shoulders sagged. His knees seemed on the point of knocking together as he stared mutely.

"Who are you?" he got out thickly.

Jerry Prince's smile had an edge of steel behind it. "I am the eagle-eyed blood hound who's run you down," he said cheerfully.

Stanley's voice, which one could easily imagine had once been rich and pompous, authoritative and arrogant when the occasion served, trembled now in a half-whine of denial. "There's some mistake!"

"Nice for you if there is."

"I'm not—my name is not Stanley! J. Milroy Parsons is the name, sir. Who are you?"

Jerry Prince leaned against the door and contemplated the other thoughtfully. He was in no hurry. There was all night to do this. He felt no compunction about what was coming. Felt only gratefulness that the gods of fortune had smiled so generously.

What else but those same elusive gods of fortune could have led him to the race track this afternoon? What else could have jogged his almost photographic memory to probe beneath the red beard, seeing there a different man from the one the world about them saw? And to see at one sweep just what it might mean?

Jerry had lost his interest in the races for the afternoon. He had discreetly trailed the red beard in its perambulations from parimutuel machines to the wide concrete apron before the stands. Lost in the crowd behind this man's shoulder he had watched a pair of fine field glasses hover over the hooked nose, and hoped generously that Red Beard would win his bets. The more cash on hand, the better, for there had been only one thought in Jerry Prince's mind from the first moment that startled recognition had come.

Now he said: "Sit down on the bed there. Let me do the talking. Don't whine about the name you're registered under. It doesn't get over at all."

IT HAD all been very easy. For Jerry had simply followed the Red Beard from the race track to the hotel, had stood almost at Red Beard's shoulder when he asked for his room key, and had been greeted by the clerk under his assumed name. Then Jerry had retired to the public library and there scanned the newspaper files for three months back. Having found what he sought in the afternoon paper where he remembered it, he drove to the newspaper office and purchased an old copy of that particular paper. There had been a picture in it of a short, corpulent man with a small, neat, black mustache and wavy black hair. Jerry had the picture in his pocket now.

This man before him was not as corpulent as the one in the picture. His red hair was thin and scanty. His entire beard was red. But the eyes were the same—small, squinting, slightly protruding.

"Now then," said Jerry Prince calmly, "where's the loot, you blood-sucking old pirate?"

"I—I don't understand you!"

And it seemed in that moment that Jerry Prince became another man. The easy debonairness he had brought to the room vanished. He became cold, harsh, threatening. "You *will* understand me," he rapped out. "Where's that hundred and seventy-five thousand dollars you lit out with before your company failed?"

"My company failed?"

"Exactly! Stanley and Company, that once respectable firm of commission brokers, just off La Salle Street in Chicago. There had been gossip you were in difficulty. You denied it emphatically, but you knew the end was in sight. And while you urged your customers to deposit cash with you, you were getting your reserves together and making plans to skip out. Three months ago you vanished with a hundred and seventy-five thousand dollars in cash."

Stanley's pudgy hand thrust out as if to ward off the words. "No!" he cried. "You're wrong! You're insane! I recall that case. I remember descriptions of Stanley, seeing his picture in the paper. Stanley had black hair and a black mustache. You fool! Look at me! Any man in his right senses would know I couldn't be Stanley."

"I see you," Jerry Prince assented coldly. "Half an eye can tell you're a crook. At that you are clever, Stanley. You almost got by with it. No one knew that you had red hair when you came to Chicago. No one knew you kept your head shaved for that bushy toupée you wore. Your customers didn't suspect your mustache was dyed. You must have had something like this in mind for years, and when the time came you threw away your black toupée, let what little red hair you had grow out, let your red beard grow naturally. And you've been walking about openly ever since."

"A fantastic story!" the man on the bed denied vehemently. But there was fear in his eyes.

"Fantastic but for one thing, Stanley. You had to buy black hair dye for your mustache. You bought it at the same place all the time. That little hole-in-the-wall drugstore on South Halstead Street."

And then the lurking fear in those little eyes flamed into horrified unbelief. "What do you know about a drugstore on Halstead Street?"

"I happened to be in Chicago at the time you skipped out. I stopped in that drugstore for some razor blades. A little weedy clerk got to talking about your disappearance. He told me that a man who answered your description used to stop in there every month or so and purchase hair dye. Black hair dye, Stanley. He wondered if it could be the same man. And so did I—until I saw you this afternoon at the race track. I knew then. Where's the cash you skipped with?"

Stanley groaned, cast a harried, desperate look about the room. "I've said enough! I'll not talk any more!" he wrenched out stubbornly.

JERRY PRINCE took a step away from the door. His face was a cold mask. He leaned forward slightly, dropped his voice to a caressing sympathetic note. "Did you ever hear of the third degree, Stanley?"

The man on the bed stared at him, wide-eyed, uneasy, mute.

"They use rubber hoses, you fat little double-crosser," Jerry Prince said gently.

The man on the bed shrank, as the vision took form before his eyes. "You people wouldn't dare do anything like that!" he jerked out thickly.

He was under the impression that he was talking to a member of the police department. Jerry Prince was content that it was so. He smiled and said nothing.

Stanley wet his lips with the end of his tongue. "I'll pay you," he suddenly offered hoarsely. "Ten thousand cash if you'll walk out of the hotel for half an hour."

Jerry lifted his eyebrows. "So you've got it here with you?"

"N—no!" Stanley stammered.

"If I saw ten thousand cash right now it might be an inducement," Jerry mused.

Stanley seized on that faint hope avidly. "I can give it to you now," he offered eagerly.

"I thought so. Lying right up to the end, aren't you? If it's here in the room I can find it. How much have you got left Stanley?"

And the man who no longer denied he was Stanley seemed on the verge of collapse as he said dully: "I've only spent about five thousand."

"A hundred and seventy thousand left, eh? Trot it out!"

Stanley heaved himself off the bed with an effort. Hope had left him and strength had followed. He fairly tottered as he crossed the room to the closet. Slowly he opened the door, reached in, brought out a stout pigskin traveling bag.

"Here," he said huskily.

The bag was locked. "Where is the key?"

Stanley's trousers were across the chair back. He went to them, fished out a key ring, selected the key and held it out silently. He seemed to be moving in a daze.

Jerry Prince felt little sympathy for the man. The price of his honor was in this pigskin traveling bag which he unlocked and opened. There it was! Packet after packet of currency. None of the bills were large. All were readily negotiable.

Jerry lifted out a package of twenties, flipped through them and put them back. He paid little attention to Stanley's dragging progress over toward the bureau—until the crashing sound of a pistol shot brought him whirling around.

CHAPTER TWO
THE GIRL ANGLE

STANLEY'S PUDGY hand held a revolver to his temple. He swayed like a drunken man there by the half-open bureau drawer from which he had taken the gun. And then with staring eyes and mute lips, already dead on his feet, he fell full length to the floor. The revolver flew from his fingers and skidded across the rug.

Jerry Prince had expected nothing like this. Mechanically he noted the little spiral of smoke still curling out of the gun barrel; saw the blood starting from the hole in Stanley's temple.

Grim, mocking justice here—for Jerry Prince had not intended turning Stanley over to the police. It had seemed justice enough to set him adrift in the world without a penny.

And it was justice of another kind, too. Stanley's act had struck back hard, upsetting Jerry's carefully laid plans. That shot had certainly been heard outside the room. It would be reported, investigated. The police would come on the scene. To think was to act with Jerry Prince. He closed the bag, dropped the keys in his pocket and turned toward the door.

And just then there was a sharp knock on the panel!

Jerry stopped short, staring at the door. He was trapped in the room. He had no gun, never carried one if he could help it. But now he wheeled back and caught Stanley's revolver off the floor; and as he did that the door opened and a girl slipped into the room.

Jerry barely had time to slip the gun in his pocket. She was in the room, the door closed behind her before she saw him. And then she stopped short, eyes widening. "Where is Stanley?" she burst out. "I thought I heard a shot along here!"

Jerry had never seen her before, but he knew the type. She was almost thirty and life had not dealt gently with her. Her clothes were expensive, stylish. Her face was carefully made up. But behind all that she was hard.

And then she saw Stanley.

Her palm went against her mouth, holding it mute. The color drained from her cheeks, leaving them haggard, rouge-stained. But she dropped her hand almost instantly and spoke, brittle accusation in her voice.

"You killed him, eh? Who are you?"

"He shot himself," Jerry said briefly. "Who are you? Where did you come from? Have you got a room on this hall?"

"I was coming up to see him," she said in a husky voice. "I heard the shot just before I turned into this corridor. Never mind who I am. What are you doing here? That's his bag, isn't it?"

Jerry spoke to her in the only language a woman of her type would understand. "I'm going out of here, sister, and one shout out of you will make it just too bad."

"You killed him!" she guessed. "You're taking his money!"

And by that she lost her role of innocent bystander. She knew who Stanley was, knew his bag was full of money.

"Get back there in the closet! I'm going to lock you in!" Jerry snapped.

Fear grew in her eyes. "I can't stay in here!" she gasped. "They'll pin it on me!" She swung around to the door, panic-stricken.

Jerry caught her shoulder, stopped her. "Don't rush out there," he warned icily.

"I'm going!" she panted. "Don't try to stop me! I'll—I'll scream!"

JERRY'S ESTIMATING glance saw that fear had swept aside her hard-boiled self-possession. There was guilt of some sort on her conscience. She did not want to face the police. If she fled in her state of mind, she could not help but attract attention. He made the best of a bad business.

"Let me go first," he ordered. "Keep your mouth shut and do what I tell you to."

As he expected, the cold note of authority in his voice steadied her. "All right, go ahead," she said sulkily, stepping back from the door.

Jerry opened it cautiously, looked out. He was just in time to see the frightened face of a woman across the hall peering through her door at him. At sight of him she closed her door and locked it.

Two swift silent steps put Jerry across the hall at her door. He heard a frightened, agitated voice saying: "Hello—hello, is this the desk?"

Jerry frowned. The lobby was blocked now. Sam Winston, the house detective, would begin to spread a net in seconds.

Jerry's eye went to that red glowing bulb at the end of the corridor where a sign said, "FIRE ESCAPE."

The strange girl was out in the hall with him. "Hurry and get out of here!" she begged, with a note of hysteria in her voice, starting down the corridor.

Again Jerry's hand stopped her. "You can't go that way," he said calmly. "Get back there to the fire escape."

And again she obeyed without question. As she went, Jerry wasted precious seconds at the door of Stanley's room. Whipping out a handkerchief he scrubbed both sides of the door knob. That was the only thing he had touched.

The girl had opened the fire-escape door and darted out. "Put a handkerchief over your fingers," Jerry warned her. He wiped off any prints she might have left on the door and stepped after her into the cool night air, closing the door behind him with his handkerchief. The girl was already on her way down. Jerry followed, bag in one hand, handkerchief covering his other hand. Down, down, flight after flight.

Down seven flights to the bottom landing of the escape. The girl halted there, peering into the dark void below. Jerry put his weight on the counter-balanced ladder before them. It slipped down with a slight creaking of cables.

Up at the ninth landing the door opened. Heavy feet tramped on the iron work up there. A powerful flashlight stabbed down toward them.

"That's him down there!" a voice shouted. "Hey you— halt!"

Jerry swung over on the ladder, gripping the suitcase tightly. His weight brought the ladder down all the way. He descended nimbly, and the girl followed.

The rough cobblestoned alley came up to meet Jerry's feet. Overhead a pistol roared. The dull smack of the bullet on the stones close by marked narrow escape. Two more shots roared out, the reports echoing loudly in the narrow alley. Jerry saw a pedestrian stop at the mouth of the alley and peer in toward the excitement. Escape that way was impossible now. The girl dropped beside him.

"Back this way," he directed hurriedly.

TOGETHER THEY ran back into the alley. The flashlight beam stabbed after them. Shot after shot roared down at them, but neither of them was struck. Jerry turned into an intercepting alley and the light vanished, the shots stopped.

A red tail-light glowed dimly ahead. Cowl-lights outlined the shiny hood of an automobile. Too late to stop now—they had to pass. But as Jerry and his companion came abreast of the machine, Jerry stopped suddenly. It was a taxi. The driver's dark form was hunched behind the wheel. His pale face peered out at them. "Got a fare?" Jerry panted.

"Waitin' for one."

"You've got another! Ten-dollar tip in it. Drive out of here, quick!"

Jerry jerked the door open, pushed his companion in. He had to keep her away from the police if possible. She had his description. As he dropped into the rear seat, slamming the door, shoving the bag between his legs, the motor spun into life. The taxi lurched ahead. They careened out into a cross street, lurched around the next corner, sped on. The driver said over his shoulder: "Want me to dodge around a little?"

He was a wise one, evidently had heard enough to guess that they were fugitives.

"You'd better," Jerry agreed, and relaxed, regaining his breath, thinking hard.

That woman across the hall had gotten a good look at his face. The elevator man would be able to amplify it. They'd have a dragnet thrown out over the city in no time. Trains, boats, exit roads would be watched and this driver—he'd be able to identify Jerry, too. He seemed to know his business. He doubled around corner after corner, rolling fast, and presently he slid back the glass window and said over his shoulder: "Where to now?"

"Where do you want me to drop you?" Jerry asked his companion.

She had been sitting in taut, strained silence. At his question she turned her head, stared at him enigmatically. "I don't want to be dropped," she said in her husky voice. "I'll go with you."

"Not with me," Jerry refused flatly.

He saw a hard smile curve her red lips. "Oh, yes I will," she told him confidently. "Do you want me to put my head out the window and yell for help?"

And she had him there. He couldn't tell whether she was bluffing or not. He dared not risk it. He swore silently to himself. "Take us back to Third and Central," he directed the driver.

A hand closed on his wrist warningly. "That's near the Royale!"

"I know it," Jerry assented curtly.

"The—the police will be around there!"

Jerry smiled mirthlessly. "All the better if you decide to scream, sister."

THE TAXI swung into the curb at Third and Central. "Get out," Jerry ordered his companion curtly. He followed her and handed the driver four five-dollar bills. "Keep the change," he said, "and drive on."

"Thanks, buddy!" the driver exclaimed. He peered wisely at them for an instant, and then the gears rasped and he rolled away.

Jerry's companion looked cynically after the cab. "He'll go for the cops now that he's got his dough," she commented.

"Undoubtedly," Jerry agreed. "Suppose we part right here?"

"No," she refused stubbornly. "I'm going with you."

Central Avenue, where they stood, was in the very heart of the theatre and shopping district. At this hour of the evening the sidewalks were still crowded, the curbs lined with parked machines, and traffic was flowing busily on both sides of the street. Jerry cast one swift look about, saw nothing menacing at the moment, and said to his companion: "All right, come along. But try not to look as if a dick had his hand on your shoulder."

"Wise guy, aren't you?" she snapped. But nevertheless she followed at his side with a slightly more leisurely air.

Jerry walked one block, turned left.

His companion gasped: "That's the Royale right ahead! What are you going to do?"

"Keep quiet," said Jerry coldly. "You asked for it. Now like it."

He walked on until they were almost opposite the hotel. Police uniforms were visible over there. A traffic man was keeping them out of the street, warning passing machines not to stop. And on the side where Jerry and his companion walked, other pedestrians stood along the curb, staring.

Indifferent glances were cast at them as the line parted unwillingly. Jerry opened the rear door of a big blue sedan parked at the curb and tossed the pigskin bag in carelessly. Smiling pleasantly, he stepped in the car ahead of his companion and thrust a key into the ignition lock.

She followed, closing the door behind her. "Is this your auto?" she asked doubtfully as Jerry pressed the starter.

"Doesn't matter, does it? We're using it." And backing slowly, Jerry steered out from the curb and drove easily down the street.

Jerry ignored her as he thought fast. The carefully laid details of his program had been smashed. First, by Stanley killing himself. Who would have thought the man would do that? And now this girl at his side....

A frown broke across Jerry's face. She was an unknown quantity. Stanley had been alone at the race track during the afternoon. His room suggested no woman—and yet she had walked in without knocking.

She knew about Stanley's money and she was deathly afraid of being arrested in connection with Stanley's death. But she had stubbornly refused to flee when she had the chance. Jerry knew her type well enough to be sure she was not staying with him for safety's sake. She had fought fear to stay with him—and the money. That was it. The money!

She spoke first, in her husky voice. "Where are you going?"

"That," said Jerry, "depends. Where do you want me to leave you?"

She ignored the suggestion.

Jerry shrugged. "Never mind. What's your connection with Stanley?"

"I met him," she said shortly. "And don't put me on the pan. I'm not talking. What I want to know is—what are you going to do with that money?"

Jerry grinned. "You wise girls all sing the same ballad. Who rang your name on this cash register?"

"I did," was the energetic answer. "And I'm staying with you until we get it added up. Does that two and two make four?"

"Five, lady. You wreck me when you talk like that. But remember the coppers. You'd make a great splash on the front pages."

"I'll tell them," she said coldly, "how I found you in the room with Stanley. I'll swear you shot him. I'll shoot the works and swear you made me come along with you when you took it on the lam. Laugh that off, wise guy."

"They boiled you for an hour," Jerry admitted. "What do you want, stranger—a split?"

And her reply was startling. "All of it, sucker. When you get ready to talk business, put it on the line." She folded her arms and sat back firmly.

Jerry turned his head and smiled at her again, thinly. "What do I get out of it?" he asked gently.

"A chance to skip town and forget about it. That's better than a murder rap, isn't it?"

"Quite," Jerry agreed politely.

She flashed him the barest glance of uncertainty. "You don't talk like a mug," she commented.

Jerry swung the blue sedan around another corner. "Thanks for the compliment," he told her.

She frowned, set her lips as she stared through the windshield.

"Did you know what you were doing with Stanley?" Jerry asked her casually.

"I did."

"What?"

She flared: "You ask too many questions! I know what I'm doing with *you*."

Jerry hunched his shoulders, blew for a car ahead, and shot around it. "You seem to," he said briskly. "Going to call the police? There's one on the corner."

Her sulky lips set tight. She was silent as they rolled past the traffic man.

"You see," said Jerry. "Now what?"

"This!" she said through her teeth. Her hand had been under her coat. It slipped swiftly out as she spoke. The gun that shoved into his side was a small derringer.

The diminutive weapon was lost in her soft hand, but the dashlight showed its two barrels calibered large. Death pressed there against his side; death absurdly small but no less certain.

CHAPTER THREE
ENTER—SERGEANT
SMITH

JERRY TOOK his foot off the accelerator and let the sedan roll slower. "Put that thing up," he said evenly. "It might go off."

Her husky voice came back as even as his. "You're telling me, sucker? What do you think I'm carrying it for?"

"Well, one wonders."

"You won't call a copper," she said. "The heat's on you too bad. Drive out the North Shore Road. And take your hands off that wheel, try any tricks, and I'll let you have it—and yell bloody murder you're kidnaping me. I'll make it stick too."

"I wonder," Jerry mused.

The little derringer shoved harder in his side.

Jerry shrugged once more. "I believe you'd do it. The North Shore Road, you said?"

"You heard me."

"Then," said Jerry blithely, "the North Shore Road it is. And if any of your friends see us riding I hope they won't think I've picked you up."

She sniffed, said nothing.

Beyond the steamship docks the lighted boulevard swept around the north shore of the bay, through the smart country-club district, finally debouching on the sea coast and continuing north. There the houses thinned out, the lights vanished; fields, patches of woodland and open country stretched under the moonlight. Now and then the open sea was visible off to the right, the restless swells glinting faintly in the moonlight.

When the last house, the last light had been left behind, and the road stretched open and deserted in their headlight beams, Jerry glanced at his companion. "Where now?" he questioned.

"Straight ahead."

He drove on, a mile—two miles—five….

She had been peering about anxiously, evidently looking for landmarks. She said now, suddenly: "Turn just ahead by that dead tree to your right."

It was a narrow dirt road cutting off toward the beach. Jerry swung into it, rolled through the black shadows by a small patch of trees and came out into the moonlight again on open meadow land with the ocean visible ahead.

"Stop here," she ordered abruptly.

Jerry obeyed.

"Now get out," she directed.

Jerry sat still with his hands on the wheel. "Are you taking me for a ride?" She prodded him with the derringer. "You're safe if you don't start anything. Get out."

"I see," said Jerry softly. He slipped from behind the wheel, left the car and looked back in at her. She was faintly visible beyond the wheel, holding the derringer on him through the open window.

"Walk away from the car, sucker."

Jerry backed up slowly, a wry smile on his lips in the moonlight.

She slid over behind the wheel, stepped on the starter. And as the motor caught one white hand thrust out into the moonlight and waved mockingly. The big blue sedan shot off down the narrow dirt road.

JERRY STARED at the receding tail-light. He sighed, lighted a cigarette, returned to the road. Somewhere back in the patch of trees they had passed an owl hooted mournfully. Jerry watched the fast receding lights of his car with growing interest. The narrow dirt road seemed to run straight into the sea. There were no houses about. It looked as if she would have to turn by the beach and come back this way to reach the highway.

Jerry sighed again philosophically and reached in his coat. His hand brought out Stanley's revolver—and he stood there waiting for the return of his car. A bullet through the gas tank or a tire would do perfectly, he decided.

The sedan rolled almost to the beach. It turned suddenly to the right and began to parallel the ocean with undiminished speed. It had gone all of a quarter of a mile before Jerry took out his handkerchief, wiped the revolver and hurled it out into the night. Shrugging with resignation he began the dusty trek back to the highway. A second road evidently paralleled the beach—one she must have known was there. Before he reached the trees he saw the now distant headlights swing back toward the highway on a third road; and presently they vanished, heading back toward the city.

The highway was dark, deserted when Jerry reached it. He turned toward the city, striding briskly. Two miles and half a dozen machines had passed him, none of them halting for his uplifted arm. The heavy rumble of a truck finally came from behind and slowed to his signal.

"Thumbin' your way pretty late at night, mister," a gruff voice called from the dark cab. "Climb in."

And when Jerry had done so and the truck was rumbling on, the stocky driver hunched over the wheel grunted: "You don't look like a hiker. Dressed too swell."

"A pretty girl took me for a one way drive," Jerry explained.

"Huh—and she dumped you out? I'll be damned!" The trucker burst into a roar of laughter.

"Quite right," Jerry agreed amiably. "I'll know better next time."

The truck was bringing baled hay to the city market. It carried Jerry to within a block of Central, in the heart of the city. While it halted momentarily for a red light, Jerry shoved a five-dollar bill into the driver's hand, swung down, and stepped to the sidewalk.

The truck rumbled on, and a huge, ungainly figure which had been loitering against the building wall moved out across the sidewalk. A vast round pinkish face grinned at Jerry with childlike pleasure.

"If it ain't Jerry Prince! Just the young man I wanted to see."

Jerry's quick frown of annoyance shaded off into a smile of delight. "Sergeant Smith, the wonder sleuth," he greeted cheerfully. "You smother me with pleasure, Sergeant. Let's see—you haven't been under foot for at least forty-eight hours, have you?"

SERGEANT PINCUS SMITH, of the robbery detail at headquarters, was a massive man, colossal. He bulged fore and aft, top and bottom. Sergeant Smith was frankly fat.

"Let's take a walk, Jerry," Sergeant Smith suggested placidly.

Jerry Prince's eyes narrowed. Some of the humor vanished from his face. "Walk? Do my ears hear right, Sergeant? Are you suggesting that I might be under arrest?"

Sergeant Smith's vast pinkish cheeks shook as he sighed and wagged his head in denial. His childlike features showed hurt; his voice sounded even more so. "Now Jerry, you oughtn't to talk like that. What could I be taking you in for? Haven't been doing anything that would land you at headquarters have you?"

Sergeant Smith's little eyes, sunk deep in folds of flesh, were bland and innocent. Here was a man, one would swear, who lumbered through life mentally as well as physically.

And Jerry Prince, meeting that bland and innocent look, hoped his own face was as guileless. For he knew as few men did what foxlike cunning lurked behind that pinkish, childlike face. Sergeant Smith for all his artlessness, his fat clumsiness, had one of the keenest brains at headquarters.

"What would I be doing that would land me at headquarters, Sergeant?" Jerry asked with pained indignation. "If I remember rightly, I never have been on your books."

Sergeant Smith slipped a massive hand under Jerry's elbow. "Let's walk," he said. "I think better when I'm moving, Jerry."

As they strolled off Sergeant Smith admitted: "I don't know of anything against you, Jerry. Far as I'm concerned you've got a clean bill of health. Honest, upright young feller. But you can't blame me for being curious, Jerry. Guess it's envy. Here I work days and nights, and just barely get by—and you never work and always have the best in town. Makes me curious, Jerry."

"Investments," Jerry explained gravely. "I've told you about those investments of mine, Sergeant. They make me—er—a capitalist." Jerry chuckled. "Ever see one of the species?"

Sergeant Smith wagged his big head. "Sure I have, Jerry. But I never seen a capitalist yet that carried a gun under his arm. You wearing your rod tonight, Jerry?" As Sergeant Smith asked the question he ran one fat hand nimbly over Jerry's coat.

"No gun," Jerry said calmly. "But I have a legal permit for one, Sergeant. Like to see it?"

SERGEANT SMITH wagged his head again. "We've been all over that permit before, Jerry. Judge Casson issued it—just before he got run out of office. But that still leaves me wondering about that hay truck."

"Always wanted to ride in a hay truck," Jerry confided. "It's the poet in me, Sergeant. Back to nature and the rugged life."

Sergeant Smith shifted his battered old hat to the other side of his head. He blinked, coughed deprecatingly. "How'd you get out in the country where you picked up that truck?"

"What makes you think I was in the country, Sergeant?"

"You don't tip a driver heavy for riding a few blocks," Sergeant Smith said placidly. "I can find out from that driver, if you're going to be coy, Jerry. I got his number."

"The fact is," Jerry admitted, "I was out on the North Shore Road."

"How'd you get out there?"

"An automobile."

"Whose?"

"I wouldn't know whose car it is right now," Jerry said dreamily. "Cars have a way of getting about."

"Who's got it now?" Sergeant Smith asked bluntly.

Jerry grinned. "Leave me a few secrets, Sergeant. You're giving me a going over right here in the street. Just what's on your mind?"

Sergeant Smith managed to look shocked. "Why, Jerry! This is only a friendly little gabfest. Where was you between nine and ten this evening?"

"Riding," said Jerry casually.

"*Hmmm,*" said Sergeant Smith in his throat. "Feller was killed in the Royale Hotel this evening, Jerry. Up on the ninth floor. Lady across the hall seen one of the guilty parties going out."

Jerry Prince stopped. He took a cigarette from his pocket, put it between his lips, lighted it. His hand was steady as he held the cigarette. "Are you accusing me of anything?" Jerry asked slowly.

Sergeant Smith eyed him for a moment, and then shrugged his vast shoulders, with all the effect of a heave running through a mountain of dough. "Not accusing you of anything, Jerry. Seems to me you're mighty touchy this evening."

"Going to take me in?"

"I should say not. Nothing against you."

"Then I'll be on my way, Sergeant. Getting sleepy. Not used to staying up so late."

Sergeant Smith nodded mournfully. "That's right. Home's the best place for a man. Makes you wealthy an' wise, Jerry. See you again sometime."

Sergeant Smith waved a massive paw, and loitered at the curb as Jerry walked on. One immense hand was caressing the sergeant's jaw as Jerry turned the next corner and vanished. Not until then did Sergeant Smith move; and then he lumbered hastily across the street toward the winking neon sign that marked an all-night drugstore—and telephoned.

CHAPTER FOUR
MURDER TO MUSIC

JERRY PRINCE might have been a debonair young man returning from the theater or a call upon his best girl when he walked out of Sergeant Smith's sight. He did not change his pace or manner as he threaded a leisurely way through the nearby theater district.

Finally he hailed a taxi, gave the address of the apartment house where he lived. He smoked thoughtfully until the cab stopped before the tall stone building. As Jerry paid his bill he looked up and down the street. Fifty yards away, across the street, a small touring car was parked at the curb, lights out, as if it might be there for the night. By looking close one could just make out two figures in the front seat.

Jerry grinned to himself. "For twenty dollars could you stay here until morning?" he asked the driver. "And for another five tell anyone who questions you that you're waiting for me?"

"For twenty-five dollars, mister," the driver said fervently, "I'd park here until you grow a beard. Can I go to sleep?"

"Snore if you care to," Jerry chuckled, taking cash from his billfold.

"O.K.," the driver agreed, taking the money. "It may be a gag, but as long as I've got the dough, I'll stooge."

The driver, small, wizened, hardboiled, watched his fare enter the building, looked at the bills in his hand, and pocketed them, grinning. Pulling his cap over his eyes, he settled down in the seat.

The elevator was automatic at this hour of the night. Jerry ran the cage up to the sixth floor, let himself into a luxurious apartment done in modernistic style. He turned on the lights, tossed his hat on a divan, began to pace the room, wrinkling his brows in thought.

Every few moments he walked into the bedroom, which was still dark, pulled the curtain aside slightly and looked down at the street.

The room was at the corner of the building. By looking straight down one could see the cab parked at the curb and the small touring car across the street. It had not moved or displayed any lights. After the third trip into the bedroom Jerry stayed by the window.

He was rewarded. A full quarter of an hour after he had entered the building a dark figure stepped suddenly from the touring car and walked to the taxi.

Down there in the street the driver was dozing as an authoritative hand clapped down on his shoulder. A gruff voice asked: "What are you waiting here for?"

"Hey, lay off that shoulder!... Oh, hello, officer. Something wrong?"

"I said how long are you going to park here?"

"Got a fare inside, officer. No regulations against parking here. What's eating you?"

"Young fellow? Slimmish?"

"Yeah, that's him," the driver nodded. "Something sour about him? You want him?"

"No. When's he coming out?"

The driver shrugged again. "Should I know that? He said to wait for him."

The interrogator stepped back, scowled up at the brace of lighted windows on the sixth floor and grunted: "All right—forget you seen me if you want to keep healthy tonight." He walked back to the patrol car where his partner sat.

And from that dark window on the sixth floor Jerry Prince witnessed what had transpired and chuckled to himself. He left the window, went back into the big living room and scooped up his hat from the divan. He was at the door when the telephone rang sharply.

Jerry halted, hesitated, went to the telephone and answered it. The gentle voice of Sergeant Smith greeted him. "Surprise, Jerry! I thought I'd call up an' wish you happy dreams."

"No surprise, Sergeant. I had a feeling you might call. How's your rheumatism tonight?"

"Kind of achy, Jerry. It twinges me fierce now and then."

"Excellent, Sergeant. I don't know when I've heard anything that pleases me more. And now I'm going to plug the bell for the rest of the night, in case you have another brain storm and wake me up. I need my sleep. Early to bed, you know."

"I know, Jerry. It was me that taught you that, wasn't it? One thing more, Jerry, did you lose an automobile tonight? A blue sedan?"

"Why?"

"Found one. It sideswiped a car at the edge of the theater district. Dodged around the next corner and was abandoned at the curb."

"What makes you think it's my car?"

"Your license number, Jerry."

"You would have that, Sergeant. It may be my car. I haven't reported the theft yet because I didn't think it would do any good."

"A woman was driving it, Jerry."

"You don't say!"

Sergeant Smith's voice was patient, almost pleading. "You don't know who she was, Jerry?"

"If I did, I'd have gotten my car myself," Jerry said calmly. "Tell headquarters to hold it until morning."

"Bring it up tonight if you want."

"No. I'll be asleep. Won't answer the door. 'Night."

" 'Night, Jerry," Sergeant Smith sighed. "See you tomorrow maybe." The receiver clicked at the other end.

Jerry turned to the table, ripped a sheet from a magazine and fashioned a small paper plug with which he silenced the bell effectively. Then he left the apartment, leaving the lights on.

The building was silent, deserted, as Jerry walked to the back and descended the service stairs to the small hall inside the rear entrance. He unlocked the door and stepped out into the night.

A carefully tended plot of grass, a cement walk, a back fence—and one came to a paved alley running through the middle of the block. Jerry walked down that alley to the cross street, turned to the right and strode off briskly.

Five minutes later he entered an all-night garage, lifted a hand in greeting to the attendant, and drove out in a black coupé that rolled with the quiet whisper of great reserve power.

THE HOUSES on Creager Street were brick, sooty, dirty, old. Two and three stories high, they lined Creager

Street in a solid scabrous wall to right and left. Here—when the wind blew right—the sweetish, sickish odor of gas came from the river gas works not far distant.

If one went along Creager Street to Haystead, and continued on five houses, then walked under the stone steps with their iron siderails, and passed a guarded door, one came into Micky Moore's place.

Micky Moore had gutted the building behind the sordid front and remade it into spacious rooms in bright colors, with wide stairs, perfect service, excellent food. In short, Micky Moore's was one of the swellest little speaks in the city. And bustling about with a grin on his face and a ready greeting to all, Micky Moore played the perfect host.

Jerry Prince passed the guarded door, walked upstairs to the big oval, chromium bar.

There was music and loud talk at this midnight hour. No one paid any attention to him.

To the white-aproned barkeep he said: "Brandy."

He stood there drinking in tiny sips, looking about without seeming to do so. The usual scattering of uptown people were present, young and middle-aged, working hard at having a hilarious time. There were men, too, whom Sergeant Smith knew well.

A few moments later Micky Moore himself bustled in, saw Jerry and came over, all five feet two inches of his stocky person radiating cordiality.

"Glad to see you, Jerry!" And Micky Moore's handshake suggested he meant it. "How's it go?"

Slow," said Jerry. "But your brandy gets better all the time, Micky."

Micky Moore nodded, smiling. He said with a trace of pride: "If there's better stuff on the market, I'll try to get it. The next is on me, Jerry."

There was no sham about the glasses they raised to each other. Micky Moore ran an honest place, gave the best service he could, and never drank with a customer unless his heart was in it.

"You know pretty much what's going on," Jerry said casually as he set his glass on the edge of the bar.

"I guess so," Micky Moore nodded. "Most of them make this place sooner or later; an' I gotta lot of friends."

"Who lands booze at Elbow Point?"

Micky Moore raised his brandy glass slowly. His eyes were shrewd, questioning as he looked over the rim. "Not turning government on us, Jerry?"

"Be yourself."

"Sure. I know. That's almost over anyway. The boys started easing into other lines months ago."

"But they're still bringing it in."

Micky smiled, looked at the soft brown liquid in his glass. "Still got to have it for the trade, Jerry. What's on your mind? Didn't know you ever mixed in the booze game."

"I don't. Just curious."

"I know you ain't a talker," Micky said bluntly. "And I guess you could find out anyway. Dave Manners' boys use Elbow Point a lot, I've heard. It's handy to town and the highway, and for some reason they haven't been bothered there. Protection's good, I guess. Anything else?"

"Ever see a girl who looks like this?" Jerry carefully described his companion of the evening.

Micky Moore closed one eye shrewdly, opened it at the finish, and said promptly: "That sounds like Daisy Dulane, Dave Manners' girl. Not falling for that dame, are you, Jerry?"

"Women aren't my trouble," Jerry chuckled. "What about her, Micky? You know most of the dirt floating around town."

"She used to be a showgirl," Micky declared. "Dave met her on Broadway and took her out of the chorus. She's straight for Dave. No horsing around."

"None?"

"Well, serious, y'understand. Dave don't keep a rope around her neck, but they're both that way about each other. I've even heard Dave married her."

"Dave Manners hangs out at the Harlequin Club, doesn't he?"

"Most nights. He owns a cut of it." Jerry tossed a half-dollar on the bar top and turned away. "I'll do the same for you some time, Micky."

THE BLACK coupé whispered its way uptown and stopped across the street from the Harlequin Club. Jerry looked about for a moment, and then leaned forward and felt under the dashboard. From a clip, above the nest of wires behind the panel, he brought out a small thirty-two caliber automatic, snub-nosed and flat. It slipped neatly into a pocket tailored in the inside of his coat and strengthened clear to his shoulder so the weight would not sag. It was practically invisible.

The gaiety was rising to post-midnight heights when Jerry strolled into the Harlequin Club. The small dance floor was jammed. The tables were all occupied. Gaudily dressed waiters darted here and there through the gay cacophony; and the blonde at the check window smiled as she met Jerry's grin.

"Dave Manners here tonight?" Jerry asked her.

"He was. I think he went out a little while ago."

"Ah," said Jerry. "And would you be knowing where he went?"

"I would not," said the blonde with somewhat less cordiality. One gathered that the employees did not touch on such matters to strangers.

And at Jerry's shoulder a suave voice said: "A table, sir?" It was the headwaiter, immaculate, affable, and, behind that first impression, hatchet-faced and brassy eyed.

"I'm looking for Mr. Manners," Jerry told him.

A brassy stare ran over him impersonally. "Sorry, sir. Mr. Manners has not been in this evening. Is there a message you wish to leave?"

"You might tell him," said Jerry delicately, "that his cousin just dropped in from Denmark. And the next time you lie like that, watch your left eyelid. It jerks when you lie."

"What's that? Me lie?" The headwaiter reddened. His veneer of politeness fractured visibly. "Listen," he said. "Don't come in here talkin' like that, mister. If it's an argument you want—"

"What is it, Gus? Something wrong. Ah, good evening— Mr. Prince, this is a pleasure. I don't believe we've ever had you here before."

The speaker was a blond, slender young man with a soft, drawling voice and a handsome, youthful face, now smiling pleasantly. The pale, tapering fingers of one hand were plucking at a button of his dinner coat as he spoke, and smiled at Jerry. Jerry remembered those fingers from previous meetings. They might have been on a woman's hand. And this young man had features so fine and pale and regular that they were almost feminine. He had soft, curly hair, a gentle, drawling voice, and an extraordinarily gentle and winning smile as he stood there.

This was Babe Regan, partner of Dave Manners; and no hardened criminal who ever walked to the electric chair in Sing Sing had behind him a more blood spotted, ruthless career than he.

"I've just been asking for Dave Manners," Jerry said gently. "How is everything, Regan? Gambling much these days?"

Gus, the headwaiter, cut in with somewhat less acrimony: "He asked for Mr. Manners; and when I said Mr. Manners hadn't been in this evening, he called me a liar. I did not know the gentleman, Mr. Regan. I thought—er—"

Babe Regan's pale eyes, blue and dreamy, rested on Jerry Prince's face. "You made a mistake, Gus," he said. "Mr. Prince is always welcome here. Glad to answer any of his questions. So you're looking for Dave, Mr. Prince?"

"In passing."

"Rather late at night," Babe Regan suggested with a slow grin. "Anything in particular on your mind?"

"Sorry, no," Jerry shrugged. "I just don't like to be lied to, Regan."

"Gus didn't know who you were. He'll tell the truth after this." Babe Regan turned to his headwaiter. "D'you hear that, Gus? The truth always to Mr. Prince."

Gus's brassy eyes blinked once. He nodded, agreed colorlessly: "Sure. I'll watch it after this. Sorry, Mr. Prince." And with a nod he left them.

Babe Regan's face had been in profile. The side nearest Jerry had remained smiling, blank, but Jerry had the uncanny feeling that some signal had passed between the two men.

Babe Regan's soft, drawling voice said: "Dave hasn't been here this evening, Mr. Prince. I'm sorry I can't tell you where he is. If you will give me an idea of what you want with him I'll see that he hears of it. He usually telephones in sometime before we close."

"It's nothing. Wasn't doing anything and thought I'd drop in and talk to Dave. I feel we should know each other better."

"Fine chap, Dave. Best fellow I ever hooked up with in business. Come back in my office and have a drink."

"Sorry. I'll dash along. Thanks just the same."

Babe Regan was standing near the hatcheck window, the tapering fingers of one slender white hand still toying with the button of his coat when Jerry went out. Standing there—watching....

THE HAT-CHECK girl, speaking casually, had told the truth. Gus, the headwaiter, had lied. Babe Regan, drawling, smiling, friendly, had lied too. Dave Manners had been at the Harlequin Club and had left a short time before. His departure was being covered up.

Jerry walked leisurely to the corner where a drugstore was still open. At the back he found the telephone directory. He found the address he sought, closed the book, went out.

Some fifty paces away a dapper young man was looking into a darkened shop window. He had not been in sight when Jerry entered the drugstore, and had no apparent reason for being there now. Jerry smiled faintly to himself, put a cigarette between his lips and touched a match to it. Out of the corner of his eye, as he did that, he saw the dapper young man glance once at him, furtively, and then return to his studious contemplation of the show window.

Jerry flipped the match away, noted that no one seemed to be loitering around his car parked across the street in the middle of the block. He turned his back on his car, stepped to the corner a few feet away and walked down the side street with all the indifference of a young man not knowing exactly what to do with his time. He walked to the middle of the block, to the black mouth of an alley that cut to the right, behind the Harlequin Club. Two steps took Jerry into the blackness of the alley mouth.

He flattened himself there against the brick wall. His hand, as he waited, went inside his coat to the automatic nestling there; and slowly drew the gun out as the soft pad of hurrying steps came along the sidewalk.

The steps slowed as they neared the alley mouth. A dapper figure moved into view, peering cautiously into the blackness of the alley. Jerry was on it instantly, one hand grabbing for a coat lapel, the other shoving the automatic rudely in the dapper young man's middle. A yank, and they were both back in the shadows, the prisoner staggering as he was jerked along, stuttering in surprise and fear.

"Shut up!" said Jerry.

"What's the idea?" the dapper young man sputtered instead. "Is this a stick-up?"

Jerry transferred his grip from coat to neck. He screwed the gun deeper in the soft stomach muscles, shook his prisoner violently. "You rat!" he said pleasantly. "Did Babe Regan say you were apt to get a bullet in your gizzard if you followed me?"

"Babe Regan? Who's that, mister?"

Jerry put the muzzle of his automatic against his prisoner's lips.

"I'm going to ram this in your teeth and pry the truth out of you!" Jerry snarled suddenly. "What did Babe Regan tell you to do?"

"D-don't do that, mister! I remember now! It's all comin' back to me! I did see Babe Regan. He said somepin' about being curious where you were goin, an' asked me if I was walkin' that way to let him know. But, honest to God, mister, it's nothin' to me. The Babe said there was a ten-spot in it. I need the dough."

"What else did he say?"

"That's all. I'll swear, so help me—"

The frantic denial cut off short as Jerry snapped the barrel of his automatic behind the dapper one's ear. The dapper one went limp. Jerry let him down to the alley cement, frisked him quickly. And in a leather shoulder holster under one arm he found an automatic.

There was a pile of ash cans a few paces further back. Jerry lifted the limp figure, carried it there, removed the cover from one of the ash cans and stuck the dapper one in, doubled up like a jackknife.

Chuckling to himself, Jerry continued on through the alley to the next street, cut on back around to the black coupé and drove off.

But he was thoughtful now as he drove. Thoughtful over that dapper shadow which had been put on him. Babe Regan would not have done that without some cause.

THE TELEPHONE directory had given the residence of David Manners as Burlingame Drive. That was in the north part of town. It was a solid, substantial residential district, semi-smart, prosperous. The householders gave bridge parties, belonged to the country clubs, drove sizable cars. Dave Manners, solidly entrenched, free from most of the menaces of rival gunmen, was pleased to aspire to respectability in his leisure hours in that environment. Jerry recalled rumors that Dave Manners even belonged to the country club, keeping the underworld side of his life well in the background.

Lights were burning in Dave Manners' house. It sat on the corner in a huge lawn studded with big shade trees, a two-story brick house with a big glass sun porch in front. An automobile was parked at the curb in front. Through an open window of his car Jerry could hear the faint strains of radio music inside the house. Callers seemed to be inside, gaiety, life. It was not what he had expected.

He turned in to the cross street, left the curb lights of Burlingame Drive behind. He parked in dark shadows in the middle of the block. No pedestrians were about at this hour. Most of the houses in the neighborhood were dark. Even wheeled traffic was conspicuous by its absence.

Jerry walked back to the corner of Dave Manners' property. A hedge bounded it, and a sloping bank some six feet high led up to the yard level. Jerry vaulted the hedge, slipped up the bank and cut through the dark shadows under the trees toward the rear of the house.

He could hear the radio music plainer now. It was turned on to heavy volume, was coming through a side window of the house, up several inches from the bottom.

The window curtains were all drawn. The radio drowned out any other sounds inside the house. Jerry walked to a screened back porch. The kitchen at least was dark. The screen door opened with slight creaks and let him on the back porch.

The back door was locked. Jerry brought out a small bunch of keys and began to fit them to the lock there in the darkness. One key finally opened the door. Food odors met him as he stepped inside. But the kitchen was silent, dark. The crashing, static-shot blare of the radio continued in the front of the house.

If there were other sounds, they were not audible. A tiny flash raked one silver sliver of light about the room, and Jerry moved across it. He made no more noise than a sliding shadow as he opened a door and passed through.

The sliver of light showed a cramped butler's pantry. Beyond that Jerry found a dining room, dark also. A door opposite him stood open an inch or so, admitting a crack of light. Jerry slipped to it, straining his ears for what might lie beyond; but only the raucous tintinnabulations of the radio came to them.

The tiny light beam in his hand swept to that door, dropped to the floor, halted, focused. Quick, noiseless steps took Jerry there. He stopped, staring, lips pursed in a noiseless whistle.

The light driving through that crack glinted on a dull crimson stream snaking under the edge of the door. Blood—fresh blood there on the floor.

JERRY PRINCE stood still for a long moment, staring at that fresh blood by his shoes. Slowly he drew the automatic from his coat. Wrapping his handkerchief about his left hand, he abruptly shoved the door open and stepped through.

He came into a library, carpeted with a thick oriental rug, furnished in heavy walnut. Book shelves lined the walls. And there on the waxed and polished hardwood, beside the costly, thick-piled oriental rug lay the source of that scarlet rivulet.

He was lying on his face, arms doubled under, one leg thrust out grotesquely. Sleek oiled hair glistened black in the overhead light. Saffron skin and slight, stocky stature marked the victim an oriental. The head lay nearest the door; and by a wound on that head he had died.

A second door, forward in the right wall, was closed. In this room, as in the others, the curtains were drawn. And through it throbbed the incessant tumult of the radio.

Jerry reached down, turned the body over. The neck he touched was limp, warm. Death had struck only recently at this Japanese house boy, struck violently at the sleek black-haired head, via some heavy blunt instrument. Struck more than once too. The saffron-hued knuckles of the right hand were bloody, bruised, as if the boy had clasped the back of his head to protect it. Straightening, Jerry saw the print of bloody fingers on the door just above the knob.

It required no great effort of imagination to bring the scene back vividly. The boy had run across the room; run from death close behind. The first blows had not felled him. His bruised, bloody hand had reached out for the door knob. And one final crushing blow had stopped him, felled him there by the door.

Jerry wondered if the radio had been playing while that happened.

He turned from the body, crossed the room cautiously; and as he passed the big walnut library table he noted a set of books on it. Books that had been held upright between heavy bronze book ends. One of them had been removed and several of the books had fallen over. The book end rested at the edge of the table—and by its heavy bronze base a smudge of fresh blood stood out vividly on the polished wood. This then was the bludgeon which had felled that slight saffron figure.

Still using the handkerchief over his fingers, Jerry opened the closed door, finding a small entrance hall, lighted, deserted. Opposite him another door stood wide.

And from that lighted room across the hall the crashing static, the raucous music of the radio blared full strength.

Jerry walked into a drawing room, suddenly no longer concerned as to who might be there before him. He knew. Death had swept through this house and the living were not around.

He was right. There stood the smart radio cabinet against the opposite wall, hurling its mechanical crescendos at him. There were the curtains stirring gently by the open window outside which he had stood. There, there....

Even Jerry, warned by the gruesome find in the library, was not prepared for it. Dave Manners, suave member of the higher underworld, lay on the floor near the radio, as still, as inert as his dead house boy. Dave Manners, wearing a dinner coat and white shirt, his hair parted neatly in the middle, a big diamond on his left hand gleaming coldly.

Dave Manners lay on his side, eyes closed. He might have been asleep. But a great red splotch stained the snowy expanse of his shirt front; and lying lax in his right hand was a small nickeled revolver. And there too on the floor by Dave Manners was a packet of twenty-dollar bills, blood-stained.

And the radio throbbed on loudly; playing for death as it must have played for life. Jerry swung to it abruptly with distaste, shut it off.

CHAPTER FIVE
"CALLING ALL CARS"

DAVE MANNERS had been shot in the chest. With his handkerchief Jerry pulled the revolver from the limp fingers, sniffed the end of the barrel. It had not been fired. Manners had died before he could defend himself.

The blood-streaked packet of money told its own story. Dave Manners had been in here with Stanley's money; must have had that packet of bills in his hand when shot. Daisy Dulane must have been here with him too. Had she done this?

Jerry dismissed the thought quickly. That stylish, sophisticated young woman had never killed the Japanese house boy. She would not have brought the money to Dave Manners, her man, and killed him too. Was she in the house somewhere, still, lifeless, too?

Jerry's eyes went to the packet of twenty-dollar bills. His lean face went hard, bitter; his mouth pressed in a tight line. The blood smeared on them suddenly seemed symbolic. Innocent investors had suffered when their money had been stolen. Stanley had died over them. Dave Manners lay here dead. Death had struck in the next room—

A dry, choked sob behind Jerry caused him to whirl abruptly.

He had put up his own gun. His hand streaking for it froze at the edge of his coat in obedience to a choked order.

"Stand still!"

"You!" Jerry exclaimed.

Daisy Dulane stood in a doorway, gun in her hand—a regulation-size automatic this time.

The girl's face was a drawn mask of grief, of suffering, out of which dark eyes blazed at him. Dark eyes, tear-wet, for she had been crying.

Her voice came thick, choked.

"So you found me?… Keep your hands away from your side!"

"I thought you were dead," Jerry said.

She ignored his words. "And you killed him!" she said in the same choked voice, brittle with accusation. The gun was steady in her hand as she took two steps forward from the doorway.

Jerry's eyes narrowed ever so slightly.

"I didn't kill him," he said. "I just got here. Where have you been? What do you know about this?"

"You're lying!" she said tonelessly, and took another step forward.

"You should know it's the truth. You've been here in the house."

But Jerry had the feeling he was talking to a wooden woman.

"You killed him!" she repeated, dully.

"Why should I kill him?" Jerry argued calmly. "I don't work that way."

"You killed Stanley for that money! You followed us here! You killed Dave!"

FOR THE first time since they faced each other, her eyes left him, dropping for an instant to Dave Manners' body between them. She glanced at the packet of bills. A visible shiver ran through her. Her eyes came back to his face quickly.

"Where is it?" she flared at him. "The money! What did you do with it?"

"Haven't seen it," Jerry denied. "Snap out of it, Daisy Dulane. If I killed him, and had that money, why should I be here? I'd be on my way—wouldn't I?"

That last sharp question, barked at her, did what patient argument would probably have failed to do. It drove through to her reasoning mind.

Jerry could see the sudden intelligence in her eyes. She stared at him for a long moment, silent; and then gradually the automatic in her hand began to quiver as she trembled.

One more dry sob escaped her, the last he was to hear that night. She swallowed, and then, "If you didn't kill Dave, who did?" she whimpered.

"I don't know who killed him," Jerry said slowly. "I found him this way. The Japanese boy is dead too. Does he belong here?"

She nodded. "Togo—Dave's man."

"What happened?"

She fought for control and somehow got it. "Dave met me here," she said through stiff lips. "We talked for a little, and then I started out to my car for my purse. On the front porch someone caught me, put a handkerchief with chloroform over my nose and mouth. I heard them open the front door and go in. A moment later a shot. And then—and then the chloroform got me. I didn't know whether Dave had fired that shot or been hit by it. I came to in the next room. I was sick, weak. I suppose," she confessed dully,

"I fainted before the chloroform put me out entirely. The radio was playing loudly. It had not been on before. I heard it turned off. I knew then they had gotten Dave. He would have been with me if he had been all right. I got this gun and found you standing over Dave. What are you doing here? How did you get here?"

"I asked a few questions and connected you with Dave Manners. He left the Harlequin Club a short while ago. I remembered he had a house. It seemed obvious you two were here."

"Who are you?"

"Doesn't matter, does it?"

"Dave said only one man in the city answered your description and would be after Stanley's money. Jerry Prince."

"Check," said Jerry. "And now that we know each other, take my word for it I didn't kill Stanley. It was suicide. What were you doing in his room?"

She stared at him silently. Without warning she began to laugh, high-pitched, mirthless laughter. "I went to Stanley's room to see when I was to leave the country with him."

JERRY FROWNED, looked down involuntarily at all that was left of Dave Manners, whom she had obviously loved. Her laugh broke off abruptly. "I was Dave's wife. I met Stanley at the Harlequin Club. He fell for me, got drunk, talked. It seemed a shame to let so much easy money leave the country."

"Leave the country?"

"Stanley had it all planned. He was financing a Central American revolution, putting up money for guns and a chartered boat. The men he was backing promised him he would be the fair-haired boy down there, and need never worry about the United States extraditing him for anything. He fell for it."

"Revolution," Jerry said slowly. "Are you sure about that?"

"Didn't Stanley tell me everything when he thought I was going with him?" she said scornfully.

"Who was he backing?"

"A greasy little ex-dictator called Doctor Juan José Alvarado who put over one revolution about fifteen years ago, lasted six months, was kicked out, and is ready for another try. It seems the country's ripe for it. There is a General Porthos y Lopez in on it too. They have rounded up a bunch of exiles, chartered a little tramp steamer and are getting ready for the blow-off. But the man," said Daisy Dulane, "who roped Stanley into it is named Dennis O'Malley."

"The devil!" Jerry exclaimed. "I've heard of O'Malley. He's fought all over Central America."

Daisy Dulane nodded. "That's the man. And he travels with a little machine-gunner whom Stanley called Brisky. Stanley was helping to finance them all. And now he's dead, and Dave is dead, and the money is gone."

"You say there was more than one here tonight?"

"Yes. I thought at first it was Babe Regan with his men."

"Dave Manners' partner?"

Daisy Dulane laughed ironically, still under the stress of taut emotion. "They were partners but it didn't mean anything. Babe Regan wanted Dave's place. He wanted me too, until I made Dave see it. They had a terrible quarrel over that. The Babe convinced Dave it was all a mistake. But he's hated me ever since."

"Did he know the money was here tonight?"

"I don't think so, but he knew we were after it. He wanted to be cut in on it. Dave told him this was our own play."

"He knows something," Jerry told her. "He had me followed out of the Harlequin Club a little while ago. He lied to me about Manners."

"Dave didn't tell him anything. I know that. But if he heard Stanley was dead, and a woman was connected with it, he could guess the rest. But," said Daisy Dulane, "if Babe Regan was at the Harlequin Club before you came here, he couldn't have done this."

"He might have had time to get back," Jerry mused. "You don't know how long you were out?"

"No," she admitted.

"He's smooth and he's dangerous," Jerry said.

"I hate him more than any man alive!" Daisy Dulane said bitterly. "And if he killed Dave, I'll kill him if it's the last thing I do in this life!"

"I don't think he did it," Jerry said suddenly. "If he had the money, he wouldn't bother much about me. Why should he? I'm not crossing his game any other way."

And Daisy Dulane nodded. "I think you're right. If Babe Regan had that money and knew Dave was dead he wouldn't have anything to worry about."

"Then," said Jerry, "that leaves Dennis O'Malley and his friends. They're probably the only others in town who knew anything about the money. They would be the only ones to follow it so quickly. Did O'Malley know you were hooked up with Dave Manners?"

SHE FROWNED. "I don't know," she confessed. "I've seen Dennis O'Malley and Brisky at the Harlequin Club. They knew I was a regular there. How much else, I don't know. They never told Stanley anything. He would have passed it on to me right away."

"Did Dennis O'Malley ever say anything to you that would indicate he suspected you?"

"We never spoke," she shrugged. "But I've caught that big red-headed mug looking at me as if he'd throw me to the sharks with a smile. He didn't like me. I think he was afraid I was chiseling in on Stanley's money."

Jerry grinned faintly. "And of course you weren't."

"Sure I was!" she flashed. "Just like you. Stanley was a sucker who stole it from a lot of other suckers. He would have lost it quickly enough anyway."

"Did it ever occur to you that the people who lost the money might be entitled to it again?"

"No. And it didn't occur to you either," she retorted quickly. "I've got your number from Dave."

"I doubt if he knew much to tell," Jerry sighed. He stepped back. "I'm going now. I suggest you get away from the house and let the police find Dave Manners. It may save you some awkward questions."

"Where are you going?"

Jerry smiled, said nothing.

"You're going after Dennis O'Malley," she charged. "Still after that money."

He shrugged.

"Then I'm going with you."

"No," Jerry refused. "I've had enough of you—"

And the next instant he dodged aside, snapping: *"Put that down!"*

For Daisy Dulane's face had suddenly blazed bitter and watchful. The gun in her hand had whipped up and was pointing directly at him. She was going to shoot. He read it in her face; he knew it.

And she shot, directly at him it seemed; one crashing report that shattered the quiet about them.

That shot was so close that tiny particles of burnt powder stung Jerry's face. The biting fumes of hot powder gasses struck his nostrils. And then it seemed to Jerry that everything went mad, unexplainable; for behind him as it happened, a second shot roared out. He felt a jerk, a cold numbing pain in his left arm as he pitched sideways.

And Daisy Dulane shot a second time. All that in a brace of mad seconds.

She was across Dave Manners' body. She was beside him, pumping another shot from her gun. But not at him. She fired past, beyond....

Jerry caught her arm. He knew only that he had been wounded. "What the devil is it? Are you crazy?" he demanded roughly, shaking her. One look showed a hole drilled through his left coat sleeve above the elbow. The numbness passed as quickly as it had come. Hot pain crawled up his arm nerves. The slow trickle of warm blood started on his skin.

"The window!" Daisy Dulane flung at him. She gestured with the automatic.

And Jerry realized as he spun about that she had not been shooting at him at all. She could not have missed at that distance. She had fired past him at something else. He had not been mistaken about that shot behind him. But the window beyond the radio at which she pointed, the window that was up some inches from the bottom, was no different than it had been when he entered the room. The curtain was still down, swaying gently in the breeze. No one was there. Nothing.

"I saw a gun shove through!" Daisy Dulane panted. "It was pointing at your back! I—I shot at it."

And there through the window shade were the two holes the bullets had made.

"Get over against the wall!" Jerry snapped at her.

Without waiting to see whether she obeyed he ran for the front hall, lunged out onto the big, glassed-in front porch.

ENOUGH LIGHT came from the house to show that the porch was deserted. Jerry jerked the porch door open, dashed down the front steps and around to the side of the house, his automatic ready.

But the gun was useless. There was no one there by the side of the house. Enough light came from the street to show in silhouette anyone running across the lawn. Jerry strode toward the back of the house, using his flashlight recklessly at dark shadows by the shrubbery and trees. Still he saw no one. And before he reached the back of the house the whir of a starter beyond the street intersection, followed by the sound of a racing motor, stopped him and drew his attention that way. He heard the crescendo of the gears as the machine departed swiftly; but it was across Burlingame Drive on the side street. He could not see it. It was gone by the time Jerry got to the front porch.

Lights flashed on in a house across the street. Back on the side street near his parked car he heard a window slide up. Those crashing shots had been heard all over the neighborhood. There would be a quick investigation. Jerry went into the house almost as swiftly as he had left it.

Daisy Dulane was in the front hall, strained, tense, gun ready in her hand. "Did you find anything?" she asked. "Did—did I kill him?"

"There was no one out there."

"Oh—I'm glad. There's blood on your sleeve. Are you hurt badly?"

"Nothing that can't be taken care of later. Let's get out of here. Those shots were heard. Before we know it we'll be under arrest for killing Dave Manners and his boy."

She clicked to it instantly. "Dave picked me up in his car and brought me here. The keys are in his pocket. I'll—I'll have to get them."

"Anything of yours in his car?"

"My purse."

"Leave his automobile there. Mine's around on the side. Black coupé. Run!"

She went without further argument. Jerry lingered briefly. With his handkerchief he rubbed the metal of the light switch he had touched; did the same to the front door knob, and that of the porch door. Certain that no marks of betrayal were in the house, he left that front porch, cut across the side yard, and slipped behind the wheel of the long black coupé. Daisy Dulane joined him there a few moments later, breathing hard from her haste. Jerry drove off swiftly.

Daisy Dulane was tense beside him, as a harsh voice came suddenly from under the dash. "Calling Car Number Seven—Calling Car Number Seven. Go to the corner of Burlingame Drive and Twenty-ninth Street. The residence of David Manners. Shots and suspicious turning on and off of lights reported by neighbors.... Calling Car Number Seven—Calling Car Number Seven. Go to—"

Jerry reached under the dash and shut off the radio. "I was looking for something like that," he said grimly. Then he swore softly under his breath.

"What is it?" his companion asked.

"I forgot that packet of twenty-dollar bills. It may be they can be traced back to Stanley, linking that up with Manners."

"I doubt it," Daisy Dulane asserted. "Stanley told me he used every precaution to make sure no one could trace the money he was carrying."

"Good. That will be some slight help." Jerry reached forward and turned on the radio again. For a couple of minutes there was nothing. Then—

"Calling all cars—calling all cars. Stop any automobile driving at suspicious speed and question the occupants. Double murder at the house of David Manners. Parties responsible drove automobile from neighborhood at high speed. Direction unknown. Examine all—"

Jerry shut off the radio again and reduced their speed. "They work fast these days," he remarked briefly.

"What are you going to do?" Daisy Dulane questioned uncertainly.

"Get this car out of sight as soon as possible, if we can make it without being gathered in. This section is clear anyway. The patrol car's at Manners' house."

CHAPTER SIX
TAILED

DRIVING AT that slow, sedate pace, they threaded a way through the dark streets. Now and then other automobiles passed them, all driving at higher speed. Jerry chuckled as the third one rushed by. "Quite a few good citizens in a hurry to get home to bed tonight will get the shock of the evening when they're stopped and questioned."

Not two blocks further on Jerry's hand clamped tight on the steering wheel. A small touring car with two men in the front seat swung out of an intersection just ahead of them and turned the way they were going.

He heard her sharp indrawn breath. "That's a patrol car, isn't it?"

"It is," said Jerry. "Sit tight."

He drove on at the same sedate pace, neither increasing nor slacking it. The patrol car slowed down. Jerry blew the horn, swung out to pass it. Slowly they crawled alongside.

The two officers in the front seat peered into the black coupé intently. Jerry didn't even look at them. His companion, sitting very still, glanced out idly for a moment and then looked ahead again, unconcerned, uninterested in those blue uniforms. The black coupé drew ahead; and the patrol car swung in behind them. For two blocks the glare of its headlights followed; then the patrol car turned north into a side street and was gone.

Jerry heaved a big sigh of relief. "That was close," he commented. "They were looking for trouble."

The strain had told on her. Her voice was slightly unsteady again. "Do you think they're through with us?"

"Looks that way. I'll get off this street and see if they turn up again."

Jerry did that. The patrol car did not reappear. And after a tortuous course which put three more miles on the speedometer, Jerry turned leisurely into an all-night garage. The lanky attendant stepped forward, grinning.

"Howdy," said Jerry, opening a door and getting out. "Gas this one up, Charlie. Get my other car out. I want it."

Charlie took an elevator to regions somewhere above. They could hear him maneuvering a car onto the elevator. He came down in a few moments with it. Another coupé, this; a light, cheap model, gray in color.

They got in, drove out in silence. Daisy Dulane spoke first. "You're like a magician. You pull things out of hats. How many cars have you around town?"

Jerry grinned. "This happens to be the last one. I change cars rather often. Nothing like having an extra or two. When you need one, you need it bad."

"What," asked Daisy Dulane sharply, "are you going to do now?"

"I'm going to find this Dennis O'Malley and see what he has to say."

"Stanley told me once that Dennis O'Malley was staying at the Capitan Hotel. And what about your arm? You haven't done anything for it yet."

"I think the bleeding's stopped. The wound can't be very deep. I can use it all right and it doesn't hurt much. Don't want to waste time with it now. We'll go to the Capitan and see what we turn up."

THE CAPITAN HOTEL was on Central Avenue not far from the point where that main artery met the water front and the bay. It was a medium-sized, medium-priced hostelry catering to the men off the boats, transient passengers and the general life of the water front. Jerry stopped openly in front, went into the dimmed lobby. Several guests were sitting in the chairs, smoking, reading. They glanced at him, paid no further attention. The clerk was busy with some records in the cashier's cage at the end of the desk. He came out, looked inquiringly at Jerry.

"Is Dennis O'Malley registered here?" Jerry questioned.

The clerk shook his head. "Mr. O'Malley checked out several days ago."

"He left a forwarding address, I suppose?"

The clerk sighed. "Just a minute, please." He stepped back into the cashier's cage, consulted a card file. Returning, he said: "Mr. O'Malley's mail is to be forwarded to the steamer *Rampa* at the Seventy-seventh Street dock."

"Thanks," said Jerry and turned away.

Just outside the door a deep voice said cheerfully: "Jerry, you'll be the death of me yet. I thought you was home in bed sound asleep—with the telephone plugged."

The speaker was Detective Sergeant Pincus Smith, looming there on the sidewalk beside the hotel entrance, his vast pink cheeks, childlike and innocent.

Jerry stopped short. His smile was a trifle forced. "I can think of no one I'd like to see less," Jerry said honestly. "You ruin my night, Sergeant."

Sergeant Smith pushed up the sagging brim of his ancient hat and beamed. "Flatterer! If I didn't know you,

Jerry, I'd think you meant that. I've got a quarrel to pick with you, Jerry."

"Pick it."

"You're running wild tonight," Sergeant Smith said solicitously. "You feeling feverish, or something like that, Jerry? Or mebbe you been drinkin' too much. You've got a taxi driver ticking off a meter out in front of your apartment building."

"I see you've been watching me, Sergeant. Naughty, naughty! A great big grown man like you running around playing peeping tom!"

Sergeant Smith's vast reddish jowls drooped. "Now, Jerry, that ain't no way to talk to me. I just happened to be driving by with you on my mind, Jerry. I was thinking about your damaged car, an' feeling sorry for you. I saw the lights on in your apartment and the hacker waitin' out in front. I figgered you might be going out, so I asked him if he was waiting for you. He said yes. And," Sergeant Smith confessed dolefully, "I waited some too. And I bet you weren't up there all the time, Jerry."

"No," said Jerry. "I went out the back way. Forgot all about that taxi driver, Sergeant. My memory's poor."

SERGEANT SMITH nodded agreeably. "I've noticed that before, Jerry. I'll bet you can't even remember where you got that car there at the curb."

"Who said it was my car, Sergeant?"

"Mebbe it belongs to the young lady, Jerry. Only why ain't she driving it? You could 'a' knocked me over with a feather when I saw you two rolling down Central Avenue a few minutes ago. 'That can't be Jerry,' I says to myself. 'He's home in bed asleep. The telephone's plugged. He told me so himself.' I said to the boys over there in the car, 'I'm calling myself a liar, boys, an' it hurts; so let's follow that little gray coop an' settle it.' An' we followed it," Sergeant Smith sighed. "An' darn if it wasn't you, after all, Jerry. It just goes to show when you go to bed early at night there's no tellin' what you'll get up with. Who's the young lady, Jerry?"

"You wouldn't be interested, Sergeant. It's a delicate matter. Er..."

Sergeant Smith's big childlike face managed to look shocked. "Jerry, you aren't philandering at this time of night? Was that what you went in the hotel for?"

"You've got a nasty mind, Sergeant. My friend—er—Miss Skolinsky—thought she had left her purse in the lobby earlier this evening. I just dashed in to inquire about it."

Sergeant Smith beamed again and thrust two fat thumbs under the belt encircling his vast expanse of middle. "Lochinvar," said Sergeant Smith admiringly to the night about them. "Sir Walter Raleigh, and all that. Jerry Prince, the ladies' delight. It isn't every girl can get her young man to run errands for her at this time of night, Jerry."

"No," Jerry sighed, "and it isn't every man who finds you back of his shoulder every time he turns around, Sergeant. You're getting to be a disease."

"You will have your little joke," Sergeant Smith chuckled. "Got your gun with you this time, Jerry?"

"I have," said Jerry, moving quickly from Sergeant Smith's outthrust hand. "Don't bother to frisk me for it. I have the permit too."

"I'll bet you have, Jerry. A nice respectable young man like you wouldn't go out with a gun unless he carried a permit to show to the first copper who asked questions. But why a rod now, Jerry?"

"I got worried, Sergeant. Stick-ups, and all that, due to the inefficiency of the police."

"My, my," Sergeant Smith marveled. "I didn't know about all that. You're a voter and one of our leading citizens, Jerry. I take a great interest in you. I'm going to see that you're protected; the rest will escort you home. You can feel perfectly safe."

"I'm not going home, Sergeant."

"Where are you going, Jerry?"

"I'm going to take the young lady home."

"I knew you'd get ashamed of yourself, Jerry. That's the place for her. Introduce me."

"She doesn't like ham coppers."

Sergeant Smith shook his head lugubriously. "You'll be the death of me yet, Jerry. I'm gettin' too old to stay up all hours of the night with my rheumatism an' be talked to like this. Where did you say you were going from here, Jerry?"

"I didn't say," Jerry replied succinctly. "Am I to understand you're going to follow me?"

SERGEANT SMITH pushed his hat forward over his forehead. "You got it wrong, Jerry," he mourned. "We're going to protect you. You might do something with that gun you'll be sorry for. So we're going to stay right behind you an' see you tucked safe in bed. You make me nervous, Jerry, running around town this late at night."

"You're getting in my hair, Sergeant."

"Now, Jerry...."

Jerry grinned. "I was just ragging you, Sergeant. Don't take it seriously. If we're going for a ride, let's go." He turned to the gray coupé.

"That was a copper," Daisy Dulane said as they drove off. Her voice was strained, jerky.

"It was," Jerry nodded. "That was Sergeant Smith. He looks like a big fat numbskull—and he can outthink anything they've got on the force. He's dangerous."

"And he's after us?"

A glance in the rear-view mirror, and Jerry said: "Not only after us, with us. He's following us in a patrol car. I bumped into him earlier in the evening, thought I'd outsmarted him. He should be home in bed now. He's stirring around tonight with more than half an eye on the Stanley case. I think he suspects I have something to do with it. He spotted us driving down Central Avenue, tailed us to the hotel in the patrol car, and now he's sticking with us."

"If he suspects you, why doesn't he arrest you?"

Jerry grinned. "Because he doesn't know anything he could make stick. He knew it was no use trying to tail me under cover, so he's doing it in the open. He suspects we're up to something and he's going to horn in on it."

"If we could have left him back there...."

"I didn't want to," Jerry told her. "He would have gone in the hotel and found out from the clerk that I was asking for Dennis O'Malley. He would have gotten O'Malley's address and been there with us, or ahead of us."

"You sound like you still intend to see O'Malley tonight."

"I do."

"I don't see how," she declared flatly.

Jerry chuckled. "Does seem kind of complicated, doesn't it, with Sergeant Smith glued on behind."

She looked out the back window. Her face was drawn, her voice troubled. "We might as well give it up."

"You watch," said Jerry cheerfully.

CHAPTER SEVEN
DEATH SHIP

TEN MINUTES—A quarter of an hour passed while Jerry drove the small coupé in a leisurely, tortuous course through the city streets. At no time did he even approach the speed limit. The headlights of the patrol stayed never more than a hundred and fifty yards behind. Daisy Dulane made one more attempt to find out what was in Jerry's mind, and failing, fell silent.

Twice Jerry drove by the freight yards near the bay. The streets were dark and shadowy down here, the houses mean and squalid. Jerry began to whistle softly through his teeth as he cruised back and forth through the neighborhood. Now and then they could hear the whistles in the yards. Jerry finally quitted that locality and began to drive as if heading for a certain destination.

Within a few minutes the street they were following ran into a highway heading out of town. It paralleled the railroad tracks. Just ahead of them were the winking red and green caboose lights of a freight train that had just pulled out of the yards. A full half-mile ahead of those caboose lights they could see the brighter glow of the locomotive headlight.

Daisy Dulane stirred in the seat beside Jerry. "Are you going to drive out in the country?" she demanded. "This is the highway south."

Jerry chuckled, "We won't go far."

"I can't see what you're up to," she complained.

"You will," Jerry assured her.

They were still inside the city limits; they would be no safer outside. The city police who manned the patrol car carried deputy sheriffs' commissions for the entire county. They could be followed and dealt with for many miles yet.

Jerry began to drive faster. They crawled up on the freight train, passed the caboose and left car after car behind. And still Jerry drove faster.

Daisy Dulane looked behind once more. "They're keeping up with us," she stated hopelessly.

"You can't beat Sergeant Smith," Jerry admitted.

Houses began to thin out as they caught up with the head of the long, lumbering train, which was picking up speed slowly.

They drew parallel with the engine, drew on ahead. The tracks were not more than fifty feet away. The glaring headlight of the gigantic freight locomotive lighted the tracks and the ribbon of cement over which they were speeding. The white painted danger signs of a road crossing stood out in stark silhouette an eighth of a mile ahead. They could see the red danger signal swinging back and forth. As they drew near to it they could hear the clangor of the automatic warning bell.

They came to the cross roads....

And Jerry slammed on the brakes suddenly, cutting their swift pace instantly. He wrenched on the steering wheel, made the car turn on two wheels, dropped into second gear, pressed the accelerator down hard. They leaped forward in gear for the railroad tracks.

The crossing was bathed in dazzling light. The onrushing locomotive was less than a hundred yards away, coming fast when they made that turn. The whistle began to shriek wild warning. Heedless of the danger, Jerry kept going. The locomotive and their car seemed to be converging on the same spot at the same instant. Daisy Dulane cried out in involuntary fear, caught the door handle as if to open it and leap out.

"Sit still!" Jerry yelled at her.

Frozen, she poised there on the edge of the seat, her eyes staring past him out the open door window at that monster of steam and steel rushing inexorably at them.

TIME SEEMED to stand still. Their automobile seemed to have lost its momentum, to be slowly crawling. Their front wheels passed over the tracks. They were suddenly square ahead of the engine; and the engine was not more than a hundred feet away. It towered high above them. They could see the spurting steam from the piston packing, the red sparks shooting high from the squat stack; and the dazzling silver headlight beam lanced the night overhead like a giant arm reaching out to hold and crush. The violent blasts of the whistle were deafening in their ears. The crossing under them was shaking, and they could feel it.

Jerry's foot jammed the accelerator hard against the floor boards. For one awful moment he knew sick doubt. It seemed they could not possibly get across it in time; that in the space of the next breath the terrible crash would come. And then they were suddenly off the tracks and the great engine roared behind them so close it seemed to brush their rear tires. The shrieking whistle fell silent. The steady rumble of the freight cars over the crossing became the dominant sound.

Jerry shifted into high once more, carefully lifted his hands from the steering wheel and drew a deep breath. "I thought for a moment we weren't going to make it," he admitted.

She sank slowly back on the seat. "You're a fool!" she said shakily.

"I know," Jerry admitted cheerfully. "I wonder what Sergeant Smith thinks about it. He'll have five or ten minutes to decide while he's waiting on the other side of the crossing. It's the only way we could lose him. Now we'll go places and do things."

They were not beyond the range of the city street system yet. Driving full speed, they entered a network of dirt and macadam roads. Twisting, turning, driving at high speed, Jerry put the crossing far behind and out of sight before that long, slowly lumbering freight train could possibly have dragged its caboose past the crossing.

And Jerry cut through toward the south shore of the bay.

The city lay in a cup around the west end of the bay. The Seventy-seventh Street dock was on the south shore, far out. Years before a grain-exporting company had run a fill through the marshy land out there and erected great concrete elevators. They had dredged the dock basin alongside the elevators. Igniting grain dust had blown the huge ferro-concrete grain towers into a mass of twisted wreckage. They had not been rebuilt.

The dock was still there, far from the rest of the harbor facilities. It was seldom used. A weed-bordered macadam road sided by rusty railroad tracks crossed the quarter of a mile of low, swampy ground to it. Jerry turned into that road with his car lights out.

Faint moonlight showed the way. Jerry drove with his engine throttled slow and silent. Weeds and cattails grew in rank profusion beside the causeway. The spot was lonely, uninhabited, desolate.

The gaunt, fire-blackened wreckage of the grain towers loomed starkly before them. In the moonlight they could see the dock basin, the ship warped alongside the concrete mole. It showed no lights.

Jerry stopped the car in the black shadows by the end of the ruined grain towers. He got out. Daisy Dulane joined him at the front of the car.

"Stay here," Jerry told her.

"I'd rather be with you. This place gives me the creeps."

Small wonder, Jerry thought. Dank air from the lower bay, smelling of fish and salt, stirred about them. Their feet scraped faintly on the concrete as they threaded a cautious way around piles of wreckage along the dock.

THE SHIP was tied at the further end. What was left of the grain towers piled up at their left to a jagged, uneven rim, sharp against the night sky. They slipped through shadows by the base of the grain towers. Beyond the dock the bay surface glinted restlessly under the moonlight. The ship's superstructure, funnel and cargo masts limned darkly against the sky. Beyond, far beyond, across the bay, the lights of the city winked and glittered around the west shore.

It was a ratty little steamer, barely big enough for deep-sea work. Leprous patches of rust showed plain as they came abreast of it. A gangplank slanted steeply up to the midships deck. Still no light had appeared. The gangway was deserted, and the deck rail above it.

They halted opposite the gangway. She whispered: "Where is everyone?"

"I'm going aboard and see. Wait here."

Jerry stepped into the moonlight flooding the concrete mole. She followed at his side stubbornly. And at the foot of the gangplank her fingers closed convulsively on his arm.

"Look at that!" she whimpered.

Jerry saw it at the same moment. From the shadows under the gangway a pair of legs thrust out into the moonlight. Jerry's companion pressed close to him, clutching his arm.

Jerry took her hand from his arm, caught the feet, moved the body out. It came face down, arms dragging limply behind the head. And Jerry, forewarned as he was, felt his pulses hammer faster as he saw the knife haft driven below the left shoulder blade.

This man had died without warning.

"Go back to the car and wait for me," Jerry ordered under his breath.

"What—what are you going to do?"

"Nevermind. Get out of here! This is no place for a woman!"

She went. Gun in hand, Jerry stepped on the gangplank and moved cautiously up the steep, cleated rise to the ship's deck.

This small tramp had no well deck forward and aft. From bow to stern there was one main deck. And on that starboard side where Jerry stood not a soul was in sight. Faint wisps of smoke were coming from the funnel. Now and then the utter silence was punctuated by the muted clank of a pump below deck somewhere. But that was all.

And then a door opened abruptly up forward.

Jerry barely had time to flatten himself beside a dark porthole. A man stepped out, closed the door, came forward several steps and crossed over to the other side of the ship, forward of the superstructure. Jerry guessed he had come out of the saloon. It should be there under the bridge.

The man had not looked aft. There had not been enough light to tell anything about him. Jerry slipped after him three steps and came abreast of a dark, yawning doorway. He could see through to the other side of the ship in the moonlight beyond. Hot air mixed with coal gasses met him as he stepped inside. This was the fire room, and by walking across the steel gratings he could reach the other side where that man had gone.

IT WAS pitch black in the fire-room fiddley. Guided only by the moonlight visible through the open door opposite Jerry felt his way across it.

The murmur of voices on the port deck met him as he advanced. Two men were talking there in ordinary tones; but only one was understandable.

"No luck so far. I never seen such a guy in my life. He's a tough egg."

Moving with half his mind on that speech, Jerry was almost to the doorway. He'd wait there a minute and listen further, he decided. There were men aboard the ship after all; men up to something out of the ordinary. And then, with no warning whatever as the voice started to speak again, a deep, sepulchral groan came from the blackness just at Jerry's feet.

He stopped short, fighting an impulse to leap back. Nothing followed that groan. Straining his eyes, Jerry seemed to make out a darker blotch there on the steel gratings. His hand streaked for his tiny pocket flash. The beam flicked for an instant.

It looked like an apparition. Something seen in a night-mare. A man was huddled there at his feet. A black, crim-son splashed caricature of a face leaped into vivid relief as the light struck it. The eyes were closed. The slack-lipped mouth was working feebly. Jerry kept the light for another moment, heedless of who might see it. The man wore dirty overall trousers and sleeveless shirt. His close-cropped head was bare. The blood that streaked his face came from a great gash in the middle of his forehead. He was, Jerry saw when all that registered, a man out of the fire room down below, black with coal dust. He had been struck down by a terrible blow and left to lie here.

Whoever had done this must have also left the corpse at the foot of the gangplank. Jerry wondered if the men talking out on deck knew it. He slipped the flash in his pocket, tightened his grip on the automatic. And in that moment, down at the shore end of the dock a woman's shrill scream of fright burst out, instantly stopped.

The louder voice out on deck broke off. Running steps pounded along the deck toward the bow. Jerry himself whirled back toward the gangway. Daisy Dulane had screamed back by the car. Jerry swore at himself for bring-ing a woman along on business like this. She had been bad luck from the first moment he laid eyes on her.

Bad luck! He learned the worst almost instantly. He was halfway across the fiddley when he tripped unexpectedly, going down full length. He struck the steel grating hard, his hands breaking the fall. The automatic flew from his fingers. He heard it fall to the fire room far below, bounc-ing, clattering against steel ladders as it went. It exploded deafeningly in midair as some projection caught the trig-ger. Jerry, weaponless, tried to scramble up, for he knew more was to come. But a leg had been out-thrust from the blackness to trip him.

He was up at arm's length when the weight of a charging body struck his back, driving him down again. Jerry twisted as he fell, trying to get his hands on the unknown. He did get his fingers on a coat. His other hand swinging around came hard against the side of a head. A hand buried in his hair at the same instant. It shoved his head down, held it there—and in the blackness a stunning blow struck him above the ear.

Jerry's strength left him. Sick, half unconscious, he struggled feebly. But he was still able to recognize the feel of a gun muzzle pressing against his neck. He heard, as if far away, yet distinct, "Pipe down, mug, before I turn on the heat!"

Jerry stopped struggling. There were two of them. They jerked him to his feet, half supporting him, and hauled him over the unconscious figure and out on the port deck. And Jerry knew that he had been within an eyelash of joining that stricken fireman. His head felt as if it had been split. He was still weak. Things were whirling. But the dank salt air out on deck cleared his head fast.

A figure came clambering up a Jacob's ladder and vaulted over the rail as Jerry was hustled forward. "Who fired that rod?" it asked excitedly.

"This guy dropped his rod."

"Who is he?" the other asked.

And the man at Jerry's right grunted: "He's a sucker who picked himself a bunch of trouble. Better go back to that boat. We won't need you."

They took him under the bridge wing, opened a door, thrust him into bright light. And as one of them slammed the door behind, the other pushed Jerry forward, keeping a gun in his back.

"This the guy you're looking for?" he asked.

Jerry stopped there by the long saloon table, staring through a thin blue haze of cigarette smoke at the assembled company. But it was on the man nearest him, who turned and faced him, smiling thinly, that his attention rested in those first moments.

Blond, slender and handsome, Babe Regan raised pale, tapering fingers in a gesture of greeting. His gentle drawling voice greeted: "Hello, Prince. I've been expecting you. This makes the evening perfect."

CHAPTER EIGHT
HORROR ABOARD

THERE WERE eight of them in that saloon. Four were sitting in chairs along one side of the table. One was standing near the door at the other end. One was standing behind the men in the chairs. Another was across the table from them. And Babe Regan, still in his immaculate dinner coat, was standing by the end man of the four seated ones.

Sheer astonishment kept Jerry speechless for a moment. Babe Regan here! It was the last thing he had expected to see.

The answer flashed to him a second later. Babe Regan had been expecting him. Only one person in all the world beside Daisy Dulane and himself knew that they had been coming here at this time. That was the man who had been standing outside the open window of Dave Manners' living room; the man who had shot through at Jerry's back.

"So you are the one who tried to pop me," Jerry said slowly.

Babe Regan's pale, tapering fingers lifted a cork-tipped cigarette to his lips. He inhaled, trickled the smoke from a corner of his mouth deliberately. His gentle, drawling voice might have been welcoming a guest at the Harlequin Club.

"Bad shock, wasn't it?" he said cheerfully. "Daisy surprised me. I couldn't see her very well. Another inch or two and she'd have planted me with the flowers under the window."

"Too bad she didn't get you between the eyes," Jerry said fervently.

Babe Regan raised his cigarette to his lips again. The fingers of his other hand played with a coat button in the old, familiar gesture. "I see you don't like me," he murmured. "I seem to be unpopular with everyone I meet tonight. But then life has its compensations. I'm looking for my compensation now. Eh, O'Malley?"

Babe Regan half turned as he spoke, exposing the man seated behind him. And Jerry saw what he had not noticed in the first surprise of facing Babe Regan.

The four men seated side by side at the table were all tied in their chairs. The one at the end, by Babe Regan, had cords around his bull chest and the chair back. His arms were under those ropes too, and his thick wrists were tied across one another in his lap. His legs were fastened to the chair legs.

The other four were secured the same way.

The fourth one at the far end was big and husky too, albeit a trifle fat; but his cheeks were dark-hued, and a fierce black mustache curled belligerently at the corners of his mouth.

Next to him was a short, thick-set, oily skinned man with a close-cropped black mustache. He was dark-skinned too.

The third man seemed like a child as he huddled there in the seat. He was thin to the point of emaciation. His face was sharp, ferretlike, and his thin nose humped in the middle and grew sharp at the end. His eyes, small and dark, seemed never still, darting here and there about the room.

Jerry had never seen them before but he knew them. That man at the end would be General Porthos y Lopez, of whom Daisy Dulane had spoken. And next to him Doctor Juan José Alvarado, ex-dictator, willing to be another. The little man was Brisky, Dennis O'Malley's sidekick and machine gunner. The big, red-headed, bull-chested man by Babe Regan was Dennis O'Malley, soldier-of-fortune, filibusterer.

DENNIS O'MALLEY'S hair was a flaming red. His eyes were blue, icy blue through the swirling cigarette smoke. He was deeply tanned, almost as dark as the Central Americans beyond him. His chin was square; lumps of muscles rippled above his jaw. From him leaped bold courage and power.

But it was not Dennis O'Malley's face or personality that held Jerry's gaze after he had scanned the others. Dennis O'Malley's cheek—the one next to Babe Regan—was scarred from the eye down under the ear with numerous red, angry burns. Fresh burns, rather horrible to look at. Babe Regan's soft, feminine fingers raised his cigarette to his lips once more—and Jerry knew where those burns had come from. That curly-headed killer had been standing there pressing the hot coal of his cigarette against Dennis O'Malley's face. This final episode of Stanley's dollars was torture.

Smiling, Babe Regan waited for O'Malley to answer his question.

And Dennis O'Malley, his face black with rage, strained against the ropes which held him in the chair. His voice rumbled out of his throat in a rasp of fury. "I told you what you could do, you lily-skinned rat! If I ever get my hands on your neck I'll snap it like a pipe stem! To hell with you and your damned questions! I've met tougher guys than you!"

"I'll bet you have," Babe Regan drawled with amusement. "I'm not tough, O'Malley. I've got a kind heart; but I don't like stubbornness. Once more—where is that money of Stanley's?"

"Go to hell!"

Babe Regan drew deep on the cigarette until the coal at the end was red hot and glowing. Then casually he put it behind O'Malley's ear where the skin was tenderest, the nerves near the surface. O'Malley's jaw muscles ridged, rocklike. The chair creaked alarmingly as his mighty muscles strained at the cords which held him. But they did not give. The rank stench of burning flesh drifted out.

Jerry Prince, whose nerves were steel, who had moved through scenes of violence unperturbed, who had faced death with a grin, felt himself growing a little sick at this. He had heard of such things, but had never seen them.

And Dennis O'Malley suddenly seemed to go insane with pain and rage. His mighty bellow filled the saloon. "I'll kill you! Damn you, I'll tear your heart out with my bare hands!"

Babe Regan took the cigarette away and puffed the dying coal red and hot once more. His faint smile was almost wistful as he ignored O'Malley and spoke to Jerry. "They don't stay hot long enough," he said almost apologetically.

Jerry's two captors were standing close at his sides, guns touching him in the back. To them Babe Regan spoke. "Are you sure no one else came with them?"

And the man at Jerry's left answered. "The two of them's all we seen. They come up to the gangplank, found the guard lyin' there. The girl went back to the car. He came in the fire-room fiddley an' we grabbed him. The boys got the dame back at the car. We heard her yelp just before we grabbed this one."

"Good work," said Babe Regan negligently. He looked at O'Malley and murmured: "You're stubborn, my friend. I know the money's on this boat somewhere and we're going to get it."

"Try it!" Dennis O'Malley defied hoarsely. Babe Regan sauntered along behind the chairs. "How about it, General Lopez?" he inquired pleasantly. "Do you feel like talking now?"

The fierce-mustached one cringed in his chair. *"Dios y Maria!"* he cried out. "If I know, I tell you! The *Señor* O'Malley knows all!"

And Alvarado, whose plans encompassed the death of many innocent citizens, shrank too, and cast a hunted look over his shoulder. "Don', *Señor!*" he chattered. "I know not'ing too! O'Malley ees the man you must deal with! You could keel me and I know notheeng!"

"You yellow-bellied swine!" O'Malley snarled at them. "What if you don't know nothing? Don't crawl because of it!"

AT THAT moment the door across the room opened. Daisy Dulane stumbled in, followed by two men. She was hatless. Her immaculate blond permanent was badly mussed. Her face was pale, haunted. Stumbling to the end of the table, she stopped, staring at the scene before her. At sight of Babe Regan she uttered a low, whimpering sound.

Babe Regan smiled at her winningly. "If it isn't little Daisy! Quite a surprise to find you out here on the bay front at this time of night. You should be at home getting your beauty sleep, Daisy. You'll need your good looks from now on. The easy-money days are over."

Her face had gone paler, if possible, at sight of Jerry a guarded prisoner. Now as Babe Regan finished speaking she burst out passionately: "So it was you who killed him!"

Babe Regan smiled deprecatingly. "Killed who, Daisy?"

"You know who I mean. Dave."

"Is he dead?"

"You know it!"

"Too bad," Babe Regan murmured piously. "Heartbreaking. If I was you, Daisy, I'd get out of town. You haven't any friend to front for you now."

Her lip curled. "Tell those gorillas of yours to let me go then."

"I'm sorry," Babe Regan sighed. "It can't be done just now, Daisy. We're busy. Mr. O'Malley here is about to turn over Stanley's money to us. You'll appreciate that since you had it tonight yourself."

She looked bewildered. "What's he doing with it if you killed Dave?"

"Ah—that's just the question, Daisy. I didn't kill Dave. Our red-headed friend, Mr. O'Malley did so. It appears that when he heard Stanley was dead and a woman had been seen coming out of his room, O'Malley put two and two together and got you and Dave for an answer. He was at the Harlequin Club, watching Dave, when you telephoned. He and two of his gentle friends trussed you up and walked into the house. Dave tried to shoot it out but they got him first. And a moment after the shot was fired the Jap boy popped into the room and saw them. He tried to run. O'Malley, realizing the consequences if the boy got to the police, ran him down in the next room and stopped that. His methods are direct, to say the least."

Daisy Dulane rested the palms of her hands on the table edge and said slowly to Babe Regan: "But if he killed Dave and got the money what are you doing here?"

Babe Regan fingered the button on his coat. His smile was winning and gentle. "The same thing, Daisy. Dave and I were partners, but he tried to chisel me out of this deal. I happened to be outside the door of his office when you telephoned him. I heard enough to be certain you had the money. I declared myself in on it. When Prince showed up, asking for Dave, I smelt a rat. I had him followed. He pushed my man in an ash can and got away. So I ran over to Dave's house to sit in the game myself. I walked up under the window and there you were, big as life, Daisy, talking to Prince. Was I flabbergasted?"

Babe Regan lifted his shoulders expressively, and waved one pale, slender hand.

"I was," he assured her. "And disappointed when I found the money was gone. You and Prince finally gave me an idea where to find it, Daisy. But since Mr. Prince seemed to be very persistent about the matter I thought it best to leave him there with Dave. Unfortunately"—and here Babe Regan smiled sadly—"you were a little too quick for me, Daisy. You almost put lead in my skull. I owe you something for that, my dear. I'll try to settle the account soon."

Daisy Dulane shivered at the gentle, drawling suggestion.

"And," Babe Regan finished, "since I missed Prince and didn't have time to wait and settle the matter there, I went on about my business. But in case you turned up here before we were through I had some of the boys watch for you. They had orders to let you come aboard before they collared you. And here we are," Babe Regan finished mildly. "There seems no doubt that Mr. O'Malley has the money here on the boat somewhere. Unfortunately he's hidden it too well for us to discover it, short of taking the boat to pieces. There isn't enough time for that. I am forced to persuade him to put it on the line."

"You'll have a beard down to your shoe tops before that happens!" Dennis O'Malley snarled.

Jerry asked: "Suppose you get it, what then?"

"Nothing," said Babe Regan modestly. "You're all in it. You won't dare squeal to the coppers. And if you do—what then?" He smiled at Jerry and Daisy Dulane. "It will be your word against mine. The coppers'll have to find the money."

JERRY SHRUGGED. His head was clear by now. Strength was back in his muscles. But he was not at ease. He knew Babe's reputation. The Babe had participated in too much tonight to make it healthy to risk the police. It was possible he would decide witnesses were not desirable. O'Malley wouldn't talk. Murder hung over his head. The Babe hated Daisy Dulane too. He knew she hated him. She knew too much about his past affairs. Would he risk letting her go, possibly to the police? It was a toss-up that he wouldn't. And if he didn't, Jerry's own mouth would have to be shut too. Babe Regan would do it without a qualm if the mood struck him.

The Babe had seven men here in the saloon—the three who had been standing guard when Jerry entered, the two who had brought him in, and the two who had come with Daisy Dulane. There was a boat alongside with at least one man in it. Big odds; too big to offer any chance at all.

The two Latin Americans seemed to realize it. They slumped in their chairs, against the ropes holding them, and made no effort to hide their distress and fright.

But Brisky, Dennis O'Malley's ferret-faced little partner, sat bolt upright, silent as he had been since Jerry first entered the saloon. During all the conversation Brisky had just sat there, his beady eyes wandering from one face to the other. And there was something about his passive, watchful silence that reminded Jerry of a runner on the mark.

Dennis O'Malley bulked in his chair like an enraged bull, wounded, helpless, but defiant. His defiance did him no good, however.

Babe Regan looked at Jerry, looked at Daisy Dulane, considered a moment and then spoke curtly to the men who watched them. "Take them out of here. I'm too busy to bother with them any more just now." He added as an afterthought: "Don't throw 'em over the side—yet. Lock them in one of the cabins. You've got the keys."

Jerry and Daisy Dulane were hustled out, two men to each of them. They were taken to an inside companion passage with staterooms on one side. One of the doors was opened. They were shoved in. It was closed, locked. The men walked away.

Jerry and his companion stood in pitch blackness for a long moment. Jerry spoke first with a dry chuckle. "Well, you would come along."

She had settled into calm, icy certainty. "They're going to kill us," she said colorlessly.

"I shouldn't wonder," Jerry agreed.

"And there's nothing we can do about it. We're locked in here. They're watching outside. They took my gun. I'll bet you haven't anything to use for a weapon either."

"Check. Not a thing," Jerry agreed.

He took out his flash which had been left on him. The beam showed them to be in a small cramped sea cabin. Locker drawers had been pulled out, contents tumbled on the floor. Even the bed clothes had been jerked off and mattresses lifted for hasty examination.

Daisy Dulane went over to the bunk and sat down. Her voice suddenly sounded weary. "I miss Dave. He looked out for me. It—it burns me up to think of Babe Regan coming out with all Dave's worked for, and Stanley's money on top of that. He'll freeze me out, of course. And there isn't a thing I can do about it."

Beyond the door, steps began to pace up and down the passage. "They've put a guard over us," Jerry murmured.

"What does it matter?" she said wearily. "We couldn't do anything anyway."

Jerry suddenly chuckled. "They only frisked me in a hurry to make sure I had no gun. They overlooked one thing. We're going right out of here."

"You talk like a cokie. Can you walk through a steel wall?"

"With these I can," said Jerry, and his hand came out of his pocket and the flash glinted on a bunch of keys. "I could get out of Sing Sing with these," Jerry chuckled.

CHAPTER NINE
RED DOLLARS

SHE **DIDN'T** believe him, and said so flatly. Jerry paid no attention. He was looking about the small cabin with the flash, looking for a weapon. He found nothing suitable, shrugged, said: "Guess I can make it all right."

And he stepped to the door and began to try the keys. The lock was simple. The fourth key he selected did the trick. The door swung in half a foot. Jerry listened.

Their guard had been pacing up and down the passage. He was at the after end now. In a moment his steps turned back. Jerry closed the door noiselessly. The man came abreast, passed without inspecting the door. Jerry had kicked off his shoes as he waited. He went out the door in soundless stocking feet. Four swift steps brought him to the man's back. Jerry caught him around the throat, yanked him back off balance, tripped him and drove his head against the steel bulkhead at the left. The burden sank limply in his hands. It was as simple as that.

He dragged the fellow back to the cabin door, across the threshold, and dropped him on the floor. Then he knelt beside the man and searched him. With a grunt of satisfaction he brought out an automatic. Slipping out the clip, he found it loaded.

Standing, gun in one hand, flashlight in the other, Jerry said: "I've got a chance now. I don't know whether you can get down the gangway or not without being seen. Better try it. If you make it, wait at the car for me."

"All right," she agreed doubtfully.

They left the cabin. Jerry locked the door. Just as they started along the passage, steps turned in at the end. A voice said: "Hey, Jack, where are you?"

"Here," Jerry replied gruffly.

"The Babe wants you in there. I'll take your place."

Jerry met him in the darkness, and when they were abreast he caught the man by the collar and jammed the gun in his side.

"Hey, what the devil!"

"Shut up!" said Jerry. "Or I'll let you have it! Your side-kick is in the cabin where you left us. How many more of you are out on deck?"

"None, mister. Don't get slippy with that gun. I'm standin' still, see? You don't have to worry about me. I know when I'm healthy."

"I'll bet you do," said Jerry. "Here, Daisy, frisk him while I hold him."

She did that, got a clasp knife and a gun. Jerry took them both. "I'll need them," he explained. "Wait a minute."

He took the second captive back, locked him in the cabin and rejoined her. Together they went to the cross companion where it gave access to the deck. They stepped out on the starboard deck. There a few feet away was the gangway. Jerry went to its head, listened there.

"Beat it!" he said.

"Aren't you coming?"

"No. I've got something else to do. Wait for me at the car."

She fled lightly down the gangway without further argument.

Jerry waited until she was safe on the mole and clear of the ship. He put on his shoes as he waited. Then he slipped forward, watching the doors as he passed. The galley, he judged, should be right back of the saloon.

The door he opened emitted a smell of stale cookery. It was dark inside, broken by one half moon of light in the bulkhead, separating the galley from the cabin. He had noticed that while he was in the cabin. Dishes were handed through there for the officers' table.

DENNIS O'MALLEY was roaring with pain and rage as Jerry stepped into the galley. The torture had evidently continued. Jerry's flashlight winked to a door that led into the saloon, put there probably for use in stormy weather. Satisfied it was there, he stepped out on deck again, closed the galley door behind him and calmly fired three shots over the rail.

While the reverberations were still echoing, he stepped back into the galley, closing the door once more.

Dennis O'Malley had stopped cursing now. Confusion reigned in the saloon, tramping feet, excited voices. Babe Regan's loud orders rose over the other sounds.

"On deck, all of you! These fellows are safe enough in here! It sounds like the coppers!"

They bolted out of the saloon in a body. Jerry could hear them tramping on the deck outside, silent now, watchful, wary.

Jerry opened the door and stepped into the saloon.

Babe Regan and his men were all on deck. Dennis O'Malley and his companions sat bolt upright in their chairs. Their faces showed a mixture of emotions at sight of him. Dennis O'Malley swore: "I'll be damned! Where'd you come from? What's going on out there?"

Jerry went around to the back of those chairs in a swift rush, opening the clasp knife.

"Nobody out there," he said to Dennis O'Malley. "I fired in the air. Only way I could get in here to you." As Jerry spoke he slashed at the ropes which held the big bull-chested filibusterer.

Dennis O'Malley swore again, dawning hope and joy in his voice. "By God, I couldn't have done it better myself! You're a wonder! Brisky, look at this! He's cutting us loose! Oh, God, give me time to get my hands on that yellow-bellied son of hell!"

And as the last word left Dennis O'Malley's lips he surged out of the chair, a free man, shaking the cords to the floor.

Jerry passed him the extra gun, went on to Brisky.

And that little silent man who had sat poised and waiting spoke now in a husky whisper, taut with venomous anticipation. "Half a minute's all I want! I was cleanin' me pepper pot this afternoon! It's all ready!"

Doctor Alvarado cringed in his chair and begged: "Don' go wild, boys."

"Close your trap!" Brisky snarled at him. "We're runnin' this show now!" And as the last cord fell away from his ankles the little man came to his feet like a cat.

He staggered for a moment off balance and then whirled to the long red-plush locker seat that ran along the forward wall of the saloon. He jerked a section of it up, dived down in the receptacle underneath, came up cradling a shining, but well-worn submachine gun. It fitted into his hands with the perfection of long experience.

"Bring 'em on!" Brisky said harshly, whirling around. He was fairly dancing with anticipation.

Dennis O'Malley's automatic suddenly crashed thunderously in that narrow room. Out of the corner of his eye Jerry saw a man stagger back through the door he had just entered. Dennis O'Malley howled: "Bad 'cess to you! Come on, you rats, an' get your medicine!"

He dodged toward the door. It slammed. Out on deck voices were raised in loud alarm.

Brisky darted forward after his partner, yelling: "Don't go out there! They'll drill you as soon as you get through the door! Out the other side quick before they get a chance to get over there!" And, turning, the little man bolted to the port door.

JERRY HAD watched calmly the sudden riot of action he had unloosed; watched while he leisurely cut the two Latin Americans free. Now, as Dennis O'Malley heeded his partner's warning and turned back, Jerry said to him sharply: "I had to round up two of the guards when I got away. One of them offered to split Stanley's money if I'd let him go. He said he'd discovered it and hid it away."

Dennis O'Malley howled with rage. "He couldn't have!"

Jerry shrugged. "That's what he said. Offered to take me right to it. I decided he was lying and locked him up. Didn't have time anyway."

"I'll look as soon as we clean these rats out! And if he's got it he'll beg to give it up before I'm through with him!" The big red-headed Irishman charged the door after his partner.

Brisky was already out on deck. The crashing crescendo of machine-gun fire burst on the night. Crashed in two blasting bursts. There was an interval of silence, and then the machine gun spoke again.

Dennis O'Malley's bull-like bellow begged: "Give it to 'em, Brisky! Cut 'em down!"

Gun in hand, Jerry strolled out on deck after them, smiling faintly to himself. It had worked, and worked well. The matter was on the knees of the gods now.

Brisky plunged into the fire-room fiddley. His machine gun spat a burst. Yelling encouragement, Dennis O'Malley went in after him. Jerry ran along the deck and ducked in the fiddley also. Behind that machine gun was the safest place on the boat. But that wasn't the reason he followed.

He heard Brisky cursing on the other side of the fiddley; heard the rasp of steps somewhere below, descending toward the fire room.

"Is that O'Malley going below?" Jerry called to Brisky.

"Guess so. He told me to watch out up here and he'd be back in a minute."

Jerry used his flash, found the top of the steel ladders and went down them swiftly, calling: "I'm coming, O'Malley! Don't shoot!" But it was doubtful if the big fellow heard him, so excited and intent was he on what he was doing.

O'Malley plunged between the two big boilers of the fire room. Jerry could hear his steps beyond; could hear the machine-gun stutter overhead too. Using his flash in intermittent winks, he slipped between the boilers also. He came out in the lighted engine room where pipes were bolted in a maze to the ceiling, and the great triple-expansion engine towered high. Several bulbs were burning dimly in here. By their light Jerry saw O'Malley's hulking shoulders in a wire cage on the starboard side.

It seemed to be a machinists' store room, for there was a work bench, a rack of tools, shelves and bins holding various articles in use around an engine room. O'Malley was stooping at the end of the cage, clawing in a pile of waste that had been tossed there. With a loud grunt of satisfaction, O'Malley straightened, pulling out of the waste a familiar leather bag. Stanley's bag!

O'Malley turned with it in his hand as Jerry stepped into the store nook. "Got it, did he?" O'Malley bellowed. "The hell he did! Here it is!"

Jerry lifted his eyebrows. "It seems so," he agreed. "Is the money inside?"

O'Malley frowned, set the bag down on the oily steel plates with a thud, thrust the gun in his hip pocket and opened the bag. It was crammed to the top with the familiar packets of currency.

O'Malley closed the bag. "That bird was lying to you!" he said jubilantly.

"So it seems," Jerry agreed. "And I was lying to you, my friend."

Jerry shoved his gun in O'Malley's middle, smiling grimly.

"Hey, what the hell?" O'Malley's face purpled as his arms rose.

"Turn around!" Jerry directed curtly. "And don't snatch with that hand. I don't want to have to empty this gun in your middle."

O'MALLEY SWUNG around, swearing luridly. Jerry deftly plucked the automatic from his hip pocket and dropped it in his own coat pocket.

"Now stand there," he ordered.

Jerry picked up the bag, backed out of the cage. The stout wire mesh door had a padlock and hasp. Jerry locked the door.

"Our friend Regan was a little crude in his methods," he said casually. "I hope the loss of Stanley's backing will not wreck your plans. Happy revolutions!"

It was awkward business getting the bag up the steep steel ladders, for even currency in sufficient amount has weight. But Jerry made it, and did not mind the effort.

Brisky had left the fiddley. His machine gun fired a burst on the port side of the ship. And then another. Jerry heard the roar of a powerful motor somewhere offside the ship. It seemed to be heading out into the bay. He stepped out of the fiddley on the starboard side, moved around a still, motionless figure there on the deck, made the gangplank and ran lightly down to the mole. It was deserted once more. The machine gun was firing no more. The speeding motorboat was fast drawing out into the bay. Jerry blended into the shadows at the base of the wrecked grain towers and ran toward his machine.

Daisy Dulane was sitting tense and oblivious on the edge of the seat when Jerry threw the bag into the luggage compartment in the rear and slipped behind the wheel.

"I thought you were killed," she quavered. "What happened?"

"That," said Jerry, "is a little too painful to touch on. But I have an idea some crooks and some killers are doing a lot of hard thinking right now. Where can I let you out? We're going to part this time you know."

"Take me to the Higland Hotel," Daisy Dulane said in a meek, subdued voice.

Jerry turned off the causeway, went toward the downtown district.

"There's a ten-thousand-dollar reward offered for the return of Stanley's money," he said casually.

"What of it?"

Jerry grinned. "I think I'll turn it in and claim the reward. The money's jinxed. I wouldn't have it."

"You talk like a cokie!"

"For ten thousand dollars," said Jerry, "I'd talk like a giraffe."

"A giraffe can't talk."

"Exactly. Honesty," said Jerry gravely, "is the best policy. That's my story and I'll stick to it."

THE GOLDEN CIPHER

IN THE PAWNSHOP OF LEO
BAKOS, JERRY PRINCE—
PRINCE OF THIEVES—HAD
SEEN THE FIRST OF THOSE
GLEAMING GOLDEN CIRCLETS,
FASHIONED IN THE FORM OF
A SERPENT, WITH DIAMOND
EYES. WHEN HE BOUGHT IT HE
NEVER GUESSED TWO MORE
WOULD TURN UP—EACH ONE
A METAL MURDER MESSENGER
MORE DEADLY THAN LEADEN
BULLETS.

CHAPTER ONE
THE MAN FROM
THE PAWNSHOP

JERRY PRINCE said gently: "If that small emerald bracelet of Miss Jeanne Cameron's is not in my hands by eight o'clock this evening, someone in this room is going to have nightmares for a long time, Leo. And it won't be me," Jerry finished cheerfully. "I sleep like a top and never dream. Think it over, Leo."

They were alone in the room.

Across the black, flat-topped desk Leo Bakos rested his stocky weight on his elbows and looked past the big oily cigar which was clenched between his teeth. His eyes were half shut. They seemed to drowse behind the blue smoke which spiraled lazily up from the motionless tip of the cigar.

With thick fingers Leo Bakos slowly removed the cigar and spoke. "If anybody heard you say that, they'd think I was a fence, Jerry."

"Hear me—in here?" said Jerry Prince with lifted eyebrows. "You're not afraid of that, are you, Leo?"

The drowsing eyes of Leo Bakos went around the room. Not large, but distinctly unusual, that room. In fact the entire pawnshop of Leo Bakos was unusual. The three gold balls over the front door were always bright with fresh gilt. The front window held a luster which matched the gleaming display behind the iron bars which backed the glass. And the shop inside was immaculate, the stock dusted and clean. Leo Bakos' place always appeared prosperous, brisk and busy.

LEO BAKOS himself came to work every morning in a five-thousand-dollar car driven by a uniformed chauf-

feur whose hard, set face was always blank, whose eyes saw nothing, whose ears heard nothing, whose mouth spoke nothing that Leo Bakos did not wish.

Two clerks and a bookkeeper handled the routine work. But if a customer asked for Leo Bakos his wish was granted instantly.

Sometimes the customer was taken back into the private office where Jerry Prince now sat. About him the walls were paneled in dark wood to the height of a tall man's

The helpless figure hurtled into space.

head. The rug was solid, thick, black, silent to all steps. Sound seemed to vanish when the door was closed and one took the single chair beside the ebony desk where Leo Bakos puffed the fat, dark cigars which he imported for his own use.

Nothing hung on the walls. No other furniture was in the room. And it was seldom that more than one person at a time sat in there and talked to Leo Bakos in an undertone. The quiet seemed to breed undertone confidences. It was an axiom that anything said in there never got beyond the walls. Leo Bakos never talked. The walls were sound-proof, without windows. The door was a double door, and the inner one was sheet steel.

It was rumored that Leo Bakos' five-thousand-dollar car and chauffeur were not supported by the profits of the shop, successful as it was. But the rumors evidently were unfounded, for no detective—and many had tried—had ever been able to find anything outside the law.

In the robbery detail at headquarters choleric detectives had sworn they would pin something on Leo Bakos, if only for his nerve in rolling luxuriously through the streets behind a uniformed chauffeur who had been pardoned from a life sentence on evidence that Leo Bakos had dug up and presented to the governor.

But nothing had ever come of such threats. No man had ever been able to prove that Leo Bakos fractured in any way the rigid letter of the law.

Something of that was in his heavy, solid face now as he pulled deep on the cigar, rolled it between his lips and slowly blew a large smoke ring.

"Me, I'm not afraid of anything," he said in the thick, slurring speech he had never taken the trouble to correct. "Shout it in here and down at headquarters, Jerry. It makes no never mind. But why you should crack I got this Cameron bracelet don't make sense. You understand?"

Jerry Prince watched the smoke ring expand and float toward the ceiling. He was a tall, sinewy young man, carefully dressed. He had an air. It was easy to believe that he belonged to the best clubs, that he was worth knowing. Features finely molded from temple to jaw, mouth wide and good-natured, he had the finely drawn look of perfect condition and steel nerves.

And yet, looking a bit closer, one never failed to sense an aloof, poised air, like that in the solitary vigil of a waiting hawk, set to swoop, strike, kill. Jerry Prince was fit—and solitary. His smile at Leo Bakos was without humor and without threat.

"Leo," he said, "I've known you a long time. Are you sitting there thinking I've come in here to bluff you?"

The pawnbroker studied him again. The quiet in that rich, ascetic room became thick and heavy. And under the quiet a certain tension lay tautly. The breath Leo Bakos exhaled was almost a soft sigh.

"No," he admitted. "I've never seen you bluff, Jerry. But listen, you can't—"

Jerry Prince leaned forward. He was still smiling. "Have you heard," he interrupted, "that Skimpy Halls was killed last night?"

Leo Bakos sat bolt upright, cigar forgotten, eyes wide. "Who killed him?" he asked. "You?"

"No!" Jerry Prince relaxed against the back of his chair, a certain sardonic humor in his smile.

Leo Bakos spoke almost feverishly. "Who killed Skimpy? Why are you telling me? I ain't interested in that little prowler. I hardly know him. What's he got to do with what we're talking about?"

"He made a statement before he died, Leo."

LEO BAKOS put the fat cigar on the brass ash tray at the edge of the desk blotter. His hand was trembling slightly. "What kind of a statement did he make, Jerry? Who killed him? The cops? Let's have it. What'd he say?"

Jerry chuckled. "Got you worried, eh, Leo? Take it easy. Skimpy wasn't shot by the police. He was struck by an automobile when he tried to dodge across the street and get away from me. I went to the hospital as a bystander. Skimpy talked to me there."

Jerry Prince's glance narrowed.

"Skimpy knew he was dying, Leo. He didn't have anything more to lose. That's why I'm asking you for the emerald bracelet that belongs to Miss Cameron. I told her I'd get it for her. It belonged to her mother. The butler was killed the night it was stolen, you remember. Skimpy was a little nervous that night. His trigger finger slipped. He confessed to that job, by the way. The confession was turned over to the police by the hospital authorities—if you're interested."

A white silk handkerchief took little beads of perspiration from Leo Bakos' forehead. His hand was still unsteady. "Nothing Skimpy Hall could say would prove I had an emerald bracelet," he said thickly. He spoke louder than necessary, as if reassuring himself as he said it.

Jerry Prince smiled again, sardonically. "Who said anything about proof? I merely asked you for the bracelet—and told you what would happen if I didn't get it. The law hasn't got anything to do with this. It's between you—and me, Leo."

Leo Bakos passed the handkerchief over his forehead twice more, reached for the cigar, left it alone, and visibly went through mental turmoil. "Suppose I had bought it?" he suggested finally. "You ask me to hand over two or three thousand dollars because you promised a girl something? Am I crazy? Do I look like a charity?"

"If you gave Skimpy five hundred for it, you sweated blood, Leo. I'll give you five hundred and we'll be friends. Done?"

Leo Bakos' lips framed an explosive "No"; but something he saw in the lean smiling face stopped it. His hands went up in a gesture of surrender. He had the grace to smile sheepishly.

"Now I think of it maybe I can get that bracelet, Jerry. I'll join you out in the shop in a few minutes."

Jerry Prince got up at once. "I knew you could—if you thought real hard, Leo. Here's five hundred."

Closing the billfold from which he had slipped five crisp hundred-dollar bills, Jerry Prince opened the steel inner door, the finely grained wooden door, and passed into the spic-and-span bustle of Leo Bakos' pawnshop.

Both the decks were busy with customers and several people were waiting with packages in their hands. A young man standing near the back dropped something on the glass case.

"How much for this?" Jerry heard him ask the clerk in a nervous voice. "It's solid gold."

Jerry had already noted that. The object had struck the glass with the dull sound of heavy metal, had twisted sinuously for a moment, and now lay there half coiled in a delicate; mobile, viciousness that was startling.

Gleaming with a dull, yellow sheen it lay there, a small golden serpent, each scale clear and distinct, with a tiny wedge-shaped head in which glittering diamond eyes stared coldly.

Jerry Prince stopped, stood idly watching while the clerk picked up the golden serpent and inspected it. And the thin, sinuous, lifelike body coiled around his fingers with startling reality.

Admiringly, the clerk said: "It seems to be gold all right."

The young man was leaning tensely on the edge of the counter. He said: "Sure it's gold. How much?"

The clerk temporized: "If you don't redeem it, a thing like this is pretty hard to sell."

"You buy old gold, don't you?"

And the clerk made no attempt to hide the amazement in his voice. "You're not going to sell this for old gold?" he asked. "It's a work of art. Chinese, I'd say."

"I need the money," said the young man.

He was thin, stooped; his old gray suit was shabby and the brim of his weathered old hat lopped down all the way round with a discouraged air. His profile to Jerry Prince was gaunt, hollow, from hunger or fever.

"We'll have to test it for fineness," the clerk said.

"Go ahead."

LEO BAKOS emerged from his private office with a small package in his hands and came toward Jerry. The clerk held up the small golden serpent. It seemed more viciously beautiful and alive than ever as it dangled and coiled from his fingers.

"Mr. Bakos," said the clerk, "this gentleman wishes to sell this for old gold. I've just told him we'll have to have it graded for fineness."

Leo Bakos looked startled. He took the serpent in his hand and scrutinized it closely.

"One hundred eighty dollars," he said without hesitation. He looked more closely at the customer. "Where did you get this?" he asked suspiciously.

"I didn't steal it," said the young man quickly. "Call the police if you think that. I can prove it's mine. And maybe if you weigh it and test it you'll know better what's it worth."

"I don't need to," Leo Bakos said promptly. "I got one like it in my safe. One hundred eighty dollars the other one came to, so this is the same. They were both made by the same man if I know my gold work. The gold ain't so fine."

"All right, I'll take it."

Leo Bakos nodded to the clerk to finish the transaction and walked to the front of the store with Jerry Prince. He handed Jerry the small package as they went. "Get it out of the store quick," he begged. "I ain't so anxious anyone should find you here with it."

Jerry slipped it in his pocket and thought that Leo Bakos looked, at that moment, a little more like the furtive crook he was than he ever had before.

"Who sold that other snake?" Jerry asked.

Bakos shrugged. "I'd have to look it up. Come to think of it, another young fellow about like him brought it in. He looked hungry too. But he thought more of his snake. He pawned it. I gave him fifty."

"Always the big-hearted business man," Jerry said admiringly. "Fifty dollars on a hundred and eighty dollars' worth of good gold. And I'll bet you squealed at it, Leo. Don't sell either of those snakes. I've taken a fancy to them. I'll see you later about them."

"Sure. Any time. Only the price ain't what I paid, and the other one ain't out of pawn for a long time. Goodby—and I hope I don't see you again, goniff."

Jerry Prince walked across the street and waited in a convenient doorway.

He was still there when the young man emerged from the pawnshop, cast a quick look about and walked hurriedly north. Jerry followed on the other side of the street.

His man walked fast at the corner, crossed the street there, passed in front of Jerry without looking toward him, and continued on down the side street. He walked with a curious shamble that covered ground at an amazing speed. It was, Jerry thought, much like the gait of a man used to long treks afoot, subordinating all extra motion to efficiency in walking. The gait seemed tireless. A mile fell behind. Not once did the other look back. He headed into a shabby neighborhood filled with old houses, some brick, some frame with the paint long since weathered away. All sat close to the sidewalk. Every other house had rooms to let.

A QUEER neighborhood to give up such an exquisite work of art as the golden serpent, Jerry Prince thought as he trailed half a block behind. More than that, he was a queer young man to be selling such a thing, with no thought of redeeming it and no haggling over the price. He must have needed the money badly, or else he had a reason for getting rid of it. And the reason was not the one that had made another young man pawn his golden serpent so cheaply, evidently expecting to get it back some day. That little mystery was what had made Jerry follow.

He was still half a block behind when his quarry entered a three-story frame house whose sagging front porch ended at the sidewalk line. The gaunt young man went in without looking back.

Jerry slackened his pace to a slow stroll as he came up to the house. On one of the square porch pillars which supported a second-story porch over the lower one, a peeling sign said cryptically—*Rooms.*

But Jerry got that with half an eye. His attention was on a large, shining limousine which stood at the curb in front of the house. Such a car in this neighborhood was an incongruity. It did not belong. It stood out against the sordidness, the grime and the wretchedness with a sleek, polished aloofness. And the uniformed chauffeur who sat stiffly behind the wheel added to the impression.

Subconsciously Jerry noted the license number before turning his head to the fat slattern who was sweeping the lower porch and talking in a loud shrill voice to a woman on the next porch.

"I says to him," she shrilled, "you can't talk to me this way! I'm a lady, I am! Better bums than you have tried to beat their rent! I'll show you—" She broke off as a hoarse, unintelligible shout sounded in the house, upstairs. It was drowned by two loud shots, upstairs also.

The two women stopped where they stood, frozen, mute. The fat one lifted her broom wordlessly, but, as the voice cried out in the house again, she began to scream shrilly: "Police! Police! Help! Murder!"

The chauffeur of the limousine started his motor as she screamed. Jerry glimpsed the man's face, middle aged, thin, pallid with fear as terror-filled eyes rolled wildly at the house. He clung to the steering wheel as if it held safety of some kind for him. Perhaps safety in flight, Jerry thought fleetingly.

The fat woman continued to scream.

Overhead a door slammed loudly. Feet stamped on the second-story porch; stumbling feet which crossed the porch with a rush.

Three louder shots, crashing against the open air overhead, drowned out the fat woman's screams.

It was all happening while a man could draw half a dozen quick breaths. Looking up, Jerry saw a reeling figure come heavily against the wooden porch railing overhead. The rotten wood at one end gave way. The rail sagged out. The helpless figure hurtled out into space, arms flopping limply.

The man did not struggle as he fell. Jerry had the instant conviction that he was dead as he went out into the air. He looked away as the body struck the sidewalk.

The fat woman saw it with bulging eyes. Her screams choked in her throat. Gagging, she dropped in a faint, the broom handle clattering to the porch beside her.

When Jerry looked at the sidewalk again, the shabby figure he had followed from the pawnshop lay sprawled and inert on the hard cement.

CHAPTER TWO
HIT-AND-RUN

QUIET HAD dropped over the street with all the smothering effect of a shroud. Stunned quiet, which one knew would erupt explosive excitement in a few moments.

The chauffeur in the big car was still clinging to the steering wheel. The motor was racing wildly. Jerry shot a wary look to see if a gun was being drawn there, and when he saw no sign of it he dashed across the porch, kicked open the front door, lunged inside—and came heavily against someone who was trying to get out.

The shock was severe. The other staggered back, crying a low exclamation. It was a woman. Jerry's arms went around her; with an effort he saved them both from going to the floor.

The front hall smelled of cabbage. Against that the soft scent of expensive perfume came to Jerry's nostrils as they stopped against the bottom stair post. He still held her close.

Small hands beat at him in fear. Against the front of his coat a stifled voice said fiercely: "Let me go! Let me out of here!"

Jerry dropped his arms, stepped back and caught her by an elbow, swinging her around so the light from the door was in her face. And sheer surprise made him whistle sharply.

If the sleek limousine were out of place at the curb, this girl was far more out of place in the dim, smelly hall. She was like an orchid on a trash heap. A small orchid, slender, graceful, dainty. But not so dainty either as she struck Jerry's hand away and tried to get past him. She was quick, strong.

He caught her again. "Did you have anything to do with it?" he snapped.

"I?" Her scorn would have withered another man. She forgot to be frightened any more. On her toes, and still falling well short of Jerry's shoulder, she looked up at him from indignant blue eyes, bright with excitement.

"I was in the other room, waiting!" she burst out. "I thought it was an accident at first. I don't know anything about it! Let me out of here!"

And when Jerry still blocked her way, she flared: "Who are you? How dare you d-do this to me?"

Her voice faltered at the last and Jerry saw that she was young, not more than eighteen, and very bewildered and frightened about it all.

He smiled at her and stepped back. There were men who would not have believed that Jerry Prince's smile could be warm, flashing, comforting as it was now. "I'm sorry," he said. "Of course you had nothing to do with it. Run along."

She was gone in a breath of frightened flight, leaving the door open behind her. The fat woman on the front porch was still quiet and the upper part of the house tense and waiting as Jerry took the steps two at a time.

The upper hall was dim, forbidding, covered with ancient, worn linoleum. It smelled of powder smoke as

Jerry came into it, panting. Not more than a minute had elapsed since those last shots, yet the hall was empty now.

A door at Jerry's left opened cautiously. A face peered at him for a second. The door slammed again, but not before he caught a glimpse of a woman's frightened face.

"Who did it?" Jerry called through the door.

Her reply was near hysteria. "Get the police! They killed him! Oh, my God, they killed him! I saw him bleeding! Get the police! The back stairs. I heard them run that way."

A REVOLVER lay on the floor where someone had discarded it. The bright nickel finish was splotched with the dull crimson of fresh blood. And plainly visible on the grimy linoleum were other splotches of blood leading out to the upper porch where death had finally caught up with the gaunt young man.

Beyond the gun an open door gave into a small bedroom, shabby as the rest of the house. Dim, too, for the curtains were pulled down. But there was enough light to show bureau drawers pulled out, clothing and papers scattered over the floor, and two suitcases slit open at the top with a sharp knife.

It was, of course, the room of the dead man. Unobserved, Jerry stepped quickly inside. He was interested in the papers scattered on the floor, mostly letters. A few seconds was enough to gather most of them up and get back in the hall again. It was still deserted. Jerry went to the back, found there a narrow boxed-in stairs that took him down to a small rear porch.

Behind the house was an untidy yard, barren of grass, enclosed by a high plank fence. Jerry ran out in the yard. A woman leaned from the second-story window of the adjoining house and, pointing, cried: "They ran down the alley an' drove away in an auto!"

"D'you know who it was?" Jerry called to her.

"Two men!" she cried excitedly. "All I seen was their backs, mister! But I knew they fired them shots for I seen one of them with a revolver in his hand! They ran to the alley an' drove away like mad!"

Jerry went back to the alley. It was deserted. The men who had fled had dropped nothing. He hesitated a moment and then turned back into the yard to a narrow cement walk at the side of the house.

He wondered as he went about the girl in the front hall and what had brought her into this neighborhood. The big limousine was not a rented car. Therefore it must be her own.

She, somehow, fitted with a limousine. Her clothes, her manner had that elusive stamp of genuine quality. The fat slattern on the front porch had known she was inside of course, and yet had seemed to take it as a matter of course. It was all very puzzling.

The street reminded Jerry of an erupting beehive. People—men, women, children—were running from everywhere, gathering on the sidewalk around the still sprawled form that was not pleasant to look at. Exclamations, loud talk, questions, answers made a bedlam. And the big limousine, the chauffeur and the girl were gone.

The fat woman was just stirring on the porch. No one had gone to her yet. Jerry pushed up the steps, helping her to her feet. Her eyes were rolling as she gathered breath for loud outcry.

Shaking her roughly, Jerry snapped: "Shut up! I want some sensible talk from you! Who was that young woman who came in the car? What did she want?"

Her eyes rolled at him. Her pent up emotion burst forth in a gurgling whimper. "What are you, a cop?" she gasped.

"Never mind about that. What about her?"

"I don't know. I never saw her before, mister. She came here to see Mr. Upton. That's all I know. I told her he had gone out for a little while but he was coming back. She said she'd wait, so I let her in the front parlor."

Her eyes rolled to the crowd on the sidewalk below them.

"An' now he's dead!" she bleated. "Oh my Gawd, I shoulda knowed better'n to let her in like that. These high-fallutin' floosies are as bad as the other kind when they get stirred up. She shot him. You seen him fall. You know I didn't have nothin' to do with it, mister! I'm a re-spec—"

She was babbling when Jerry shook her again and stopped it. "Answer my questions!" he said savagely. "How did you know this Upton was coming back?"

She swiped at her eyes with the back of a big red arm. "I'd give him notice about his room," she snuffled. "Him and a coupla others that was behind in their rent. I'm a poor woman, I am, an' I can't afford to take chances with strangers. I said I'd have to have the money by noon, an' he said he'd get back in less than an hour with it. So I told her to wait in there for him. I tried to talk to her too, but she was snooty an' toney. So I left her in there an' come out to sweep the porch, an' when Upton come back he handed me a twenty-dollar bill an' I told him she was in there."

Jerry said coldly: "That girl wasn't upstairs. When I went in the front door she was coming from the other side of the lower hall."

"I dunno about that. Upton said he'd talk to her private, an' slammed the door when he went in, so I didn't pay no

more attention to him. I could see he was all right. He had
a roll of bills when he paid me."

"Not a bit of doubt that he was all right then," Jerry said
dryly. "And that's all you know? She ever been here before?"

"So help me, mister, I never seen her before. An' I never
had anything like this happen in my place before. It'll
give me a black eye. Every hussy on the street'll be telling
around how I'm running a joint here. An' I got the clean-
est, most respectable rooming house in this end of town.
I can prove it."

"Were any strangers in the house?"

"I didn't see none. If they got in, they come in the back."

"How long has Upton been here?" Jerry pressed while
he had her talking.

"About two months," she gulped.

"What did he do?"

"Nothin' I could see, mister. He didn't have company.
He spent most of his time in his room. He looked sick to
me. Some nights he was out late, but it wasn't none of my
business."

A POLICE siren wailed around the corner and a
patrol car raced up to the front of the house. Its wheels had
hardly stopped rolling when a second siren came around
the other corner; one of the bigger squad cars from headquarters Jerry saw as he went down the steps and mingled
with the growing crowd.

To leave now would invite notice. Jerry waited in the
crowd while the police took charge. He was thinking of
the girl when a hand fell on his arm from behind. In his
ear a genial voice said: "As I live and breathe—Jerry Prince.
Fancy finding you around a murder like this. Let's get out
of this crowd, Jerry."

Jerry felt the back of his neck crawl as he turned slowly. That bland voice was the last thing he wanted to hear at this time. He would have left quickly had he known this was going to happen. In his pockets were the package he had gotten from Leo Bakos and the letters he had scooped off the floor of the dead man's room. Either would make trouble if found on him.

Jerry Prince's face was debonair, cheerful, however, as he went with the speaker. "I was wondering if they'd send you out to take charge," he said. "And how is my old friend, Sergeant Pincus Smith today?"

Jerry's hand was engulfed in a huge paw which looked fat and had an iron grip. The great, bland, pinkish face of Sergeant Pincus Smith broadened in a modest grin. "I'm not in charge, Jerry. Just came along to see what all the fuss was about. Unusual neighborhood to find you in, Jerry. Business around here, I suppose?"

"I was walking," Jerry said easily. "Walking for my health, Sergeant. A little exercise might help your own waist-line."

"There goes my vanity again," Sergeant Smith said mournfully, as they stopped in the street. "Didn't I see you leaving the house as we drove around the corner, Jerry?"

Sergeant Pincus Smith was a large man, in height and breadth. His middle bulged far out. His huge pinkish face was innocent as he laid the trap and waited.

Jerry silently damned Pincus Smith. Behind that big, bland countenance was the keenest brain in the department.

"You did," Jerry admitted. "I was passing and heard shots inside. Then a man fell off the porch up there. I ran in to see what I could do. The landlady there on the porch will verify it."

Sergeant Smith looked slightly disappointed. "What luck did you have inside, Jerry?" he asked.

"None. A woman upstairs said two men had done the shooting. They ran out the back way and left in a car which was waiting in the alley. A woman next door saw them leave. One carried a gun in his hand. And there's a revolver on the upper hall floor."

"Hmmmm," said Sergeant Smith thoughtfully. "You aren't carrying a gun by any chance, Jerry?"

Jerry managed to look shocked. "Of course not, Sergeant. Why should I be carrying a gun?"

"Search me," Sergeant Smith sighed. "Why doesn't a snake have rabbit ears? Sure you ain't kidding me, Jerry? Mind if I have a look?"

Sergeant Smith made a quick movement with his hands. He was half through a frisk before Jerry managed to step back.

"Am I under arrest?" Jerry demanded.

Sergeant Smith's big bland face was aggrieved. "Of course not, Jerry. Just a little friendly curiosity, you might say. What's that lump in your left coat pocket?"

"That," said Jerry, "is a package I'm taking home." He displayed the small package which held the emerald bracelet, and put it back in the pocket. "If I'm not under arrest," Jerry said severely, "don't be so curious. If I am under arrest, take me along and do it legally—and give me a chance to start some fireworks under you, Sergeant. I've always wanted to see you squirm. Just out of friendly curiosity, of course."

Sergeant Smith was wounded and showed it. "If I thought you meant that, Jerry," he sighed, "I think I'd take you in just to see what would happen. Smooth your back fur down. If you don't know anything about this, you don't. Mind coming along in the house with me?"

"No," said Jerry. "But I've some business to do. Plenty of people around here can tell you as much as I can. You're not going to be nasty, are you, Sergeant?"

"Good lands no, Jerry," Sergeant Smith assured him hastily. "Run along."

THE SERGEANT waved a big hand cheerfully and turned away with the flat-footed lumbering movement of a man whose feet had been punished by years of walking a beat. He headed into the house. Jerry walked easily to the corner, turned right and left the excitement behind.

But in less than half a mile Jerry became aware that an automobile was trailing him. He smiled thinly to himself. He had expected it. Sergeant Smith was never so dangerous as when he cheerfully dismissed a matter.

Jerry walked with long strides to the edge of the business district, hailed the first empty taxi he saw and had the driver take him into the thick of the mid-town traffic.

Following Jerry's directions the taxicab zigzagged here and there through the crowded streets; and just as it turned one corner Jerry thrust a bill into the driver's hand and said sharply: "Keep going."

He left the cab while it was still in motion, slipped across the sidewalk, entered the first doorway and watched.

The police patrol car turned the corner a moment later and kept on after the taxi. Beside the driver Sergeant Smith bulked with his eyes glued on the traffic ahead.

Smiling to himself, Jerry waited until they were past and then walked the opposite way. Shortly thereafter he entered a cigar store and, from the telephone booth, called Leo Bakos.

"Leo," Jerry said, "look on your record and get me the name and address of that first chap who pawned his gold snake with you."

Leo Bakos snorted. "A smart business man, huh? You want to buy his ticket in cheap?"

"I won't try to buy his ticket," Jerry promised. "My word's good for that, I guess."

"Uh-huh," Leo Bakos grudgingly admitted. "Wait a minute." And presently he said: "The name is Harry Duval. He gave his address as the Windsor Hotel. But you can't tell about them names and addresses they give. Half the time they ain't right."

"This chap probably told the truth," Jerry said. "He evidently intended to get it back. The Windsor isn't a half bad place either. I know it. Quiet and respectable. Thanks, Leo."

THE WINDSOR HOTEL was located in a side street where the business district merged into a section occupied by residences and apartment houses. Five stories of gray limestone, it's small lobby was cool, quiet and heavy with an air of sedate respectability. Not at all the place, one would say, for a young man to be staying, unless he also was ultra-respectable and quiet.

The clerk at the small desk in one corner of the lobby was elderly, fussy in little movements. He wore an alpaca coat and rimless glasses, over which he peered with a startled look when Jerry said: "Do you have a Mr. Duval staying with you?"

The elderly clerk asked a queer question, almost eagerly. "Are you a friend of Mr. Duval?"

The clerk's manner was not unfriendly. Jerry smiled. "I could be a closer friend," he said. "Does it matter?"

"Very much so," said the clerk, bobbing his head with such vigor that the glasses slipped on his nose and he had to replace them. "Will you talk to Mr. Haworth, our manager, sir? I'll get him down here at once."

Jerry's smile grew a trifle forced. "I'll talk to him if it will make you feel any better," he agreed. "But I can't see that my interest in Mr. Duval calls for a consultation with the manager. Just ring Mr. Duval's room."

"That is impossible, sir."

"I see. He's left, eh?"

"Not exactly," said the clerk, lowering his voice and straightening the pen by the register pad with a nervous gesture. "Mr. Duval is dead. He was—er—burried by the city because we could find no trace of his home or people. We are holding a piece of luggage filled with his things. Mr. Haworth would like very much to speak to you, I'm sure."

"I'll see him," Jerry agreed.

The clerk ushered him into a little cubby hole office behind the desk. The manager hurried in a few minutes later. Elderly too, he was short and plump and round. His face was bright with good nature and lack of worldliness. His story was brief, after introductions.

"Mr. Duval was with us a matter of three months, I should say, Mr. Prince. We hardly knew he was around. Just the kind of a young man in which we delight, for our guests are older and quick to complain if they are disturbed. I noticed at the last that Mr. Duval seemed rather worried and nervous. He dropped behind in his account with us. But," said the manager earnestly, "we did not press him unduly. Frankly, I liked what I saw of him. It was a great shock when he was killed."

Jerry's face showed none of the emotion he experienced. "Who killed him?" he asked calmly.

The manager lifted a quick, protesting hand.

"It was an accident. A hit-and-run driver, the police decided. Mr. Duval's body was found about three miles from the city limits, just off the North Shore Boulevard. It was—uh—badly bruised about the face and had been lying in some bushes below the edge of the road several days. Identification was made by one of our statements which was in the coat pocket."

"What proof did the police have that it was a hit-and-run driver?" Jerry asked. "What was—er—Harry doing out there? The street cars don't run beyond the city limits. Rather a queer place for him to be, I'd say."

"Now that you speak of it, I'm inclined to agree with you," the manager admitted. "But Mr. Duval's watch and billfold were not taken. The bruises about his face and body were those that would have been inflicted if he had been struck violently by a speeding car and hurled down the rocky bank at that point. It is possible he rode to the end of the car line and walked into the country for a bit of fresh air. He registered from New York. I believe the police got in touch with New York, but were unable to obtain any information about him."

Jerry made his decision on the spur of the moment. "You're holding his luggage against the bill?" he said.

"One piece," the manager admitted. "Mr. Duval had two bags when he arrived. But we found only one in his room, and very few other effects."

"I'll pay the bill and you can give me his bag," Jerry suggested. "You'll find no relatives."

The manager looked doubtful, but the thought of the unpaid bill evidently forced his nod of agreement. The bill came to thirty-eight dollars. Duval's bag, a worn leather kit bag of good quality, had seen much service. Foreign steamship and hotel labels had been scraped off, so that it was impossible to tell in what parts of the world the bag had been.

"One thing more," said Jerry as he prepared to leave. "What papers were found on him?"

"Our statement only, as far as I know," the manager replied. "The police have the billfold. It only contained three dollars, poor fellow. You can question them."

Jerry smiled, said nothing and left.

CHAPTER THREE
STICK-UP

A SHORT time later a taxicab let Jerry out before a high, smart apartment house. An elevator whisked him to the fifteenth floor. He let himself into one of the apartments, locked the door and emptied the kit bag in the middle of the living-room floor.

It contained only old clothes. Two pairs of khaki shorts were all that he showed interest in. They were stained, worn, had not been washed since the last wearing. They were the type of clothing a white man would wear in the back country of the tropics.

Thoughtfully Jerry repacked the clothes in the bag and took out the letters from Upton's room. He was not surprised to find them addressed to another name—John Lambert. And they had all been sent to foreign addresses, ranging from Peiping, China, to Singapore. They were dated over a space of eight months and written by a woman who signed herself Jane.

Mailed in America, at several different points over the eight months, they bore no return address. Jerry skimmed through them with a growing sense of guilt. Jane, whoever she was, loved the man whose name was John Lambert. She worried in those letters about fever, danger and trouble he might encounter. She wrote without enthusiasm of trips here and there, light social affairs, mentioned people by their first names and spoke often of her father who was evidently with John Lambert part of the time, begging Lambert not to quarrel with him. Bad blood evidently existed between Lambert and her father, but the cause was not mentioned.

In no letter did she give a definite clue as to who her father was, who John Lambert was, what he or her father were doing in China. The last letter was dated several months before.

The remaining item was a small, strong manila envelope which contained a woman's white linen handkerchief with a J worked in one corner. The envelope was crinkled, soiled, as if it had been carried a long time. The handkerchief itself showed signs of much handling. A faint scent clung to it. Jerry put the handkerchief to his nose.

And his mind returned to that dim, smelly rooming-house hall. For a moment there, as he had held the girl in his arms, the same scent had been in his nostrils. She must be the Jane of the letters.

Jerry looked at his wrist watch. It was after four thirty. He telephoned the Motor Identification Bureau, gave a certain name; and a moment later said: "This is Jerry Prince, Bill. I know you're closed there but will you look up a number for me?... Thanks. Here it is...."

The search took some time, but Jerry waited by the telephone patiently, his brows creased in thought.

"Michael Madison," he repeated as the name was finally given him. "Sixty-seven Forty-three Laguna Road, Huntley Park. Thanks, Bill. I'll do the same for you some day."

Jerry went down to the street, stepped in a taxi, and within two blocks was able to assure himself that he was being trailed again. Sergeant Smith was evidently devoting the afternoon to an idea.

It took Jerry fifteen minutes, afoot, in the home-bound rush of the shopping district, to assure himself that he had lost this latest follower; and shortly thereafter he walked into the pawnshop of Leo Bakos.

Leo Bakos himself was behind one of the cases. "I've come to have a look at those gold serpents," Jerry said to him.

"Too late," Bakos grunted. "I only got one left." He seemed in an ill humor.

Jerry smiled noncommittally. "That's strange, Leo, after I asked you to hold them for me. I suppose one of them crawled out of your safe and wriggled away?"

"For such a wise crack I ain't even got a laugh," Leo Bakos said peevishly. "I know you'd figure I was running a hot one on you. The fellow who pawned his came in a little while ago, put down the cash an' his ticket an' got his property. He was out the door before I heard about it. I gave the clerk hell."

Jerry put his palms on the edge of the counter, leaned toward Bakos. His smile had an edge, his voice even more of a one. "Do you mean to tell me," Jerry said, "that the man who pawned that serpent with you, the Harry Duval who lived at the Windsor Hotel, came here and got it?"

"That's right."

"You're lying," Jerry said softly. "Duval is dead, buried, gone, forgotten. You'll need a better story, Leo, or, so help me, I'll make you sweat tears for doublecrossing me."

LEO BAKOS put his hands on the counter edge too. He appeared to need the support. His eyes were not drowsy now. Horrified was nearer the word.

"You're kidding me, Jerry!" he said.

"Am I?"

Bakos fished one of the fat, oily cigars from his coat pocket, and then forgot to light it. "Sure you're kidding me," he repeated as if trying to convince himself. "It was the same guy who pawned it. The clerk said so himself. He had the ticket an' knew what he wanted."

"Duval is dead, Leo."

"Maybe some other guy pawned it an' used Duval's name," Bakos suggested eagerly. "You know me, Jerry. I wouldn't lie to you. Hell, ain't we done business too often? Would I cross you on a lousy little deal?"

"You'd cross your mother on a five-cent piece," Jerry said calmly.

Leo Bakos' broad face turned red. But despite his anger he kept his voice low, leaning over the counter to keep his words between them. "You can't talk to me like that, Jerry. I got your number, but it ain't aces with me when you go too far. You may be the slickest crook in the country—an' I got an idea you are from the funny stuff I've handled for you—but I ain't takin' too much from you."

Jerry Prince's face went hard. His voice did not change. "Leo," he said, "you're a rat. I was wondering when you'd get such ideas in your head. Any transactions I've had with you can be reported to the police at any time. I never trusted you. But business is business. When I make a deal with you, I expect it to be carried out. What happened to that other gold snake? And don't alibi."

Leo Bakos himself didn't know why he cringed. He always had done it when Jerry Prince looked at him in that way. He had heard things about this lone young man which were not conducive to easy sleep. Jerry Prince—Prince of Thieves—if rumor had it right, made no idle threats.

"Jerry," said Leo Bakos, "it ain't an alibi. So help me, the same guy that pawned that snake came in and got it. I don't want no trouble with you. I'm doing the best I can."

Jerry looked at him closely, nodded slowly. "I believe you are telling the truth," Jerry said. "Let's see the other one."

Leo Bakos went back to the safe, returned and put the golden serpent on the case.

It was more life-like than ever. The tiny scales, the graceful sinuousness of the body and the perfection of the head with its cold diamond eyes carried the very essence of life. Evil life. It was uncanny. The master goldsmith who had made the serpent had with his art injected into the hard cold gold a lurking evil, a threatening viciousness that was startling to see.

"Does this mean anything to you?" Jerry said.

Leo Bakos shook his head. "Two hundred dollars' worth of gold it means to me. And another hundred for the work that's in it. And the trouble you make over it with me."

"Three hundred you want for it, eh?" Jerry asked briskly.

Leo Bakos hesitated, nodded slowly. "That's right."

Jerry dropped the golden serpent in his coat pocket. "Sold," he said. "I'll send you a check for it, Leo. If you see or hear anything about the other one, or the chap who redeemed it, let me know at once."

Down the street Jerry stopped in an optical shop and purchased a small but powerful magnifying glass. He walked four blocks to a garage, drove away from there in a modest blue sedan, which might have belonged to any man on the street.

Beyond the business district he parked at the curb and, unobserved, took the snake, turned it over and inspected its belly through the magnifying glass.

In the pawnshop he had caught a glimpse of what he now saw more clearly. The tiny belly scales bore an inscription, etched faintly, barely discernible. Each scale held a Chinese character. They ran from throat to tail, done as carefully as the rest of the gold work. Their faintness was clearly to escape attention. Only a student of Chinese could decipher them.

JERRY DROVE on out north to Huntley Park. It had been an exclusive suburb before the city reached out around it. It still was. Laguna Road was on the outskirts. With no trouble Jerry found the address he had gotten from the motor bureau.

He was not surprised at the size of the grounds or the big house back among the shrubbery; or the high iron fence that surrounded it. But the locked gate, the man patrolling inside with a gun at his waist did surprise him.

When the blue sedan stopped before the gate the guard made no move to unlock the chain which secured it.

Jerry got out and spoke through the bars. "Is this where Michael Madison lives?"

"Yeah." The answer was surly and a scowl went with it.

"Is Miss Jane Madison at home?"

"Maybe."

"I'm asking a civil question. Is she home?"

The guard topped six feet. He was powerful, rough-looking, able to give a good account of himself in trouble. His reply was a grunt. "She's home," he said. "What about it?"

"I'd like to see her."

"You can't."

Jerry spoke calmly. When anger rose in him he always grew calm; it was a lesson he had learned at some cost long ago.

"Why," Jerry asked, "can't I see her? What have you to do with it? Is this an institution?"

"It's private property," the guard told him. "Private—get me? No strangers wanted in here."

"How do you know I'm a stranger?" Jerry asked.

As he spoke, he was looking past the guard into the grounds, mapping them in his mind. The high iron fence seemed to enclose six or seven acres. Trees, shrubs, bushes, cut off most of the view of the house. Off to the right he glimpsed a second guard; armed also, walking watchfully; and at the man's side, a big police dog.

The man inside the gate spat, answered promptly. "It doesn't matter who you are. No one gets in here. We've got orders."

"Who has orders?" said Jerry.

"The guards. Day and night."

"Why," Jerry begged, "do they need so many guards? What's wrong?"

"Beat it!" said the guard coldly.

Jerry made one last effort, looking at a small brick gate-keeper's lodge inside the gate.

"Call the house and tell Miss Madison that I'd like to talk to her about an important matter connected with Mr. Upton. She'll understand. Tell her I'm the man she spoke to before she left the house."

The guard said curtly: "We got orders not to call the house about anybody. That's flat, see? No one gets in. Now scram."

Returning to his car, Jerry drove off. He should have been annoyed but he was not. Rather he was cheerful. The curiosity which had led him to follow a single thread of mystery was being rewarded as it led into an ever widening web, grimmer and more ominous with each new discovery.

He had not been able to put out of his mind the look in Jane Madison's eyes, or the helpless terror on the face of her chauffeur. She walked with fear, that slender girl with her big car, her fine clothes and the guards about her house.

And the one man who could perhaps have helped her, the man to whom, across the world, she had written her love for long months, was dead, shot down, murdered in cold blood.

Gruesome too was the death of Harry Duval and the reappearance of the man who had pawned the other golden serpent under Duval's name. It was impossible to doubt that the manager of the Windsor Hotel had told anything but the truth. What, then, was the answer to everything; where the connection, Jerry asked himself.

The street lights were on when he parked the blue sedan in front of his apartment house. He opened the door, started to get out—and found himself looking into the barrel of an automatic pistol.

"Back in and drive on," a gruff voice ordered.

The man must have come from one of the parked automobiles. A soft hat was pulled low over his face. The automatic was held in against the front of his body, invisible to anyone who glanced casually at the spot.

He was a stranger, medium-built, well dressed; and there was no doubt that he meant what he said.

Jerry slipped back behind the wheel.

A second man got in the seat from the other side at the same time. From the corner of his eye Jerry saw a second drawn gun. He had little time to think. The first man jumped in the back and slammed the door. The man beside Jerry snapped: "Let's go! Straight down the street!"

JERRY DROVE off, trying to place the one beside him. The thin, sallow face was vaguely familiar. He had covered several blocks before he got it. His companion had been a body-guard for one of the notorious liquor racketeers several years before. The racketeer was dead, his gang broken up, scattered in the swift changes that had come over the underworld. But this man had been a killer then; he was undoubtedly so now. He'd probably kill quicker now. Money was no longer easy for his kind to get.

Neither of the men had said anything more. Jerry was still driving straight ahead. He spoke first. "What," he said, "is the idea? If you two want my billfold, take it and get out. You don't need to go to all this trouble to get it. I'm in a hurry."

"Lay off the wisecracking, smart guy!" the man in the back seat said in Jerry's ear. "We'll get your dough when we feel like it. Don't drive so fast. You might draw a speed cop—and then it'd be too bad for you."

Against Jerry's neck the cold end of a gun muzzle pressed warningly.

And the man said: "You'd better frisk him, Jack. He's supposed to be hot stuff. I'll keep the rod on him."

The frisk was quick, thorough. Sergeant Pincus Smith couldn't have done better.

"He ain't heeled," said Jack.

From Jerry's pocket he drew the golden serpent, held it to the faint radiance of the dashlight, whistled loudly.

"Geeze—lookit this!" he exclaimed. "If it ain't all gold I'm a liar! Feel it. I thought it was a real snake at first. I can't stand snakes."

The man in the back seat did not bother to look. At least the pressure of the gun did not alter on Jerry's neck. "Yeah, it's gold all right," he said, as if already aware of the fact. "Never mind that. He got anything else on him?"

"I'll see. Where's your billfold, guy?"

And the man in the back seat swore impatiently.

"Get that later too! See if he's got a bracelet on him."

Jerry had all he needed to know by now. He said slowly: "So Leo Bakos is behind this?"

And his companion said, "Who? That fence who runs a hock shop?"

"Cut out that talk," said the man in the back seat. "Frisk him good, Jack."

"Hell, I am! He ain't got no bracelet on him!"

"All right. We'll find out what he did with it."

"I'll save you the trouble," Jerry said calmly. "It's in the left hand dash compartment. I haven't time to argue with you two. Take what you want and get out."

The small package was retrieved from the dash compartment, opened by the man in the back and examined. "It's a honey!" he said with satisfaction. "Worth five grand if it's worth a dime. Gimme that snake too. Get his billfold."

That done, neither man made a move to get out. Jerry was still driving north. The boulevard they were on was a through street running into a state highway at the edge of town.

Jerry said shortly: "If you two want a joyride, take the wheel and let me out. I told you I was in a hurry."

"Now ain't that too bad," the man behind him said sarcastically.

For the first time since the sudden surprise of a gun in his face Jerry's nerves went tight. This was no common stick-up. These two were leisurely, as if robbery was only a part of the job.

And, suddenly, Jerry knew what the rest of it was.

Leo Bakos was behind it, of course, since only he knew that Jerry had the valuable bracelet. Bakos had evidently decided to take no chances on reprisals. A gunman, down on his luck, needing money, would not ask much for a killing these days.

Jerry silently swore at himself for not wearing a gun after he began to get an inkling that murder was connected with the mystery into which he had been penetrating.

Silently he drove straight ahead as he had been ordered. The street was well lighted. Cars were constantly passing, people were on the sidewalks and front porches. And, instead of being a comfort, the life all about was a mockery.

Silently they passed the edge of the city and rolled out into the country, where there was no lights, fewer cars.

Jerry's nerves grew tighter each moment as he wondered just when the end was coming. Either of them might slug or shoot at any second. It was almost a relief when the man in back, who seemed to be giving orders, said: "Turn off at the next road. And take it easy on the turn, fellow!"

The next turn was a dirt side road. In a few minutes they were far from the world, between fields and patches of woodland and an occasional farmhouse well back from the road.

No better place for murder could be found around the state. Jerry recalled that the victims of various gang killings had been found down this road.

A small white concrete bridge showed up in the headlights. Jerry took a chance. Quick thinking and disregard for the consequences had worked before.

The sedan leaped forward as his foot pressed hard on the accelerator. A wrench on the wheel at the last instant—and Jerry braced himself hard.

Crash—

CHAPTER FOUR
SERGEANT SMITH
DRAWS A BLANK

THE FRONT of the car struck the thick concrete end of the bridge. Glass cracked. Jerry heard the man behind him yell as he catapulted over the back seat.

The car slued around, rolled down the embankment, grinding and crashing, and came to rest on its wheels again.

Bruised, battered, the breath knocked out of him, Jerry let go of the steering wheel. The other two were crowded in the seat beside him. One was sitting up, groaning, swearing. The dashlight was still on. Jerry glimpsed a hand coming up with an automatic. He grabbed for the gun, got it, wrenched it free as a shot shattered the stillness which had fallen about them.

The shot went through the front of his coat, just missing his chest. The next moment Jerry struck hard with the gun palmed; struck hard to the head which dodged too late. One blow was enough.

The man he had hit was the one who had been sitting in the back. The other had been knocked out against the shatter-proof windshield, which was a mass of cracks.

Jerry shut off the ignition, recovered the unwrapped bracelet, the golden serpent and his billfold from the man's coat pocket and got out. He ached in half a dozen spots, was dizzy from the shock, but otherwise he seemed all right.

The front of his car was a wreck. It would have to be towed back to town. Gun in hand, Jerry started to climb the weed-grown bank to the road.

Panting, he reached the top—and stopped short as a blinding spotlight played over him.

From behind the light a voice called: "Put 'em up! You're covered!"

Another car must have been following them to be sure that nothing went wrong. Jerry dove out of the light, down the bank, dodging as he went. He couldn't risk luck a second time. Better chance fighting it out now than cold-blooded murder with a gun against his back.

He escaped the spotlight for a moment, but it swerved down the bank and picked him up at the bottom. Instead of a burst of gunfire, a voice called:

"Jerry Prince! You're under arrest!"

And at the sound of that voice Jerry stopped, turned, and climbed back up the bank into the bright light. He was smiling wryly now. "Fancy meeting you out here, Sergeant," he called. "I didn't interrupt a necking party, did I? Why didn't you say who you were? I might have taken a shot at you."

Sergeant Pincus Smith lumbered out into the light, cradling a sawed-off shotgun in his arm. "If I live to be eighty, I'll remember it, Jerry," the sergeant said. "You went down that bank like a kangaroo. What are you doing out here with a gun in your hand? Give it to me."

"A slight accident," Jerry replied as he surrendered the gun.

Sergeant Smith looked down at the wrecked car and shook his head wonderingly. "Slight?" he said. "I'd hate to see what you'd turn out if you tried real hard, Jerry. Ain't there someone in that car of yours?"

"Two old style gunmen," Jerry said. "They brought me out here to look at the stars. We—er—got so interested that I ran into the bridge."

The sergeant tilted his head to the sky. Clouds hid all the stars. "And I'll bet you ran up the bank with that gun to shoot a star," the sergeant said admiringly. "Come on, Jerry, what's it all about?"

"I wish I knew," Jerry admitted. "I was getting out at my apartment when they materialized out of the air, forced me back in the car and made me drive but here. Things began to look a little serious so I ran into the bridge for a change."

They were climbing down the bank to the wreck as they talked, two plainclothesmen with drawn revolvers following. The two men were still unconscious in the front seat.

ONE OF the plainclothesmen directed a flashlight in on them. Sergeant Smith looked, said: "Jack Hall. There's a 'want' out on him. Either of you know who the other one is?"

They didn't answer.

"Must be a visitor," Sergeant Smith decided. "Bring them up to the car. We'll give you the keys to the city when they come to. Your story checks, Jerry. We happened to be passing and saw them walk to your car."

"You were probably parked across the street looking for me," Jerry corrected amiably. "But let it pass, Sergeant. You will waste your time. Here—what are you doing?"

"Frisking you legally," Sergeant Smith sighed. "You're under temporary arrest now you know. Great snakes— what's this?"

Sergeant Smith held up the gold serpent; and in the light of the electric torch it writhed and wriggled in his fingers realistically.

"Exquisite, isn't it, Sergeant?" Jerry asked.

"Funny thing for you to be carrying around in your pocket, Jerry."

"There's no accounting for tastes," said Jerry. "Suppose you stop going through my pockets. I've no other gun."

Sergeant Smith's hands were already probing. A moment later it came out with the emerald and diamond bracelet.

"All kinds of tastes, haven't you, Jerry?" Sergeant Smith said with a mildness that did not hide an exultant satisfaction. "And I guess this is where you finally put your foot in it. Take a look at this bracelet, boys. If this isn't part of that Cameron jewel robbery, I'll eat my hat. Here, let me look at the list."

Sergeant Smith took a folded paper from a small notebook, held it in the torchlight, scanned it, and studied the bracelet again, counting the emeralds and diamonds.

"It is!" he said. "By the Lord Harry, I've got you this time, Jerry! It's been a long time, but I knew you'd slip finally. I—I can't understand your killing the butler though. I never thought you were a cheap gun." And there was honest regret in the sergeant's voice.

Jerry warned calmly: "You're on the wrong track, Sergeant. I don't know what you're talking about. I was going to return that bracelet to Miss Cameron."

"Sure you were," Sergeant Smith said. "We'll return it to her right away. Did you get the snake in the same place?"

"Look at your lists," Jerry advised. "Was there any such article stolen and reported?"

"Not that I know of," the sergeant admitted. "But we'll probably get a report on it. Come along, Jerry. And no tricks. I don't want to have to put the cuffs on you."

Jerry said nothing as he stood on the road with the sergeant and watched the two detectives bring the limp forms from the wreck to the patrol car.

"You pulled a slick trick on me today," Sergeant Smith said suddenly. "Why didn't you tell me everything about that murder, Jerry? If I'd known you were covering up, I'd have taken you in."

"Covering up, Sergeant? You're wrong, aren't you? How could I be when I was just passing?"

"You didn't say you went in the house and met a girl in there who probably shot that fellow."

"I didn't meet a girl who did that," Jerry said calmly. "She didn't have anything to do with it."

"Why didn't you tell me about the girl, Jerry? And why did she run away if she was innocent?"

"Can't tell you why she did anything. I never saw her before. If she didn't want to stay, it was her own business. Don't know that I blame her with the place sounding like a battle field and a corpse on the sidewalk in front. For all she knew, she might have been the next one."

Sergeant Smith pushed his old slouch hat on the back of his head and turned abruptly.

"You knew her, didn't you, Jerry? You had an idea what was going to happen—and that was why you were there at the house when it did!"

Jerry laughed. "Try again," he invited.

"Mighty funny you took the trouble to run through the house, Jerry."

"It looked like a man was needed in there. As a public-spirited citizen I did what I could until the police got around. I was hoping you'd praise me for that," Jerry said wistfully.

SERGEANT SMITH passed a hand over his big bland face. What thoughts were running behind it no man could say. The sergeant himself grew thoughtful and let the subject drop.

A few minutes later they started off. The patrol car was heavily loaded.

"We'll drop them at Emergency Hospital," Sergeant Smith decided. "And then go to the Cameron's and get the bracelet identified."

Jerry said nothing. On the way to the hospital Sergeant Smith tried to draw him out about the Cameron jewel robbery.

"I don't know anything about it," Jerry said goodnaturedly. "You're making a terrible mistake, Sergeant."

"You made a terrible one when you shot their butler," Sergeant Smith retorted. "I'm sorry, Jerry. It looks bad for you."

"Doesn't it?" Jerry agreed.

He let the matter stand while they dropped the two prisoners at the hospital and then drove to the dignified town mansion of Augustus Cameron, a leading banker. As they got out of the car Jerry brushed as much of the debris from his suit as he could with his hands.

Sergeant Smith took him by an elbow. "Your looks don't matter now, Jerry."

"They always matter," Jerry corrected as he went to the front door with the sergeant. A butler admitted them after hearing their errand, left them in a drawing room, saying: "I will inform Mr. Cameron, sir."

Sergeant Smith planted his feet stolidly on the thick rug and looked around. "Pretty swell," he commented under his breath. "I'd like to live here. I guess it looks familiar, huh?"

"Nice," Jerry agreed. "I've always enjoyed coming here."

The sergeant wagged his head. "You will joke about it. How did you get in the night you knocked the house off?"

"I wasn't here that night," Jerry said. And he turned as a clear voice behind him said with amusement: "What are you doing here, Jerry? Heavens, your suit looks as if you've been rolling on the ground. Stevens said it was about my bracelet."

Jeanne Cameron was twenty-two, pretty, blond, frank and friendly as Jerry said: "Sergeant Pincus Smith, of head-quarters—Miss Cameron. We brought your bracelet back, Jeanne. The sergeant has it. We wanted to be sure it was yours. *Ummm*—Sergeant, the bracelet."

Sergeant Smith looked slightly dazed as his eyes went from Jerry to Jeanne Cameron. "I didn't know you knew Jerry, Miss," he mumbled.

Jeanne Cameron laughed. "Everyone knows Jerry. We've been friends for years. Ohhh! That is my bracelet! Jerry you're a duck. I didn't believe you when you said you'd get it back for me. How in the world did you do it?"

"Yes," Sergeant Smith prompted quickly. "How, Jerry?"

And Jerry's smile at them both was quizzical. "That," he said, "is one of the advantages of knowing people. I couldn't get everything that was stolen, Jeanne. Our efficient police will have to do that."

Jeanne Cameron's smile at Sergeant Smith was dazzling. "I'm sure they will," she said. "This was the most important piece. Here's daddy."

Augustus Cameron looked more like a polo player than a banker. He had been a polo player of note some years before. He seemed almost too young, too vigorous, too cordial to be a banker as he shook hands with Jerry and Sergeant Smith.

"Good work, Jerry," he said, looking at the bracelet. "I suppose there's no use asking how you got it? Some of your queer friends, I suppose?"

"Something like that," Jerry smiled.

And his smile grew broader as Cameron smiled at Sergeant Smith and said: "Mr. Prince is rather an unusual young man. He's told us some tall stories of his queer friends. I've often wondered if half of them were really true."

Sergeant Smith's eyes were slightly glassy. He rallied with an effort, an edged meaning in his voice. "I'll bet Jerry hasn't told you the half of it. He—uh—interests me too. Some day I hope he'll tell me a lot of things. Uh—nice he was able to get your bracelet back. We'll do the best we can on the other things, I guess we'd better get along now, Jerry."

Jerry said easily: "Run on, Sergeant. Nothing more you can do for me this evening. Thanks for coming. I'll stay on here a few minutes and see you in the morning."

"Uh—well—all right," Sergeant Smith agreed meekly.

He lumbered out, hat in hand, still glassy-eyed and rather dazed. The sergeant looked somewhat like a small boy whose firecracker had exploded in his hand.

JERRY WAS smiling as he remained with the Camerons; although he knew that Sergeant Smith would not soon forget the chagrin he had just undergone.

"Do either of you know a Michael Madison who lives in Huntley Park?" he asked the Camerons. "There's a daughter named Jane I believe."

"Two daughters," Jeanne Cameron corrected. "Jane and Caroline. I've heard friends speak of them. The father inherited his money and that place out at Huntley Park from the Philadelphia branch of the family. He's an explorer or something of the sort. Always away in queer parts of the world. Do you know anything about them, daddy?"

"Can't say that I do, except that Madison's credit is very good," Cameron replied. "I'll have to get back to my study, Jerry. Glad you stopped in. Do it again."

When he was gone Jerry turned to the daughter. "I was hoping you knew Jane Madison well enough to get her on the telephone," he said. "I tried to get in touch with her this afternoon and couldn't. The place was guarded and the man at the gate refused to tell her I was there."

"A romance," Jeanne guessed.

"Nothing like it, child. I want to see her on business. If I can get her ear for a moment I'm sure she'll see me."

"You've made me curious," Jeanne Cameron confessed. "I'll telephone her and ask for Betty Thornton's address. Betty's in Europe and they're friends. I never heard of a person being guarded so well that a man wouldn't be announced to them."

But Jeanne Cameron's intentions helped little. No one answered the call she made. "I don't understand it, Jerry," Jeanne said, puckering her brows. "Can I do anything more?"

"Thanks, no." Jerry said lightly. "I was merely curious, too. I'll run along now."

CHAPTER FIVE
PRINCE OF THIEVES

THE POLICE car was not in sight when Jerry came out on the street. He walked some distance, making certain that he was not being followed. Sergeant Smith had evidently given up for the evening in disgust. Jerry finally hailed a taxi, rode a mile across town, paid it off, walked some more to be certain no one had followed him, and ended at a garage.

The attendant recognized him on sight, and brought out a powerful, speedy black coupé. The motor purred almost inaudibly as Jerry drove it away. He turned a dial and a short-wave radio began to pick up police calls. With one hand he opened a compartment in the top of the seat and took from it a small automatic, a pair of light suede gloves and a ring of keys which he slipped into a pocket tailored inside his coat.

Driving leisurely he skirted the business district through the quieter streets. The evening was still young. Late diners were little more than away from their tables.

Leo Bakos lived in a sedate brownstone house within walking distance of his store. One of the oldest parts of town, the neighborhood was still occupied by many well-to-do people who did not wish to live further out. Bakos lived alone with the ex-convict who drove his big car, the only person he fully trusted.

And tonight, as Jerry drove slowly past the house, he saw Leo Bako's limousine parked at the curb. The window shades were pulled down but the lights were on behind them. Parking near the corner, Jerry walked back to the house and went on the porch noiselessly.

For a moment he listened at the front door. No sounds were audible inside. Ignoring the bell button at the right of the door, Jerry pulled on the suede gloves and turned the knob carefully. The door was locked.

He took out the keys and began to try them. Half a dozen slipped in and out of the lock without a sound that could have been heard more than a foot inside the door.

The lock clicked gently. Jerry eased the door open, stepped inside and closed the door in a breath. He wrinkled his nose at the stale odor of incense which filled the overfurnished hall. It had offended him before.

In one corner a tall clock ticked loudly against the silence. To the left a living room was empty. Leo Bakos must be upstairs in his study, where so often at night he had received visitors in whom the police would have been interested. Jerry had one foot on the stairs when a muffled groan from the back of the house held him there.

The groan was not repeated.

Jerry hesitated, drew the small automatic and went back in the house on his toes. The rear hall was not lighted. He had been in before and knew his way roughly.

A small cross hall cut across the back of it. In there he tripped on a body and almost fell. As he groped for matches Jerry heard hoarse breathing at his feet, but no movement.

The match flared in the blackness.

Jerry said, "Damn!" very softly.

The ex-convict chauffeur was lying on the runner of rose-colored carpet, face down, hands outstretched with the nails digging into the pile of the carpet, as if seeking to pull himself forward.

Beside him in the corner a small telephone stand was overturned. The telephone lay on the floor just beyond his hands. He had been trying to pull himself to it when he collapsed. By his neck the rug was damp with blood.

All that Jerry got in a glance. As the match burned down he looked for a light switch, found it, clicked it on.

The chauffeur was near coma, breathing heavily. On the rug behind him bloodstains were still damp. Turning him over, Jerry found slits in the front of the gray uniform where a knife had stabbed again and again.

"Poor devil," Jerry said gently.

The overturned telephone and the man's position told their own story. Wounded badly, dying, almost helpless, he had tried to get help.

Leaving him, Jerry searched quickly, watchfully. Leo Bakos was not in the back of the house. He went up the stairs at a run; and got no further than the top. There in the upper hall, wearing slippers and smoking jacket, Leo Bakos lay on his back, dead, with a useless gun in his hand. His throat had been slit.

AGAINST THE stale incense Jerry smelled the faint odor of powder smoke. He brought Bakos' gun up with his gloved hand. The thick fingers of the pawnbroker clung to the weapon even in death. The gun had been fired at least once.

Before Jerry could look further the scrape of a step sent him melting back in the hall. The front door opened as he went. And Jerry's nerves crawled for the second time that evening as he heard the voice of Sergeant Pincus Smith say: "Doesn't seem to be anyone in here."

JERRY PRINCE didn't have to reason it out. Sergeant Smith had all he needed for a case. Breaking, entering, murder, robbery—it might have been made to order for the sergeant. And the way out front was blocked. Jerry kept on to the back of the house, where Leo Bakos' big den was located.

It was a huge room, that den, extending clear across the back of the house. In it were books, chairs, couches, liquor, everything to make one comfortable, welcome, unwary. The business from which Leo Bakos had derived most of his profit was conducted by word-of-mouth negotiations. Hospitality helped.

One thing only was different about the room. It had no windows and only two doors. Jerry knew about the other one.

The study was lighted, quiet, peaceful. One of Bakos' fat, black cigars was still burning on an ash tray. From the length of the ash Jerry judged it had been lying there for ten or fifteen minutes. That short a time had elapsed since death had visited the house.

One look was all that Jerry cast about as he closed the hall door softly and turned to the left corner of the room. He was partway across the floor when an object caught his eye. He turned back and picked up a woman's small glove, dropped evidently after Bakos went out of the room to his death. Bakos would have picked it up himself if it had been there before. His neatness was known to everyone acquainted with him.

A woman, here, again. Jerry brought the glove to his nostrils automatically as he continued on across the floor.

And, somehow, as he had expected, this glove had been worn by the same girl; by the Jane Madison who kept herself barred, locked and guarded on her father's estate; that slender, graceful, dainty girl whose expensive perfume seemed to be at every point Jerry turned. It was on the glove.

Three long steps took Jerry to the end of the room. A rug lay awry on the polished floor where it had been pulled aside. Faintly discernible in the floor, now that the rug was off, was the outline of a small trap door.

Bending, Jerry pressed a plug in the floor beside it. A hidden spring raised the door up an inch or so at one end. Jerry lifted it the rest of the way. Narrow dark steps went steeply down. Carefully he descended, closing the door overhead, leaving himself in pitch darkness.

He knew where he was going. There was no great secret about the trap door or steps. Set in the floor that way it was merely one of Leo Bakos' precautions against surprise, and a way for surreptitious visitors to leave without discovery when someone was at the front of the house whom they did not wish to see.

The steps went down in a little square shaft and as he felt his way Jerry heard voices through the thin wall which separated him from the lower floor. Sergeant Smith and the men with him had discovered the body of the chauffeur in the back hall.

Sergeant Smith was speaking loudly. "It's going to be murder all right. This fellow can't live long. And I'll bet there's more of it around the house. Look the place over as quick as you can, boys. Bakos never got very far from this man of his. He must be the one who made the funny noises over the telephone. Guess he was passing out when he did it. Brown, call an ambulance."

And the steps went on down past the first floor to the level of the cellar. At the bottom Jerry felt with his hands, turned a knob and a close-fitting door swung noiselessly out. He stepped through, held the door a moment while he listened and then closed it carefully. It had no knob on the outside. Once closed no man could get in to those steps. The whole arrangement was an exit only. Anyone who entered the upper part of the house did so by the front stairs—after passing inspection by Leo Bakos or the man who had guarded him.

ORIENTING HIMSELF in the darkness, Jerry felt a way to the back of the cellar, finally being forced to strike one match which he extinguished almost instantly. The light however had shown him the door he wanted.

It was not latched. Someone had come out this way in a hurry. The cool freshness of the night was against his face as he stepped out. He ducked his head, went up steps to the back yard, kept on toward the alley at the rear of the property.

The back door of the house opened suddenly, letting out a shaft of light. Jerry heard footsteps, then the voice of Sergeant Smith saying loudly: "I'll have a look around the outside."

It was too late to get back to the cellar. The yard had no place to hide. Jerry ran for the back gate as Sergeant Smith lumbered down the steps.

The sergeant heard him, sensed him or started his search at that moment. The bright beam of an electric torch swept over the back yard, passed Jerry, came back to him.

"Stop!" Sergeant Smith yelled.

Jerry kept on. Nothing else for it now.

Sergeant Smith shouted again—and then the loud report of his revolver smashed the quiet of the neighborhood. Jerry heard the bullet *plunk* into the wooden planks of the fence ahead of him.

He did not fire back. Perhaps he would have done it with another man; but not Sergeant Smith. They had, in a way, been left-handed friends for a long time. The sergeant, suspecting him of various nefarious things, had worked assiduously to prove them.

With satisfaction the sergeant would go into court with proof and send Jerry Prince to prison for a long term of years. But somehow Jerry could not shoot at the big lumbering detective with his bland and innocent face. He would, he knew, regret it ever afterward, if his bullet went home.

Sergeant Smith had no such scruples however. His service revolver crashed twice more on the night as he ran across the back yard in pursuit, keeping the dancing beam of his flash on Jerry as much as possible.

Both bullets came closer. The neighborhood was being aroused, the other detectives called out from the house. Jerry swore as he sprinted for the gate. He made it, kicked the gate open and ducked out into the alley as a fourth bullet drove splinters from the wood at his shoulder.

To make matters worse as he went out he heard the sergeant yelling: "Jerry Prince! Stop or I'll kill you!"

Jerry gave vent to an oath as he sprinted along the alley. He was in for it now. Without additional proof no power on earth would convince Sergeant Smith that Jerry Prince had not invaded the house of Leo Bakos and committed murder.

The sergeant would work until he had proved the case around that; and the facts which he would quickly turn up would only bear him out. The evidence of the clerks in the pawnshop would help mightily. They would tell about Jerry's visit there, about his getting the golden serpent—which the sergeant had found on Jerry.

Circumstantial evidence, of course—but many a man had gone to the chair on evidence no more conclusive.

Before the sergeant reached the alley Jerry came abreast of a lower fence on his left. He vaulted over into the back yard of the third house down, raced toward the street and his car. For a few moments all the attention of the sergeant and his men would be concentrated in the alley.

And it was.

Jerry ran past the side of a dark and quiet house and at the front, paused, breathing heavily, while he looked up and down the street.

Down the street to the left the police car stood before Leo Bakos' house. At the right, near the corner, Jerry's own powerful coupé stood waiting.

DOORS WERE opening along the street as people looked for the source of the excitement. At the moment they could do no harm. Jerry ran for his car, jumped in, started the motor and, in second gear, raced around the corner and sped out of the neighborhood.

He drove fast, turning a corner now and then, and finally slowed somewhat and turned on the radio. His heart was still pounding. It had been a close shave. And—the whole thing was just beginning. The manhunt would be on in a few minutes.

It meant flight—and continuing flight, with a murder charge ever dogging him; disgrace and probably prison and the chair at the end. Years of that—or quick discovery of the murderer to satisfy the law.

A decision had to be made in brief minutes. Flight meant the need of money, certain things to be taken and destroyed in the apartment, quick exit from the city.

From under the dash the announcer's voice at headquarters droned impersonally.

"Calling all cars.... Calling all cars.... Pick up on sight black coupé driven by one Jerry Prince.... Wanted for murder.... This man is probably armed and will resist arrest.... He has just driven out of the fourth district, heading east when last seen.... Calling all cars... Calling all cars...."

Jerry turned the next corner, worked through the dark streets toward the west. The man hunt was on. He was little better than a fly slipping through the ever tightening strands of the police web. If they snared him, guns would probably blaze without warning. Mentally he chalked up that little score against Sergeant Smith, being forced at the same time to admit that the sergeant was only doing his duty as he saw it.

Jerry made up his mind. In escape he would find no escape. Always the thing would dog him. He headed out toward Huntley Park. There, guarded and inaccessible, was the only person who could give evidence that would help him. Jerry's face set in hard grim lines as he drove.

She would be accessible tonight.

CHAPTER SIX
THE GOLDEN CIPHER

HUNTLEY PARK was a dark tree-filled section of the city. The estate of Michael Madison was even more isolated. Jerry parked the coupé in a dark lane half a block from the north side of the estate. Here he had noted the trees and shrubs were thicker, and garage and outbuildings lay between the fence and the house.

From the hidden compartment in the top of the seat Jerry took a small flashlight, an extra clip of cartridges for the automatic inside his coat, a light and powerful steel jimmy that folded for easy carrying, a pair of wirecutters and another ring of keys.

They did not bulk greatly in his pockets as he walked out of the lane, crossed a dark cinder road and came to the high iron fence around the estate.

The one thing that would have made access to the grounds dangerous, lights spaced inside the fence, had not been installed. Jerry smiled slightly, grateful to whomever had overlooked that, and walked up to the fence without hesitation.

A heavier, clumsier man, one in less perfect physical condition, could not have done what Jerry did then. He had the build of an athlete, steel muscles, wiriness. By sheer strength of arms and wrists he drew himself up the fence bars, caught the top, levered his weight gingerly over the sharp iron spikes and vaulted into space.

He landed lightly, staggered a few steps and came upright, listening.

A breeze rustled the leaves of nearby trees; an automobile horn blew in the distance. Those were the only sounds. He judged that his entrance had made no alarm. Walking carefully he set off toward the house.

He had seen one dog that afternoon. There must be others. They were his chief concern. Once they scented him they would arouse everyone on the property in a few minutes. And, if trained well enough, they might easily be dangerous. They would have to be risked however.

Quiet lurked about the two story garage to which Jerry came. Past it he could see several lighted windows in the house, but the garage itself was dark.

He went on—and not fifty feet in front of the garage stumbled over a soft and yielding body on the ground.

No cat could have recovered balance and crouched for trouble quicker than Jerry did then.

The form did not stir. He moved to it, put down a hand, felt the short hairs of a dog's coat. The dog was dead.

The quiet had subtly changed. The peace was gone, driven away by the discovery of that dead dog. Almost as warm as in life, it had been dead only a short time.

Wrapping a handkerchief around the end of his flashlight, Jerry held the light low and winked it once. The faint glow showed blood on the gravel of the driveway—and a pair of boots a few feet away. A man lay there.

Jerry was at his side a moment later, using the light again. It was one of the guards, still wearing a gun belt around his waist. But the gun was gone, and the side of his head was covered with blood. He had been felled by a terrible blow.

In the wrist a faint pulse beat steadily. Jerry left him there, got off the gravel and skirted the side of the house on grass damp with dew.

The trees and shrubs that had promised to be a help to him were abruptly menacing. They hid now the thing which had struck down the guard and dog.

The house was brick, two stories with wings, with the driveway sweeping before a big front porch. At the steps stood the black limousine which Jerry had seen that afternoon before the rooming house.

The parking lights were on, heading the other way. In the radius of their rays two traveling bags were sitting on the gravel in front of the machine. A quick departure was evidently to be made. But no one at the moment seemed to be around the machine. Jerry went to it on the balls of his feet, looked in, made certain it was empty.

And as he did so a shot sounded in the depths of the house and a woman screamed.

SKIRTING THE front of the machine Jerry ran to the front porch—and dodged the moment he stepped on it. A dark figure had lunged out at him from the left.

The blow would have crushed the side of his head. It missed, due to his quickness, and glanced off his shoulder, numbing the shoulder; and as Jerry dodged again, swinging around, a gun roared close to his side.

He saw the flash from the muzzle, felt the hot blast drive through the fabric of his coat, and breath for an instant was driven from his chest as the bullet struck a rib with a sledgehammer blow.

Jerry shot as he staggered back, twice, as fast as his finger could pull the automatic trigger. And then stood on widespread feet, gasping, as his attacker pitched down to the porch floor, stirred there a moment and lay still.

Abandoning caution, Jerry used the flashlight.

The man had been shot through the middle. A revolver and leather-covered blackjack had dropped from his hands. He lay on his back, clenched fists pressing in against his middle. About thirty, well dressed, stocky, his features were stamped clearly with the mark of the underworld. Jerry had never seen him before but he knew the type. A killer, ruthless, desperate. He'd kill even now if he was able. His eyes opened, closed; he continued to breath harshly and hold his middle. He was almost unconscious.

Jerry's breath was back again. Strength too. The hemorrhage of blood inside did not come, but he could feel blood trickling down his side. When he moved pain stabbed through his chest. He judged correctly that a rib had been cracked or fractured and the bullet had been deflected from the chest cavity. He could still move normally; and he did, swinging to the front door, throwing it open, stepping inside in time to face a man plunging down wide curving stairs with a gun in his hand.

The man opened fire on sight and tried to stop. His first shot splintered the door glass behind Jerry. His second clipped Jerry's coat sleeve. Close shooting for a moving man. Jerry fired once, carefully; and hit his target as he intended. The man fell forward, tumbling and rolling to the bottom of the steps.

Jerry was past him before he was quite at the bottom, running up the steps. The trouble was upstairs, the girl must be up there; to hesitate now might double odds which Jerry had no way of counting. One thing only he was certain of. He could not go back. The girl, and only the girl, could help him; and she herself needed help now.

In the hall above an excited voice called: "Joe, what's the matter down there?"

The speaker ran toward the head of the stairs.

They met at the top, almost colliding. The other was the most surprised. His jaw dropped. Fear ran over his face. He dropped instinctively the golden serpent which dangled from his left hand and raised the automatic in his right.

And Jerry clubbed hard with the gun he carried, smashing true to the back of the other's hand. He saw, as the automatic dropped and the fellow cried out in pain, the little golden serpent writhe for a moment on the floor and then lie still.

The man was young, in his late twenties, thin-faced, gaunt, sallow, as if his frame had been racked by fever and privation. His face could have been frank, open, likable, but at the moment it was dark with fear, hate, apprehension as he backed off holding his injured hand.

"Hold it," said Jerry. He kicked the automatic behind him and stood watchfully, listening.

Down the hall behind a closed door a woman was sobbing loudly. At the foot of the stairs the man stirred, groaned. The rest of the house was quiet.

"Who else is up here?" Jerry asked the man before him.

And the fellow shrugged. His eyes, deep-set, dark, shifty, Jerry saw, darted here and there as if seeking escape. His fear made him more desperate. He did not answer.

"Who else?" Jerry rapped at him. "And don't try the jump you're figuring on. I'll drop you at the first move."

The other looked at the gun, at Jerry's face. The watchfulness drained out of his own face. His shoulders drooped a little and he shrugged.

"No one," he muttered.

"Just the three of you come here?"

"You've—got the others?"

"What does it look like?"

The young man considered him for a moment, and shrugged again. "I guess you have," he admitted. "That's all there was. The three of us."

JERRY STIRRED the little golden serpent with his foot. His mind was working fast. Sergeant Smith had taken the serpent Jerry had gotten from Leo Bakos. And the second one had been taken out of pawn by the man who had pledged it, by the man who called himself Harry Duval—who had been found dead beside the North Shore highway.

"Where did you get this snake?" Jerry asked.

He got no reply to that question. Stooping, with his eyes on the other, Jerry picked up the snake, dropped it in his pocket and said curtly: "Back down the hall. We'll have a look."

Jerry stopped him at the door where the woman was sobbing. It was unlocked. Gun against the other's side, Jerry threw the door open and looked in the room. A pretty girl in a maid's apron and cap was lying on the bed. She started up fearfully, peering from swollen eyes. She was alone in the room.

"Where is Miss Madison?" Jerry asked her.

She wailed: "I think they killed her! I d-don't know. Who are you?"

Jerry smiled at her. "I dropped in to call on Miss Madison," he said. "And I was forced to join the party. What were they after?"

"I d-don't know!" she sniffed. "We were packing to leave when they burst into the house with guns in their hands

THE GOLDEN CIPHER 253

and held us all up. The s-servants are locked downstairs in the pantry. They threatened to k-kill us if we made any noise."

"And so you cried as loud as you could," Jerry said.

"I c-couldn't help it, sir."

From the hall behind Jerry a voice he remembered well said: "Are you looking for me?"

Jerry made the mistake of turning his head. His prisoner was on him instantly, grabbing the automatic and trying to wrench it away. The maid screamed. And Jerry fought for the gun and, he realized his life.

Natural strength or the frenzy of fear made the other almost a superman. Using both hands he twisted the automatic from Jerry's fingers. And as it went out of his grasp Jerry struck with his other fist, crossing hard to the jaw with all his weight behind it.

His man staggered across the hall, struck the wall and weaved there in a daze, trying to bring the gun up. Jerry was on him a moment later, tearing the weapon away, jerking the fellow around by the coat collar and running him along the hall with the gun against the back.

The girl who had spoken was standing there to meet them. She wore a traveling suit now, but she was as slender, as graceful and as dainty as ever. Pale, nervous, she seemed to be forcing herself to stand and face them.

And her look at Jerry was a mixture of astonishment, fear and relief. "Where did you come from?" she asked.

"Outside," Jerry said, shaking his prisoner by the collar. "Sorry I had to let this fellow break out that way again. He seems to be dangerous."

She said: "Who are you? What are you doing here?"

"I dropped in to talk to you," Jerry said, smiling slightly. "You made a bit of trouble when you left so quickly this afternoon. And the guards at the gate didn't seem to want to admit me when I called shortly after."

"Why did you call? What business was it of yours? How did you find me?"

She put the questions with forced calmness, and back of that her hands were tightly clenched at her sides and there was enough light in the hall to show the quick pulse throbbing at the side of her throat.

"My name is Jerry Prince, Miss Madison. I'm a friend of Jeanne Cameron, who knows Betty Thornton, who knows you."

"I don't know Betty Thornton."

"I understand she was a friend of Jane Madison."

"I am Jane's sister," she said. "Jane is in Europe, ill. And I still don't see why you came here."

RELEASING HIS prisoner's coat collar, but keeping the gun against his back, Jerry took the little golden serpent from his pocket.

"I came here about this," he said.

"It's mine. He took it away from me by threatening me with a gun. Give it to me."

She reached for it and Jerry let her have it. "How could he take it away from you when he's had it?" he asked.

"He hasn't had it."

"He pawned it, and then redeemed it this afternoon," Jerry said.

"Not this one," she said. "He had another one. That must have been the one he pawned."

And, weakly, Jerry demanded: "How many of those gold serpents are loose around town?"

"Three," she said. "I had one, he had one and—and—"

"And the man who was killed this afternoon had the other one?" Jerry finished for her. "He sold his outright—and was killed as soon as he got back to the house. Why was he murdered, Miss Madison? You know."

"No!" she denied.

"I'm afraid you do. Would I be close to the truth when I said you went to the pawnbroker's house tonight to buy the serpent from him?"

She swallowed. "What do you know about that?"

"Bakos was murdered while you were there," Jerry told her bluntly. "That makes the score two for you today."

He felt the prisoner stir uneasily against the gun muzzle, and gave no indication he noticed it.

"Killed?" she whispered. "While I was there? No!" And her face was white now and her denial wrenched out with fright. "He wasn't dead when I left," she said. "I did go to see him. John told me he had just sold the serpent at that pawnshop. He had no money. He had to live, and he wouldn't let me give him money. He ran upstairs to get something and—and he was killed up there. When I got to the pawnshop it was closed, so I went to see the owner this evening and buy it back from him. While I was talking to him someone called downstairs. Bakos raised up a door in the floor and told me to get out. I—I think he expected trouble and didn't want me there. Just as I started down I heard a shot—and—and I got out of the house as quickly as I could."

"And left your glove there," Jerry said.

Startled, she said uncertainly: "Did I?"

"You did," said Jerry. "Who is this man?"

"His name is Harry Duval."

"That right?" Jerry asked his prisoner.

The man kept a sullen silence.

She said: "Why shouldn't he be? I know him. He was with my father's party in the Orient. I've seen him in pictures of the party my father sent back. John Lambert told me over the telephone some time ago that he had seen Duval on the street, and Duval saw him and hurried away. John was afraid there would be trouble. He warned me to be careful."

"Why careful?"

Duval burst out abruptly: "The police aren't looking for me. If they mistook someone for me, it isn't my fault."

"They'll have something to say about your billfold and hotel bill in the pocket of that dead man," Jerry remarked dryly.

"They were stolen."

"Of course. And you didn't report it—and the man was careful enough to keep the hotel bill. They believe fairy tales at headquarters—sometimes," Jerry said. "But not as raw as that one, I'm afraid. Miss Madison, you're holding out. Where is your father? What about these three snakes that seem of such interest to everyone?"

SLOWLY SHE said: "I guess you might as well know. Father is dead. He was killed in the hills of Annam, in the country behind French-Indo China. Stabbed. They were hunting for the ruins of a lost city supposed to be hidden back there in the jungle like Ankor-Wat was for centuries. They found it, and in one of the temples they unearthed those gold serpents. They were so striking that my father, John Lambert and Duval each took one. Father sent his back to me by the first post, without saying anything about it to the others. Two nights later he caught Duval ransacking his tent. Duval stabbed him and fled from the camp with a rifle and his own gold serpent.

"John Lambert came back to the coast at once. On the way he heard a rumor that Duval had been killed by a tiger but could not verify it. He cabled me, wound up the expedition and sailed for home with what little money he had left.

"On the way he managed to decipher characters on the belly of his snake and realized that they were part of directions for reaching the buried temple treasure. Each snake apparently had part of the directions engraved on it, and all three of the snakes had to be deciphered to get the full directions. Duval must have stumbled on the truth and, thinking father probably knew it too, killed him to get him out of the way and get his snake and the directions it held. John Lambert would probably have been next. John came back here, told me the story, got the directions off the snake father had sent me, and found that he still had to have the one Duval had carried away.

"And the next day," she said soberly, "John saw Duval on the street and realized that Duval must have come here to get father's serpent and the one John had. John warned me. I had the place guarded. John wouldn't stay here. He began to search the city for Duval. I didn't know his money was so low until I went there today and he told me he had sold the serpent for the gold in it. And then—he was killed."

She hesitated, and then said: "That pawnbroker—Bakos, seemed to know more than he should. He asked me what I would pay for both snakes, and when I said any reasonable price, he laughed and said they would come pretty high as he knew a thing or two about their value now."

"*Ummm*, so Leo said that?" Jerry commented softly. "That means he talked with this man then. He didn't know a thing about them this afternoon. But shortly after that he sent men to hold me up and kill me. It makes sense now. Leo made a deal with our friend here."

And abruptly Duval broke out with thick rage: "That swine! He had me followed from his store and forced himself on me. He said he was the only person who could get the other snake back. He promised to have it this evening. I thought he knew more than he did."

"And so," said Jerry, "when you went to get the snake, you removed Bakos, and then came to finish up with Miss Madison."

"I didn't say that, damn you!"

"You did," said Jerry, "only you didn't mean to. There's such a thing as circumstantial evidence." Jerry drew a soft breath and smiled past his prisoner's shoulder at Miss Madison. "I should know," Jerry said to her. "I've become an expert on circumstantial evidence this evening. Suppose we get to a telephone? I know just the man who will know what to do with it, and with our slippery, greedy friend here. He'll be chagrined, but he'll be honest about it. I think your troubles are over, Miss Madison."

She smiled doubtfully at him. "I hope," she said, "you are telling the truth. You—you seem so honest."

Jerry chuckled as she went along the hall by his side, with Duval walking dejectedly in front of the muzzle of Jerry's gun.

"When my friend gets here," Jerry said to her, "I want you to tell him just that. How honest you are sure I am."

"Of course," she promised. "But—but I don't see why."

Jerry chuckled again at the vision the idea brought up. "I merely want to be there watching his face when you do," he said.

HOUSE OF DREAD

OUT OF ONE CRIME MAZE
STRAIGHT INTO ANOTHER—
THAT WAS THE JUMP PRINCE
MADE THAT NIGHT WHEN
HE RACED AFTER THE TAIL
END OF THE CONTINENTAL
EXPRESS TO ELUDE THE
CLUTCHING FINGERS OF THE
LAW. FOR THE GIRL SITTING
THERE ON THE OBSERVATION
PLATFORM AS HE SWUNG
ABOARD, HAD MYSTERY AND
MURDER WAITING FOR HIM
READY-MADE.

CHAPTER ONE
PRINCE TAKES A WIFE

IN CERTAIN well informed police departments over the country there was no doubt that Jerry Prince was a thief. But, as Jerry Prince had amiably told more than one, "What a thief!" To which the records held no adequate reply. Jerry Prince had been "mugged," fingerprinted, and the records scattered broadcast. It was devoutly and profanely hoped they would do some good.

Legally Jerry Prince was honest, upright—and for all anyone could disprove—noble. Although Jerry would have been the first to deprecate the last.

Which brings us to Albuquerque, and the thirty-two thousand dollars in bonds and the three missing letters of Colonel Jefferson K. Carson.

THE COLONEL had missed the bonds and letters ten minutes after his amiable and charming party guest had departed from the Carson mansion in Beverly Hills. Being somewhat shady in his own dealings, hence facing complications if the bonds and letters fell into the right hands back east, Colonel Carson had cursed the impulse which had warmed him toward the affable young man whom he had met only casually the day before, and had immediately retained a famous detective agency.

"Get him!" the colonel had roared to the agency manager. "I don't know who he is and I don't give a damn! One of the maids saw him leaving my study. There's no doubt that he got the bonds and—er—the letters. I'll prosecute, of course—but first of all I want the bonds and letters. I'll file complaint. Go after him with a John Doe warrant. His alias is Prince. Jerry Prince, he called himself. I haven't the slightest idea what his real name is."

The agency manager had gasped.

"Jerry Prince, did you say?" he had asked.

"That's the name."

"Youngish man? Looks like a clubman? Tall? High cheekbones—"

"That's the man!" Colonel Jefferson had exploded. "I see you know him! What's his right name?"

He clawed futilely as he dropped in a shower of dirt.

"Jerry Prince," said the agency manager. "He's an ace. Never taken a conviction. Usually uses his right name. Hell—I beg your pardon—Jerry Prince could get away with your pants while you were holding your suspenders. They call him the 'Prince of Thieves.'"

"I'll get his scalp this time!" the colonel had sworn. "No cheap, petty-larceny crook can come into my house and make a fool out of me. Go after him. I don't think he knows the maid saw him."

The agency manager forebore to point out that thirty-odd thousand dollars was not exactly petty larceny and that the man who had earned the title of Prince of Thieves was nothing less than exactly that.

"Now that we know who your guest was it should be easy," he assured the colonel. "If we can make this charge stick, it will be something to shout about. He won't have the bonds or letters on him, of course."

"Doesn't matter," the colonel said grimly. "That door had been locked ten minutes before. The fellow was wearing gloves when he walked out. Gloves!" snorted the colonel, "when the thermometer is registering seventy-eight degrees tonight! If he hasn't the bonds on him, make him tell where they are before you turn him over to the police!"

Which puts us in Albuquerque, that small metropolis lying on the steel highway of the transcontinental railroad and under the invisible highway of the transcontinental plane service.

Jerry Prince had the colonel's bonds and letters. Furthermore he had them on his person, where, for reasons known only to himself, they would have to stay until he delivered them personally.

In addition, Jerry had seen the door just down the hall move slightly when he emerged from the colonel's study, and knew that trouble had perhaps caught up with him. He could have reentered the study, replaced the bonds, let the matter drop.

He had elected to stroll on out of the house with them. In a week, ten days, it wouldn't matter who had taken them. The colonel would be cornered then, and in no position to press any charge. But, until then, the colonel was dangerous, the bonds damning, and there was nothing to do about it without wrecking a carefully planned attack by others on the highly respectable and eminent Colonel Carson.

Knowing he would quickly be recognized by the law, Jerry had left Los Angeles at once by a cross-country bus. Trains and planes would be checked, wires sent ahead. But no man in his right senses would suspect Jerry Prince of traveling east on a bus.

Which shows the fallibility of man, even a prince of thieves.

JERRY LEFT the bus at Albuquerque. He was soiled, unshaven, utterly weary. He had days of time to kill. Albuquerque was as good a place as any. Who would think of looking for him here in this small oasis in the vast reaches of southwest mountain and desert country?

He checked in at the Harvey House, beside the railroad station; and in the Spanish mission luxury of its interior he bathed, barbered, sent his suit down to be pressed and dropped off into dreamless sleep.

When he awoke, thunder, lightning, sheets of rain were dinning in the darkness. He had slept ten hours. Calling for his suit, he dressed leisurely.

A train arrived while he was doing that. Jerry looked out the window, saw a fresh engine coupling to glistening Pullmans. The train was heading east. He grinned as he thought of the scrutiny to which eastbound trains were probably being subjected at strategic points.

He was adjusting his cravat when someone tried the doorknob furtively. Jerry heard the soft sound, swung around, stood poised, while the knob went gently back and forth. A moment later someone knocked on the locked door.

"Who is it?" Jerry called absently.

"Bellboy, sir."

Jerry's smile was thin. Bellboys didn't try doorknobs furtively. In fact a bellboy had no business at his door. "Wrong room," he said. "I don't want you."

"Package for you, sir."

"Not mine," said Jerry. He was thinking fast. The only exit from the room was out that door. And, granting that a man could get out of the hotel, he'd be no better off in the town. Outside, the locomotive bell began to toll. The train was getting ready to leave.

And beyond the door politeness gave way to gruffness. "Open up, Prince! I've got a John Doe warrant here for you an' a local man with me."

Jerry pocketed his billfold and the heavy manila envelope containing the bonds and three letters. "Who is talking?" he asked.

"Hertz, of the Globe Agency. That bus idea wasn't so hot after all. C'mon, open up before we bust the door in."

Steam blasted up through the rain outside as the train moved; and Jerry said amiably: "Why run up a bill for damages? Wait until I get some clothes on."

And he donned his hat, stepped noiselessly to the partly opened window, pushed it carefully up. He was on the second floor; the ground looked a long way down; but without hesitation Jerry removed the screen and slid out over the window sill.

As he went he heard Hertz, of the Globe Agency, wrathfully say: "Bust that door in! He's up to some trick! Hell, I'll bet he's trying the window! Watch here while I beat it outside and see."

Jerry lowered himself to full arm's length, kicked out hard from the stucco wall and hurtled down over the bushes planted below.

THAT DROP would have injured a man whose body was not in perfect shape, trained for just this sort of thing. Jerry's shoes struck hard on soft, wet turf; his legs jack-knifed like flexible shock absorbers and his palms slapped hard on the slippery grass, taking up the last of the shock.

He came up with a spring, turning to the moving train with rain spatting down the back of his neck. The long, open station platform was deserted. No one had seen his drop from the second-story window. A high hedge separated the little strip of lawn from the brick platform. Jerry measured it with his eye, sprinted several steps and went into the air as if catapulted, landing neatly on the platform bricks beyond.

In front of him the last Pullmans of the long train were slipping past with rapidly accelerating speed. All doors were closed; a fly could not have gotten into that train. But an observation car was coupled on the rear.

Running over to the second platform, Jerry sprinted hard, hurled himself at the rear step of the observation platform, swung up over the brass railing—and tumbled into the lap of a young woman seated by the railing.

Disaster hung by a thread as the chair toppled. Her arms went around Jerry. His arms went around her. Then he caught himself and staggered up.

"Sorry," he apologized. "I didn't know the railroad furnished such assistance to late passengers. Hurt you?"

She was ruffled, irritated. "You did not," she said, ignoring the smiles of the other passengers on the platform. "But if you intend to do this at the next stop, will you please give some warning, young man?"

She was all of twenty-two, perhaps younger, from what Jerry could see under the low-turned brim of her hat and the enveloping collar of her wool sports coat. Younger than himself by years; and yet she spoke with the cool disdain of extra years, or assured authority.

"I'll remember," Jerry promised with a smile. He turned, looked back along the lighted platform as faint shouts came through the storm.

Out from the hotel a man had dashed, running through the rain after the train, shaking his fist, shouting unintelligible words. Jerry leaned over the back rail and waved cordially as the train sped off into the night.

He was chuckling as he turned to the cold gaze of the young woman and the somewhat astonished regard of the other passengers.

"Next time," Jerry said to them, "he'll know better than to wait so long."

And wiping his damp hands on his handkerchief, Jerry entered the dry warmth of the observation car and went forward in search of the conductor.

WHICH WAS all well enough as far as it went. But that was not far. Jerry was aware as he walked forward through the train. Hertz, of the Globe Agency, was evidently not a man to be settled so easily.

Hertz would undoubtedly send wires ahead. Jerry had been over this line many times before. This was a through train. The next stop was Lamy, where passengers for Santa Fé took the bus. A sheriff or deputies could easily meet the train and search it.

Lamy, as Jerry recalled the place, consisted of a few houses, a station, a small hotel and a coaling tower. A man leaving the train there would find nothing but wild country about, miles from a highway, little better than a trap to a stranger.

He considered pulling the emergency cord and stopping the train before it reached Lamy—and dismissed the idea for a good reason. The country was wilder if anything between Albuquerque and Lamy.

"It looks," Jerry admitted to himself, "as if we're as bad off as we were."

The conductor proved to be dour, sour, suspicious. "Berths all taken," he said. "You shoulda asked at the ticket office, young man."

"Sorry. I was in somewhat of a hurry."

"This is an all-Pullman train," the conductor told him. "No coaches."

"I'll sit in a smoker or the club car then. Sell me a ticket and reservation to—er—La Junta. That's the junction point for Denver, isn't it?"

"Seems to me you don't know where you're going," the conductor grunted.

Jerry grinned at him. "I've a good idea where I'm trying not to go. La Junta it is."

"Can't sell you a reservation when I haven't one to give you," the conductor said testily.

Jerry waved it aside. "Don't then; just a ticket."

"You can't ride this train without a Pullman ticket."

Jerry put a hand on the conductor's shoulder. "I *am* riding this train," he said. "And I intend to continue riding it, to the next stop at least. I suggest you get used to the idea. You wouldn't put me off in the rain, would you? I might catch pneumonia and sue the railroad."

The conductor was scanning his car cards. "A young lady's getting off at Lamy," he said. "Her stateroom will be vacant from there on. But it'll cost you three full fares for that."

"Done," said Jerry. "Three full fares to La Junta it is. By the way, how quick could a man get from Santa Fé to Lamy if he were in a hurry?"

The conductor was handling with suspicion the fifty-dollar bill Jerry had landed him. His manner indicated that if it were metal he would probably have bitten it to test it. At the last question he peered over the tops of his glasses with a frown.

"Twenty minutes, I reckon, if he was in a hurry. It's about eighteen miles."

"Not very far."

"Eh?"

"Nothing," said Jerry. "Nothing that matters to you. And now that I'm a passenger in good standing, do you suppose I could get something to eat in a hurry?"

"Dining car closed just before we got to Albuquerque."

"You're killing me with kindness," Jerry sighed. "Good night, until the young lady gets out of my stateroom at

Lamy. If you see the train butcher, please tell him to look me up back on the observation platform,"

SHE WAS still sitting there, the brim of her felt hat pulled low, the collar of her brown coat turned up, hands in her pockets and her gaze fixed on the wet glinting rails and streak of roadbed unwinding back into the night. Damp gusts were swirling across the platform and she was alone now. She did not look up as Jerry sat down across from her.

The train butcher came out with his basket. Jerry bought three apples and a banana; and when the butcher went forward again Jerry ate one of the apples, bit into another, glanced over and caught her looking at him.

He smiled, leaned across. "Have an apple?"

She said coldly: "Do I look hungry?"

"I can't tell under that coat."

Instead of ignoring him, she studied his face. Jerry saw that her face was small, finely formed, sensitive.

"What," she asked, "were you running from?"

Jerry bit into the apple, masked with a grin the surprise her question produced. "What makes you think I was running from anything?"

"I was looking forward along the platform as the train pulled out. I saw you drop out of that second-story window. You were running from something."

"Hobgoblins and nightmares."

"I suppose that was a hobgoblin who ran out on the platform after you?"

"In a way," Jerry chuckled.

"I think it must have been a detective."

"You never know," said Jerry. "They turn up in the unlikeliest places, don't they? For instance, you might be a lady detective."

"I might," she agreed calmly.

"But I don't think you are," Jerry decided critically. "You're much too pretty for a lady detective. They're usually—*ummm*—more on the efficient side."

"You seem to know quite a bit about detectives."

"I've read stories," Jerry chuckled. "Can I interest you in a banana?"

"You cannot."

She retired into the enveloping collar of her coat, resumed her contemplation of the receding roadbed, dismissing him more completely than if she had used words.

Jerry finished the second apple, peeled the banana thoughtfully, scanning her from the corner of his eye.

She had an air of wealth, of self-assurance. His tuned senses had caught more than casual curiosity in her manner. What it was he couldn't guess. What he was sure of was that she was troubled. Her casualness had not been able to keep it off her face, out of her voice. She sat there now with her shoulders slumped in an attitude of dejection. Once when the dim light had struck her face just right faint circles had been visible under her eyes. In that moment she had looked exhausted—almost frightened.

"Lovely night, isn't it?" Jerry asked presently.

She stood up and went inside without looking at him. Jerry turned, watched her walk through the observation car. Not very tall, she held her shoulders well back, balancing perfectly to the lurches of the car floor without removing her hands from the coat pockets.

"Perfect," said Jerry to himself. "And—I wonder why she wanted to know if I was running from something? She's not the curious type."

He was still wondering when the engine whistled long and loud, and the pounding forward drive slackened and the train began to coast to a slow stop. Looking out, Jerry saw the switch lights of Lamy ahead.

He remained on the platform. Just before the train stopped, he swung down to the ground on the side opposite the station, crossed to the platform, walked slowly forward toward the station.

IT WAS not raining here in Lamy. Strolling passengers quickly thronged the platform. Mixing with them Jerry went to the station. The conductor was standing by one of the station windows talking to a stranger who wore a Stetson hat. The conductor nodded, pointed to the train and back at the observation platform.

The story was there plain to read. The stranger had that air of the constabulary; his manner had purpose as he left the conductor and walked back toward the observation platform.

The Los Angeles detective had done the obvious—got in touch with Santa Fé at once, and there was now no chance of Jerry getting out of Lamy on the train.

Or out of Lamy at all unless he walked down a lonely country road on foot. Undoubtedly the sheriff would look in the bus before it started.

Jerry walked around behind the station in search of an idea. The bus stood there, lighted, waiting. Two big covered trucks were loading express. And on beyond, several cars were parked. The lights of one flashed on as he looked; the motor started, the machine backed under an overhead light into the road.

Jerry vaulted a low wire fence and ran forward under the light. The machine was a large sedan, holding only the driver, a man. The front car window was down.

"I say," Jerry called as the car stopped for a moment before swinging around up the road. "Can you give me a lift?"

The man looked at him, shook his head, answered shortly: "No. Take the bus." And shifted into gear, started forward, and then stopped abruptly. He leaned over nearer the window.

"Where do you want to go?" he asked.

"Down the road. Santa Fé—or what have you. You see," Jerry said cheerfully, "I can't afford to take the bus."

"Get in. No, the back."

The driver pushed the door open. Jerry was inside, closing the door after him before he became aware of a suitcase on the floor and a third person sitting low in the other corner of the seat.

"Nice of you," he said, relaxing. "I was—er—dreading the walk."

"I'm sure you were," she said coolly. "But you needn't have lied about lacking the bus fare. I saw the bills from which you bought the fruit."

Jerry sat very still for a moment. She, then, was the girl whose stateroom he had taken to La Junta. "I didn't mention money. I said I couldn't afford to take the bus. It was true."

"Where do you want to go?"

"It doesn't matter," Jerry said cheerfully. "Although I would like a bed tonight. More or less of a habit."

"Still running?" she asked from the corner of the seat. She had not moved except to turn her head.

"More or less," Jerry admitted.

"From whom this time?"

"I judge he is the county sheriff. I didn't stop to make sure. I thought," Jerry chuckled, "that while he was searching the train I'd move along."

She said: "It must be serious."

"Rather."

"Murder—or anything like that?"

"Sorry to disappoint you."

"Do you live in Albuquerque?"

"Hardly."

"Where?"

JERRY SPOKE truthfully. "All over the country." He was enjoying her cool cross-examination, enjoying her while the car swept smoothly up a steep winding grade and the driver paid no attention to their conversation.

She said: "I need help." And added stiffly: "I'm willing to pay for it of course.

"Suppose we leave that out," Jerry suggested.

"Very well—for the present. Are you afraid of death? I mean—being killed?"

Jerry laughed again. "Certainly. But never worried about it."

She sat up, turned on the side lights, studied him gravely. And he saw again the faint shadows under her eyes, the look of strain and lurking fear. She made an inner decision, nodded.

"I think you'll do," she said. "You wear the right clothes fairly decently and carry yourself with rather an air."

Jerry laughed. "I'm glad I seem to suit. Were you looking for a tailor's dummy?"

Her reply left him speechless. "I am looking for a husband," she said calmly; and amplified it quickly: "Someone to pose as my husband for a short time, I mean."

Jerry put the Santa Fé sheriff out of his mind as he chuckled again. "Nothing I'd like better. But first, are you married? No, you couldn't be and carry through an idea like this. What's behind it?"

She had turned off the lights. From the dark corner of the seat her reply came soberly. "My life, I think."

"Not that bad?"

"And yours also," she said calmly. "Your life before mine, probably. You're going as my bodyguard. Only we two and the chauffeur will know. If there is trouble, you will draw it first."

"Cigarette?"

"No, thanks."

Jerry lighted a cigarette. The brief flare of the lighter showed her large dark eyes watching him.

"Where are we going?" he asked her.

"That needn't concern you."

"Mean to tell me you were heading alone into something which might cost you your life? And doing nothing about it?"

With sudden irritation she said: "Don't ask questions. I've told you all I'm going to. You can leave the car any moment you wish."

"I'm going through with it of course. What about my lack of luggage?"

"It could have been delayed."

"Is the chauffeur dependable?"

"He'll say nothing. The chances are he won't be able to help you. And I'm sorry I have no gun."

"Never use one if I can help it. Now that we understand each other, my name is Jerry Prince."

"I'm Sylvia Breamer," she said calmly.

"Charming name."

"You can dispense with that."

The end of Jerry's cigarette glowed in the darkness. "I think I'm going to enjoy this."

"I hope you live long enough to do so," she said with an utter lack of emotion.

CHAPTER TWO
MOUNTAIN VIEW

JERRY HAD no idea where they went after that. The car turned right off the dirt road onto black oiled pavement. There were grades, up and down. Rarely a house, only occasionally another automobile passing.

Then the car turned left on a narrow dirt road and bored into wild country. No houses here at all. Tall pines beside the road presently. Steep grades. Once, far ahead, the flashing form of a deer through the headlights. They forded a small shallow mountain stream tumbling over water-worn boulders.

Jerry said: "Charming country for a murder through here."

"You talk too much," said Sylvia Breamer.

The car began to climb again, in gear this time, up—up, until it seemed there was no end to the ascent. Suddenly the road leveled off, curved through tall, stately pines and came out in front of a low stone house.

Jerry stared. The headlights, sweeping to the house, seemed to thrust past it into empty space. An instant later the house cut off the illusion. They stopped.

The girl at his side said in a tense voice: "Here we are. Keep your eyes open. Say as little as you can. Don't be surprised. And—and be ready for anything. *Anything.*"

"Righto," Jerry said in a low voice. In spite of himself he was impressed. If ever a voice held warning dread, hers did in that moment.

The big front door of the house, planks studded with bolts, opened inward. Warm light streamed out to her side of the car, where the chauffeur was just opening the door. And to meet her bustled a short, round, rolypoly man with a broad smile of welcome. Others followed, but he reached her first.

"Welcome back, my dear Sylvia," he cried, catching her hands. "You look more charming than ever. Doesn't she, Annette? Come in and meet everyone. We're having a small houseparty this week."

She withdrew her hands, said: "Just a moment. I want you to meet my husband."

The rolypoly man froze there, smile and all. From the corner of an eye Jerry saw that fleetingly. His attention was fixed on the woman addressed as Annette. She was fluffy and blonde—probably peroxide—a cuddly, carefully corseted young woman.

She froze too; and as Jerry stepped off the running board and looked straight at her he saw as if by magic a different woman standing there. An older woman, by twenty years, with haggard lines at her eyes and a hollowed, shrewish face.

A swift smile wiped it away; and magic happened again, for youth and a measure of beauty moved to meet him.

"Sylvia, you're not married to this handsome young man? Introduce me."

"His name is Jerry Prince," Sylvia Breamer said coolly. "Jerry, this is Annette Craig. Aunt Annette."

The last two words held ghosts of sarcasm and dislike. The small hand Annette Craig put in Jerry's was wrinkled and aged on the back, and Jerry knew that in that brief earlier instant he had seen the real Annette Craig. She was a generation older, worlds harder than this soft little woman who smiled up at him.

"When did it happen?" Annette Craig begged reproachfully. "Why didn't you two let us know?"

"Secret," said Sylvia. "Jerry, this is Annette's brother, John. Dear Uncle John."

Jerry doubted that she meant the last. But the handshake of rolypoly John Craig was hearty, the fringe of gray hair around his pinkish bald pate seemed to bristle with welcome.

"Happy to have you with us, Mr. Prince. Come in, both of you. Carl will bring your bags in. Ahhh—my son, Dwight. Mr. Prince, Sylvia's husband, Dwight."

The young man who saluted Sylvia Breamer indifferently and gave Jerry a limp hand was tall, bony, slack-shouldered and long-faced. He murmured a word of greeting and went into the house with them.

SEVEN OR eight others were in a long, low-ceilinged living room. They were mostly young people, hilarious, cordial. Gay Navajo rugs had been moved back and they had been dancing. Jerry noticed one girl at once. Twenty-odd years earlier Annette Craig must have been as fresh and softly blonde—and selfish—as this girl. Her name he found out later was Rena Craig. She was a sister to the gangling, rather vacuous Dwight.

And Jerry knew before he was introduced to her that she did not like Sylvia Breamer.

The whole thing was puzzling. He had been warned against danger and then taken into the midst of a house party. She had spoken of death and they both had met warm welcome from close relatives.

Annette Craig showed them to a bedroom and Sylvia said: "We'll want adjoining rooms. We're used to them."

Annette Craig lifted thin eyebrows. "You don't act as if you're married, Sylvia."

"I'm sorry," Sylvia said, turning a small white-gold wedding band on her third finger. "Jerry's bags didn't come on the train either. We'll try not to make any more trouble."

The ring had not been there on the train. Jerry had looked then. Annette saw it and seemed satisfied as she went out, saying at the door: "We're so anxious to hear all about your travels, Sylvia. Join us as soon as you can."

The door closed behind her. Sylvia shrugged out of her coat, tossed it and her small felt hat on the bed. She half closed her eyes. Her face was tired.

"I've been wondering how right you are," Jerry said.

She put a finger to her lips, stepped quietly to the door, opened it quickly and looked out. The hall was empty. She closed the door and turned back, saying: "I expected you to feel that way."

"You're in danger here with your relatives?"

"They are not relatives. I've merely known them all my life."

"I see. What next?"

She shrugged, went to the mirror and arranged her hair. "We'll be here for a day or so. Stay alive if you can. That's all."

"Sounds slightly fantastic. These people seem friendly enough."

She looked at him from dark, brooding eyes. "I hope you're not as credulous as you sound. Shall we go to the living room? Hiding away in here won't help us."

"I think I'll look around a bit," Jerry decided. "Can you give me any pointers?"

"I've never been here before. They leased it for the summer, I believe."

Jerry had noticed one peculiar thing about the hall outside their door. It curved in a semi-circle. Sylvia Breamer went left to the living room. Jerry followed the semi-circle on around. At the end, out of sight of their rooms, a door let him out into a crisp, cool breeze on an open porch.

Jerry stepped to the railing and stopped there, staring. The automobile headlights had seemed to glance off into space. He looked into space now, into an abyss falling away into fathomless blackness. Far, far off in the lower distance, tiny twinkling lights marked other houses; fifteen, twenty miles away, Jerry judged. Perhaps more.

It gave him an eerie feeling to look down. The house had been built on the curving rim of a precipice. This side followed the curve. And the edge of the wide front porch fronted on incalculable space. In the faint starlight, far down, he could make out the dark tops of trees.

Midway, by the living room, the porch jutted out farther, hanging over into space at that point. Light streamed from open glass doors. Jerry walked toward the doors and radio music and voices and laughter. Stepping silently, as was his custom, he came within sound of a sharp, suppressed voice; and he stopped, flattening himself against the wall, and listened to Annette Craig saying—

"...yes, *married.* He's here with her. Leave at once! Take the next plane." She was silent a moment, and then in suppressed anger said: "The plane is safe! You get off at Albuquerque. I'll have the car meet you. Catch the next one and wire me. They'll telephone it out."

THE MUSIC lulled. Jerry heard the receiver slap on the hook; heard a deep, indrawn breath of emotion.

He stood there after she left the dark room. His doubts were gone. Sylvia Breamer had been right. That long distance call had been urgent, desperate, with an undertone of harshness.

Behind him a door opened. Someone stepped out of the hall he had just quitted. Jerry was moving toward the living room doors when a cheery voice hailed him.

"That you, Mr. Prince?"

Jerry stopped. John Craig came up and cheerfully reproved him.

"Your drink is waiting, my boy. This is the last place I expected to find you, with a pretty bride like Sylvia waiting in the living room," Craig cleared his throat. "I'm looking for my sister, Annette. Do you know where she is?"

"I haven't seen her out here," Jerry said truthfully as he let himself be guided into the living room.

Annette Craig was there with a glass in her hand, laughing animatedly. Looking at her, and at the pinkish, beaming face of John Craig beside him, Jerry found it hard to hold that sudden, sure feeling of danger which had gripped him out there on the porch.

The sharpest suspicion could not find fault with the remainder of the evening. The young guests made their own amusement. One servant appeared briefly now and then to refill glasses.

The one older couple among the guests sat beside a stone fireplace in which large chunks of wood crackled and blazed. They were a Mr. and Mrs. Kernan. The man was stocky, red, with short black hair and a bulging lower jaw. His greeting to Jerry had been brief, his hand moist, lax.

During the rest of the evening Kernan sat beside the fireplace and said almost nothing. But his eyes were bright and restless behind glistening nose-glasses. Now and then, as his left hand moved, a huge diamond set in a massive gold ring gave off cold glints of light.

Kernan and his wife were in their middle forties. She had been pretty once; but it had been a cheap prettiness and now she was merely hard. Jerry noticed her eyes went more often to Sylvia than anyone else in the room. The glances were speculative.

Presently he steered Sylvia off into a corner. "Don't look surprised," he said under his breath. "I think we're being watched. Just wanted to tell you your charming aunt put in a long-distance call. Someone's taking a plane at once to get here quickly. She seemed greatly disturbed over your showing up with a husband."

Sylvia smiled; but her voice held no laughter. "I knew they would be upset. I can guess whom she called. Did you hear anything else?"

"No. I eavesdropped from the porch. She left the room at once. John Craig came out a moment later looking for me. I think he knew what she was doing and halfway suspects I may have overheard her."

Still smiling up at him, Sylvia said: "Lock your door tonight." She turned from him to smile at Annette Craig who came to them.

"Sylvia, dear, I want to hear all about it," Annette said. "Where did you meet this charming Jerry?" She smiled at Jerry.

"In Singapore," Sylvia said. "It was love at first sight."

"Isn't it romantic? You might at least have cabled us."

"I wanted to surprise you."

"You did, my dear," Annette Craig said.

It had the ring of sincerity.

Sandwiches and coffee were served and the evening ended.

PAJAMAS AND a dressing gown had been found for Jerry. He sat on the edge of his bed and smoked, reviewing the events of the evening. Here on this isolated mountain top he could dismiss Hertz, of the Globe Agency, and the Santa Fé sheriff. Good enough so far. But that left plenty to think about.

Starting as a bit of adventure, this business was shading more to the sinister side. That extra sense of danger, so finely developed by the life he led, was warning now of danger close and certain. The quiet house seemed loaded with it.

The smiling hospitality of these respectable people made it all the more forceful. Long ago Jerry had learned there was nothing more dangerous than respectability gone wrong and desperate. You never could tell what might happen.

He turned off the light, opened the casement windows, went to bed. The windows were not screened, the door not locked. Jerry's nerves were taut. He had long ago found that he came awake almost instantly when his sleeping quarters were entered.

That faculty brought him out of the first drugged sleep. As his eyes opened, Jerry swept off the covers and poised alertly. The room was black, silent; but something had awakened him.

A slight draft blew across the bed. A door was open. Jerry came off the mattress in one swift flow of movement and crouched at the foot of the bed.

A tense whisper reached out to him.

"Jerry—Jerry Prince. Are you awake?"

It was Sylvia Breamer. She had entered through the connecting door between the rooms. Jerry relaxed.

"What is it?"

She moved close in soft-soled slippers.

"Someone is prowling outside! I thought he was coming in my window. Then he went on. It's—it's started already."

Jerry put out a hand, touched clinging silk on her arm.

"Does Craig have a watchman?" he asked.

"I'm sure not."

"Go back to bed. I'll look into it."

She was more troubled than frightened. "I'd feel better if you had a weapon," she whispered.

"Don't need one. You've probably been having a nightmare."

"I was wide awake." She left obediently.

Jerry slipped into his clothes silently. He had done this sort of thing before. He left by the window without a sound.

No moon tonight. Jerry's illuminated wrist watch showed fifteen minutes past two. The wind had died. The bright stars seemed very close in the thin, clear air. An owl hooted mournfully somewhere off in the trees. And far off in the lower country a faint, ghostly yapping put an eerie pulse into the waiting night. Coyotes, Jerry knew.

He had forgotten to ask which way the prowler had gone. On a chance he went toward the center of the house.

Grass had been planted along here, for which he was thankful. It made silent progress easier. But, by the same token, it muffled the movements of any prowler.

He passed the circling bit of drive and the wing of the house beyond. From one or two open windows he heard lusty snores. Peaceful enough. Dread, certainty of danger seemed to exist only in the minds of Sylvia Breamer and himself.

He rounded the end of the house and stopped at the edge of the abyss. A step put him on the curving porch at his right.

The boards did not creak as he stood there listening to the ghostly coyote-clamor drifting up from the lower country.

"Lonesome sounding beggars," Jerry thought.

And a woman screamed in terror. Just once.

CHAPTER THREE
CRISTOPHER CRAIG

JERRY BOLTED along the porch toward the living room doors. She had screamed inside the house. His first thought was of Sylvia Breamer. Had death found her while he searched?

The glass doors were standing ajar. The living room inside was dark, quiet, although he had seen bedroom windows lighting up as he raced along the porch.

Groping across the room to a floor lamp he stumbled over a body. Swearing softly, Jerry stooped, felt. Relief surged through him as his fingers touched cotton fabric and his searching hand found a work-hardened palm. This was not Sylvia Breamer.

Doors were opening. A hall light went on. The floor lamp was two steps away. Jerry yanked the chain.

On a gaudy Navajo rug lay the Mexican housemaid who had been in and out during the evening. Her hair was up in curlpapers, her feet in sleazy red carpet slippers. Under her flower-printed cotton dressing gown was a nightgown. No blood, no sign of violence; she simply lay there inertly.

Sylvia hurried into the room. Her eyes were wide with apprehension. "Jerry, are you all right?"

"Quite," said Jerry.

He was on his knees examining the woman. He searched for a pulse in her wrist, and as he did so her body jerked, quivered, and her other arm struck him in the face. She screamed and came alive fighting him.

That was how John Craig found them. The rest of the house had gathered quickly in various stages of undress.

Craig was in a bathrobe, holding a revolver. "What is happening here?" he demanded.

The maid was sitting up, sobbing wildly.

"Wonder what she was doing here in the living room?" Jerry said, looking down at her.

To John Craig, Sylvia explained: "I heard someone prowling outside my window and Jerry investigated. Then this woman screamed. Jerry—got into the living room ahead of me."

She hesitated at the last. Jerry read her mind. She was not sure just what had happened. He explained: "I was on the front porch when she screamed. I ran in here and stumbled over her. The room was dark."

The maid fingered her throat. "Hees hand!" she wailed. "On my throat! *Madre de Dios,* he keel me!"

Craig slipped the revolver in his bathrobe pocket. He was uneasy, uncertain, as he questioned: "Who got you by the throat, Trinidad?"

The maid hesitated, then pointed at Jerry.

"Heem," she said. But it was half a question and did not stand up when Jerry snapped: "Be sure what you're saying. I wasn't in the room when it happened."

"Somebody," the maid amended. She stood up, explaining nervously: "I go for drink. Wind she ees blowing down the hall. I theenk the door he ees open an' I come see.

An' in the dark—*Madre de Dios*—" She caught her throat graphically.

Jerry said: "Did you close the door?"

She shook her head. "No. *Señor.*"

"It was unlatched when I came in," Jerry said.

John Craig frowned in perplexity. "I was the last one in the room tonight. I bolted the other door and those doors were latched before I turned out the lights."

Jerry looked about the room. All who had been present earlier in the evening were there. No one was fully dressed. All were excited. Yet, somehow, he was certain one of them had been prowling about the house. But he spoke casually.

"Whoever it was is doubtless halfway down the mountain by now."

John Craig nodded. His fringe of gray hair resembled a benevolent monk's tonsure.

"I think you're right, Mr. Prince," he said. "It would probably be a waste of time to search now. I'm sorry this happened, but I think we're safe in retiring again. I'll see that the doors are locked."

They all began to talk at once. Several laughed as they drifted back to their rooms. Jerry went to his room, closed the door, and when he heard Sylvia Breamer enter her room he knocked softly on the connecting door. She opened it at once.

"Did you hear anyone in the hall?" Jerry asked her.

"Not a sound."

"I was at the other end of the porch when she screamed," Jerry said. "No one came out the front door. The driveway door was bolted. That leaves the other wing of the house for him to have escaped into."

She nodded, watching him gravely.

"The dining room, the kitchen, the maid's room, seem to be in that wing," Jerry said. "And a bedroom or two occupied by the young men. None of them mentioned anyone passing. And yet," said Jerry, "someone got out of that living room in a hurry. It wasn't any casual prowler."

"Why at this hour of the night?"

"I have no idea," said Jerry.

"Neither have I," Sylvia said. "But I think if we had not arrived tonight there would have been no prowling. I shall lock my door and windows and hope for the best."

But the rest of the night was peaceful.

AT BREAKFAST there was much discussion of the incident. Jerry let them talk, left the house afterwards. In the bright sunshine the place more than ever resembled an eagle's nest perched atop a cliff. The view was breath-taking.

Sheer for a full thousand feet the cliff dropped, and steep, forested slopes went down farther. Over the next ridge, miles away, one looked off into the purple haze of limitless distance.

Tall pines grew behind the house, and, half a mile away, the mountain rose higher. Back in the trees was a stone garage. Beyond it was a horse corral and saddle shed. Still farther were two adobe huts occupied by Mexicans.

The place seemed to be purely a luxury retreat with no indications of ranching, mining, or mountain farming.

Some of the young guests rode off on horses. The big car which had brought them the night before was gone when Jerry returned.

Sylvia was reading in a deck chair on the front porch. "Everything under control?" Jerry asked her.

"So far," she said gravely. They were on that wider part of the porch jutting over into space. Sylvia's eyes wandered past the railing.

"It's a long way to the bottom," she said.

Jerry smiled. "Thoughts like that will keep you awake. I'm anxious to see whom that long-distance call is bringing."

Sylvia said slowly: "If it's who I think it is, I shall not sleep well tonight." She shivered, made no effort to explain why.

Late in the afternoon the sedan returned. John Craig and his sister hurried out to meet it. From the living room Jerry saw the lone passenger coming in with them, and he understood why Sylvia had shivered.

Tall, six feet and a half at least, this new arrival towered. An enormous, lean, stoop-shouldered figure, he had to bend his head as he entered. The hand which swept off a broad-brimmed, flat-crowned, black hat was big, lean, corded. And the stranger's head was as bald as John Craig's, but the skull was higher, the circling fringe of gray hair shorter. Head, face, long bony neck were leaner, longer, sharper.

Dwight Craig resembled this man. But it would take long years and experience to make young Dwight's eyes so sunken and glittering, to make his eyebrows harsh and bushy, to draw in his cheeks and make his mouth such a hard determined gash. Jerry doubted whether young Dwight's mouth ever would be so hard and forceful and cruel as the mouth of this huge old man.

"My brother, Cristopher, Mr. Price," John Craig said. "This, Cristopher, is the young man Sylvia married."

"Indeed?" said Cristopher Craig. He nodded once. "Mr. Price," he said in acknowledgment.

And Cristopher Craig's voice was as unusual as the rest of him. His vocal cords had suffered at some time. He spoke in a dry, harsh wheeze.

"I am fortunate," he said, "in being able to get here and meet you."

From another man that comment would have been merely polite. Wheezing from the hard, cruel mouth of Cristopher Craig it had a sinister inflection.

"Thank you," Jerry replied. And by the sharp look which followed he knew that Cristopher Craig suspected his sincerity.

That was all for the moment. Later Jerry heard Annette Craig tell others her brother's arrival had been unexpected.

John Craig and his sister were closeted for some time in private with the new arrival. When Jerry next saw Annette Craig before dinner she was pale and her eyes were red, as if she had been weeping.

JOHN CRAIG looked uneasy. The towering Cristopher was grim, unfathomable. He took John Craig's place at the head of the table, as if it was his right. Silent and aloof in his high-backed chair, he apparently paid little attention to what went on around the table. But his presence cast a pall over the younger guests. Conversation languished, there was no laughter. They all seemed relieved when the meal was over and they could get off to themselves.

The man's very presence did that. Even Sylvia Breamer, so competent and cool, looked pale and had little appetite.

And Jerry became aware of growing irritation. He wanted to ask her angrily why she came here, why fear lay so heavy on her, why she didn't come out in the open. But he had no chance. After dinner Cristopher Craig bore her off. She went beside the tall, stooped figure like a small, unwilling prisoner.

They went, Jerry noted, to a study at the opposite end of the house. The house was only one story high but it spread over a large area. During the day Jerry had investigated it thoroughly. There were two enclosed patios, innumerable bedrooms, at least three servants living in the house.

The driveway was on the east, the abyss on the west, the study where Sylvia had gone on the southeast corner. Jerry had no inhibitions about strolling out in the dark and drifting to the study.

The windows were closed, curtains drawn. Sheltered by a tall spirea bush Jerry put his ear close. Sound escaped in some quantity from even the most carefully closed room.

Sylvia was speaking angrily.

"I won't sign anything. You should have known better than to ask me!"

Cristopher Craig's wheeze was not understandable. But her next angry words were defiant.

"I won't. I came here because I was forced to. I'm helpless. I want to know what he intends to do. How long must I stay here?"

Again Jerry could make nothing of Cristopher Craig's reply. He heard Sylvia say: "I don't believe a word of it!"

A door slammed. Silence followed. The light went out a moment later. Jerry straightened, stepped from behind the bush—and the back of his head seemed to explode and that was the last thing he knew.

SOMETIME AFTER that Jerry became aware that he was cold and his head hurt. Wind soughed lonesomely through pine branches overhead. He got to his feet painfully. The entire back of his head was tender and sore. But it was not cut or bleeding.

Thinking back, Jerry decided he had been sandbagged or dropped with a weapon wrapped to diffuse the shock, and carried some distance from the house.

A moment later he swore bitterly under his breath. His pockets had been emptied of everything but a package of chewing gum and a pocket-knife. Billfold, cigarette lighter, small change were gone. The thick manila envelope which held the bonds of Colonel Jefferson K. Carson was gone. Until now his status had been no more than that of a spectator.

Jerry's jaw was set and his manner had purpose as he followed the downslope of the ground. Within fifty yards he came to the road. From that spot the lighted windows of the house were visible not far off. By his watch he had been unconscious almost an hour.

Halfway to the house a girl's voice in the darkness ahead sent him off the road. Two of the younger guests strolled past. Vehemently the girl was saying—

"Just the same, I'm going to make an excuse and leave in the morning. So are Dot and Jim. Dwight and Rena can think anything they please. This place is giving us the jitters since the old man came. He—he looks like an old buzzard. I get goose-flesh when he's around."

"Feel the same way myself," the young man said. "Dwight's running out on us this evening is pretty thick too. I wonder where he went."

"I don't care—or how long he stays. I'm going to...." Her voice faded out down the road.

The radio was playing in the living room as Jerry came up to the house. No one else was outside that he could see.

A light burned inside the curtained windows of Sylvia's room. His own casement windows were latched inside.

Popping three sticks of gum into his mouth, Jerry took out the pocket-knife which had been left him. To groping fingers that knife was cheap and ordinary. It had, in fact, been made at some cost for especial purposes. In one end of the handle, for instance, was set the best glazier's wheel money could buy.

Working methodically and with sureness which could have come from long practice only, Jerry etched a circle in one of the panes of glass. He stuck the gum in the center of that circle, tapped the round piece of glass free and pulled it out with the gum. Reaching in, he unfastened the catch, opened the window and went over the sill into his room without a sound.

THE CONNECTING door was locked but, when he knocked softly, Sylvia opened it immediately. In her hand was a magazine she had been reading, on her face worry, strain, and also open relief at sight of him.

"I've been worried," she said. "Where have you been?"

Jerry knocked pine needles from his suit. "Out," he replied. "Just wanted to let you know I'm back. Where is everyone?"

"Scattered around. No one seems to be at ease this evening—since Cristopher came."

"Who was in the living room when you came out of the study after dinner?"

"Why—no one," Sylvia said. "I noticed that. Mrs. Kernan and Annette were talking on the porch."

"Where was John Craig?"

"I don't know. When I came into my room a few minutes ago he was talking with Cristopher. A little while ago he went out and called you, but you were evidently out of earshot."

Her look was searching. "You're hiding something."

Jerry smiled.

"What are you going to do?" Sylvia asked.

"I don't know," Jerry told her truthfully. "But I'll be busy. Run along and forget about me."

She closed the door without further questions. That was one of the things he liked about her. She acted without waste motion.

With the pillows, in the darkness, he made a realistic dummy under the bed covers, and then left by the window, latching it behind him.

Moments later, Jerry entered the dark study through a window he had found slightly ajar. This same window had been closed tightly an hour ago. Someone had been interested in it then, before himself. No prowler. No common thief. Such would never have carried him off into the trees, left him, probably, for dead.

The radio was audible in here. But a listening ear would have heard no sound in the dark study as Jerry moved across the room. A ten-second look that afternoon had mapped the room in his mind. He went to the small, flat-topped desk in the corner first.

Jerry's pursed lips formed a silent whistle as his exploring fingers, masked by his handkerchief, tested the desk front. The drawers were all closed, all locked; but the front of one drawer was scarred, broken where it had been forcibly pried out against the lock.

The interior of the drawer was empty.

That drawer had been intact earlier in the day. Jerry's hand was just coming out of the drawer when the door opened.

The radio had covered up quiet steps outside. The sudden intrusion trapped Jerry fairly. Few men could have moved as quickly and silently as he did. Only perfect nerves and bodily coordination could have closed the drawer and put him crouching behind the desk in the short seconds it took the door to open and the intruder to enter. A switch clicked, the room filled with light.

The next instant even Jerry started as a piercing shriek filled the room. Following shrieks receded as the woman fled toward the living room.

CHAPTER FOUR
TWIN MURDERS

THE VOICE sounded like Annette Craig's. Jerry didn't see whoever it was. She was out of the room, out of sight as he came to his feet and saw what she had seen as the light went on.

There on the floor, not two feet from where his feet had passed, lay the body of young Dwight Craig. His head had been beaten in by terrific blows. The sight was not pleasant. One look and Jerry knew there would be the devil to pay if he were discovered here in the room. After the law checked his record, his reasons for being here, a local jury might well convict him of murder and let it go at that.

But even in the sudden shadow of the electric chair, Jerry's quick moves were calm, logical. First the light, in case anyone outside could see in through the study window. Then out the window, closing it behind him as running steps came along the hall.

Jerry came out from behind the spirea bush on his toes, listening. Running steps on the driveway marked the young couple which had been strolling. Through the open window the scream had reached them.

The study light went on as Jerry ran out from the house. He was beyond reach of the window lights, crouching on the grass, as the two ran past, breathing hard. Crossing the driveway behind them, Jerry ran to the window of his room, opened it again and entered his room.

In the darkness he stripped off coat, necktie, unbuttoned his shirt, unlaced his shoes and rumpled his hair. And then snapped on the bed light and reached for the pillows.

His hand stopped in mid-air and he stared at the bed.

In the dark he had smoothed the covers carefully. Now they were disturbed, rumpled. Someone had been here in the room while he was in the study.

Tossing the pillows in place, Jerry punched a depression in one where his head would have lain. Rumpling the bottom sheet, he whirled as the door was flung violently open. The giant figure of Cristopher Craig loomed in the doorway.

Jerry masked a yawn.

"Hullo," he said. "Thought I heard a noise. Woke me up. Anything wrong, or was I dreaming?"

The high, bald head gleamed in the light. Craig's sunken eyes glittered as he snapped: "Woke you up? What do you mean?"

Jerry nodded at the bed. "Felt bad," he said. "Went to sleep. Didn't Sylvia mention it? I told her to convey my regrets."

Cristopher Craig stared at the bed. His hard mouth was set. He was excited, shaken, and yet so great was his control he appeared calm. Only the fingers of his big, corded hands were slowly working.

"Sylvia said you were asleep," he commented harshly. "We came to wake you up. My brother's son, Dwight, was murdered while you were—asleep."

IN SPITE of all his control, Cristopher Craig could not help snarling out the last word. His sunken eyes had a baleful light as he stepped inside. Behind him in the hall was one of the young house guests, pale and shaken now. And Jerry knew without any more being said that Cristopher Craig was aware he had not been asleep—had not indeed been in the bedroom.

This enormous, sinister old man was the one who had disturbed the covers. And Jerry was conscious of a cold chill as he thought of what might have happened if he had really been in bed, asleep. Those powerful hands were working too suggestively.

Craig had evidently rushed to the room with a witness who could swear that Jerry had not been in the house as Sylvia Breamer had stated.

Testimony like that would go far toward a conviction. Cristopher Craig must desire a conviction. Was it, Jerry wondered, because Craig wanted the guilt for that cruel and rather ghastly deed pinned on someone?

No hint of that was on Jerry's face, however, as he countered stupidly: "Murdered? Dwight murdered? You don't mean that?"

Cristopher Craig did not answer. Brushing past Jerry, he strode to the window. Turning, Jerry saw a breeze stirring the curtains. Cristopher Craig's big hand pulled them aside, exposed the hole in the glass.

Pointing with a long finger, Craig demanded: "What made this hole in the glass?"

Jerry walked to it, buttoning his shirt, frowning as he looked at his handwork.

"Wonder how that got there?" he said. "I don't think it was there this afternoon."

Craig answered harshly. "I'm sure it wasn't. It has been cut there this evening."

"Queer," said Jerry—and then he slapped his fist into his palm. "It's by the latch! I wonder if someone was trying to get into this room? Perhaps while I was asleep? Great heavens!" Jerry gasped. "Perhaps trying to get in at me! You don't suppose anyone was trying to kill me this evening, do you?" he said to the baleful gaze of those sunken eyes.

"Why?" Cristopher Craig countered, moving slowly away from the window, "should anyone wish to kill you?"

The excited young man in the doorway saw only two men talking casually to each other. Yet electric currents of tension were playing in the room. Jerry had the feeling that all enmity between Craig and himself was out in the open; that the sinister old man was aware Jerry knew he had been in the room. Whatever the enmity between them, it must come to an end quickly. And there would be, Jerry knew as he looked up at Craig—he had to look up, so tall was the old man—no quarter given from now on.

Jerry turned to the door, speaking briskly. "I don't know why anyone should want to kill me. Perhaps for the same reason your nephew has been murdered—if there is a reason. Shall we look into that? Where is the body?"

"In the l-library," the young man stuttered. He was barely twenty, round-faced, fair-haired, tanned; pale and shaken now by this sudden blast of tragedy.

IN THE low-ceilinged living room the household was gathered. Several of the women were crying, Sylvia was standing by Annette Craig with a vial of smelling salts. Mrs. Kernan, her face hard and controlled, was trying to comfort the plump, pretty Rena Craig.

When Sylvia's eyes fell on Jerry she started. Color rushed into her face.

Several of the men were in the hall which led to the study. But Jerry halted and turned, finding Cristopher Craig's eyes on him, as if the old man watched to see if he went to the body without guidance.

"Where is he?" Jerry inquired.

"This way," Cristopher Craig said, moving past.

Jerry lingered a moment to tell Sylvia: "Someone evidently tried to get into my room while I was asleep. You'd better stay in here with everyone."

She nodded. He didn't know whether she got the full import of his warning or not. He hoped so as he followed Cristopher Craig. If she had been in danger at all since entering the house, she was doubly so now.

The men were grouped about the doorway helplessly; even Kernan, who should have taken charge. John Craig's rolypoly cheerfulness had given away to flabby, drawn grief. His manner was dazed as Cristopher Craig came up, demanding: "Did you get in touch with the sheriff?"

Kernan replied: "The line is dead. I couldn't get any kind of an answer." His face and bulging jaw were redder than usual from the emotion he was laboring under.

A low oath of fury came from Cristopher Craig. "Something would have to happen at a time like this!"

Kernan spoke thickly. "I don't think it was an accident. Look at that." His hand shot out, indicating the scarred, chipped front of the desk drawer which had been forced. "John tells me that was done this evening. You've been robbed. Dwight, poor boy, evidently walked in on the thief. The telephone line has been cut so the fellow can get away before an alarm is sent out."

Cristopher Craig yanked the drawer open. Another oath came from him. "John, did you take anything out of this drawer this evening?"

"No," John Craig replied huskily.

"I'll drive down in one of the cars and report it," Kernan offered. "There may still be time to catch the fellow."

"No," said Cristopher Craig gruffly. "We'll all stay here. Young man, you get Carl, the chauffeur, and tell him to drive down the mountain and get word to the sheriff." A long finger stabbed at one of the young men in the doorway.

"Where does the sheriff live?" Jerry asked.

Cristopher Craig scowled at him. "I'm sure I don't know. What does it matter?"

"It will have something to do with the length of time it takes him to get here," said Jerry; and that was as close as he came to voicing his real reason.

John Craig was drawing life and spirit from his older brother. "The sheriff will come from Las Vegas," he stated. "That is the county seat."

And as the young man hurried off to tell the chauffeur, Jerry breathed a huge sigh of relief. The Las Vegas sheriff might have his description, but he would not be as dangerous as the man from Santa Fé. That problem could be met when the sheriff appeared.

At least, Jerry thought, Colonel Jefferson's bonds were out of reach. That brought back the question of where they were. Had one of those bright young men turned thief, lost his head, chosen violence? Youth was rushing in these days where older, wiser heads would never dare enter.

"How about the chauffeur?" Jerry questioned. "Are you certain he had nothing to do with this?"

"Certainly not!" Cristopher Craig snorted. "He has been with John nine years."

"The Mexicans who work on the place here?"

John Craig said: "They were all vouched for by the owner. They've lived in this section all their lives. Their characters are excellent."

Jerry looked at Cristopher Craig speculatively. Evil he looked, evil he might be, but he had hardly done this. He could have entered the room openly, taken anything.

But Craig had entered Jerry's room furtively, found it empty and now suspected Jerry of this murder. Why didn't he, Jerry wondered, voice his suspicion? Was it because Craig was afraid to admit he had been in the room?

The big diamond on Kernan's stubby hand flashed as he fingered his bulging jaw uncertainly.

"I'd suggest we search the house and look around outside the windows," Kernan said.

"Why outside the windows?" Cristopher Craig rasped.

"I'm surmising the—the intruder entered that way. He could hardly have come in through the house without being seen."

That drew a grunt from Cristopher Craig. He went to the windows, lifted the curtains, found the unlatched window. "John, these windows were latched, weren't they?" he inquired.

"I—I think so," John Craig assented uncertainly.

"I want to know. Ask the maid who cleaned this room."

John Craig slipped out, returned quickly. "The maid says she is certain all these windows were latched this afternoon," he declared.

"*Ummmm,*" said Cristopher Craig. No more.

Jerry was certain the old man was thinking the same thing he was. Unbroken, that window could have been unlatched from the inside only.

Then John Craig offered: "He could have come in by the patio door here. And the patio wall is only a little over seven feet high."

John Craig opened a door Jerry had not; investigated. One of the small flower-filled patios lay beyond, dark and deserted now.

Jerry pointed out: "A ladder would be necessary to get over that wall. It would leave marks in the ground."

Cristopher Craig said harshly: "Is there a flashlight in this house? We'll settle this."

RELIEF SEEMED general at an opportunity to do something. While a flashlight was being procured Sylvia took Jerry aside in the living room. He had not seen her more serious.

"What do you know about this?" she asked directly.

"Nothing."

"Where were you while—when Dwight was killed? What were you doing?"

Tenderly, Jerry touched the back of his head. "Busy," he said. "I'd like to know what everyone in the house was doing at that time. The men particularly."

For the second time she accused: "You're hiding something."

Jerry gave her a crooked smile. She was uncertain about him also. Like Cristopher Craig, she was wondering if his unexplained absence outside had any connection with the boy's death.

"You're not sure I didn't kill him," he said bluntly.

Equally as bluntly she answered. "After all. I don't know anything about you. And I certainly don't know what you have been doing this evening."

Together they could see this through; at odds, misunderstanding, it was hard to tell what might result. So Jerry told her what he had been doing.

"Someone in this house has those bonds I was carrying," he finished. "But please don't mention it."

"You stole them?"

"That," said Jerry, "needn't worry you. We took each other on faith, in a way, didn't we?"

Sylvia nodded, troubled but determined. "We did," she admitted. "What do you want me to do?"

"Ask as many questions as you can. Find out where everyone was within the last hour. I'm going outside. The sheriff will be here shortly. I haven't much time to find out who killed young Craig. But I've got to do it."

"And if you don't?"

Jerry's smile was rueful. "Give a dog a bad name—and hang him." He left her there as he followed Cristopher Craig and the others outside.

Two flashlights had been obtained. Cristopher Craig had one. Kernan the other. They made short work of searching outside the study windows and the patio wall.

Indistinct footmarks were found outside the window, none beneath the patio wall.

Kernan, at the wall, summoned them with a cry. "These look like the fresh marks of a ladder!"

Kernan was right. Someone had used a ladder here. The marks were plain.

They were looking at that when running steps came from the garage. The young man who had been sent to find the chauffeur dashed up to them. He was almost incoherent.

"Carl's dead!" he gasped, breathing heavily.

CHAPTER FIVE
ONE MAN MISSING

CRISTOPHER CRAIG caught the young man's arm as the latter explained. "I couldn't find him at first so I went over to the Mexicans' houses. He wasn't there. The men came back with me. We turned the lights on and looked around. The cars were all there. Then one of the Mexicans found him outside the garage. He's been—brained."

For a brace of seconds stricken silence greeted that. Then the younger men made a concerted rush toward the garage. The lights inside streamed out through the open doors. And at one corner of the garage two dark-skinned Mexicans were standing by a body on the ground.

In the flashlight beams Jerry saw a step-ladder lying on the ground nearby.

"There's your ladder," he said to Cristopher Craig. "Whoever used it brought it back and evidently met the chauffeur, who recognized him. So he killed the chauffeur."

Carl was quite dead, from several terrific blows on the head.

Out here in the night the spectacle was even more gruesome than the other in the lighted study. And in a momentary pause which followed, Jerry heard once more the far, faint howling of coyotes, which now sounded more blood-curdling than ever. It had its effect on the younger men and the two Mexicans, short, stocky, wearing overalls, who stood close together uneasily.

Cristopher Craig addressed them harshly. "Do you men know anything about this?"

The nearest one shrugged, spread his hands, thumbs up, answered in broken English: "No, *señor*. We have go to bed early."

Behind their rather forbidding, unshaven faces they were simple men, frightened now. Jerry dismissed them as suspects. Petty thievery they might be guilty of, but not cold murder.

Cristopher Craig addressed the young man he had sent to the chauffeur.

"Drive down yourself, young man, and get word to the sheriff. Watch your driving, too. You won't help matters by getting excited and running off the road."

And as he left, Cristopher Craig said curtly: "A club of some kind was used. I see some oil lanterns back there in the garage. Each of you get a lantern and help search for the weapon. It should be around here somewhere."

"Unless the man carried it off," Jerry said.

Cristopher Craig's facial expression was indistinct, but his voice was baleful. "I don't think the man could have carried it very far, Prince. We'll look for it."

So lights began to move about through the night. Carrying an oil lantern, Jerry participated, but he had small hope of finding anything.

Only a fool would have tossed a club down carelessly. The guilty man was not a fool. He would have had to walk only to the edge of the abyss and hurled it out into space.

Jerry went back to the study windows and along the patio wall. Then he walked on beyond the house, set his lantern down by the precipice and lighted a cigarette. He wanted to think here in the quiet alone.

BUT AS he flicked the match away and stared out into space, a swift movement behind drew his attention. Jerry never finished the turn. Two hands clamped on his neck from behind. A violent shove carried him to the edge of the abyss.

Thought of the awful drop into space drove Jerry lunging back from the edge. One foot remained against a post of the crude two-foot fence skirting the edge.

Never had he thought fingers could have such vise-like strength. Deep into the bulging cords of his neck they sank stopping breath and voice. The man behind him was invisible.

Another shove pushed his legs against the low fence. Inches more and he would be overbalanced and helpless. His shoulder was against the man's chest. Only Cristopher Craig could be so tall. Only Cristopher Craig's huge bony hands could have such crushing power.

Breath was whistling between the man's lips. Jerry's eyes began to bulge from the strain. In seconds now his strength would begin to go. His lungs seemed on fire, about to burst. He clawed futilely at the hands about his throat. Struck back wildly over his head, glancing blows which did no harm. His fingernails raked down over a smooth bald head—and then the night began to whirl.

He was forced hard against the fence, over—over—until he unbalanced. And that was the end, Jerry knew. He dropped, managed to grasp the top rail of the fence as his body went out into space. His hands were torn away from the wood; his fingers clawed futilely over the earthy edge and he dropped in a small shower of dirt.

Life held no agony like that first flashing second of fall. Jerry had read that one's mind cast back over a lifetime. He thought only of the dizzying chasm below.

Then in a cruel, scraping rush he struck the cliff, bounced off, struck again lower down and slid, dislodging rocks and dirt which cascaded in a small avalanche down ahead of him.

The cliff looked almost straight up and down. Actually it sloped outward slightly in a series of small ledges and slants. Stunted trees and bushes clung to the inaccessible sides. Jerry crashed into one bushy tree and tore it loose, struck another a few feet below.

Pine needles slipped through his clawing hands. He stopped. The small avalanche of rocks and dirt cascaded on down, gathering in size and sound. With it went his oil lantern which had arched briefly through the air and gone out when it struck.

The falling sounds died away far below. Silence held above as Jerry lay, half stunned. No one else had been near the spot, doors and windows of the house were closed. He moved, found himself on a small sloping ledge. The little trees seemed rooted firmly enough. He crawled to his knees and took stock.

Bruises, lacerations, and a painful throat seemed to be the list. No broken bones, no muscles strained beyond use. Jerry smiled coldly. From above it must have sounded as if his body had rocketed clear to the bottom. No man could survive that.

He was, then, supposedly dead. Shouts might bring help. But who knew what "accident" might happen while he was being rescued? A rock dropped right, a rope released, might kill him after all.

He could make out the dark cliff from perhaps a hundred feet above. Most of that distance he had slid down the steeply sloping cliff face. Had he been shoved out into space nothing could have saved him. Painfully Jerry began to inch upward.

A dozen times in the next two hours he almost gave up and called for help. His name had been shouted. Men had walked near the rim above, voices had spoken on the overhanging porch of the house. Like a fly Jerry had crawled a diagonal course up the cliff face, seeking one spot he vaguely recalled as not plunging straight down from the rim. Finally, with heart hammering, he made it and staggered over under the trees and dropped to the ground.

All during that tortuous climb he had waited for another body to plunge down. Sylvia's body. But she had evidently heeded his vague warning and remained in the living room with the others.

Racing automobile engines drew near. Jerry was on his feet watching when two cars rushed up the driveway and stopped before the house. Three men left the second car and entered the house. That would be the Las Vegas sheriff and two deputies.

It occurred to Jerry that he could walk off and vanish. They would think him dead. That would give Hertz, of the Globe Agency, something to think about when he got the report. But it wouldn't account for the bonds and letters of Colonel Carson. It would leave Sylvia Breamer in the lurch when she needed help. He started toward the house—and the sheriff who probably wanted Jerry Prince.

THE STUDY window was ajar. Jerry saw them in there, heard them. The officers were typical Westerners, holding broad-brimmed Stetsons styled differently from the flat-crowned black hat which Cristopher Craig now wore.

Listening to Cristopher Craig's harsh voice, Jerry noted again and again the glitter of the big diamond as Kernan absently touched lapel and breast of his coat.

With deep emotion Craig said: "It must be a madman. A third man has since disappeared."

The tallest officer answered thoughtfully. "I'll have a look at your chauffeur, an' then ask you all some questions."

By the time the men were leaving the house, Jerry was around the corner, at a bedroom window he had ignored until now. He had one stick of chewing gum left. With that and his pocket-knife he opened the window and entered.

He lighted the room for a second, located every object, and then in darkness went to work. Only the Prince of Thieves could have searched that room as thoroughly, quickly and skillfully as Jerry did in the next ten minutes. Suitcases and bags were locked. Three keys serving as blades of that extraordinary little pocket-knife made short work of the luggage locks.

Beneath silk lingerie Jerry found papers. The manila envelope was not among them, but he carried them to the bed light and in thirty seconds investigated their contents. In darkness once more, smiling to himself, he replaced the papers, relocked the bags, left the room. And behind him the little knife lay among the papers.

They were all gathered in the living room when Jerry came in. Annette Craig was the first one to see him. Her mouth opened silently. Her eyes grew wide, terrified. She lifted a hand, pointed soundlessly.

The sheriff looked inquiringly.

"Jerry!" Sylvia cried with relief.

But Jerry was looking at Cristopher Craig. The huge, stooped figure had turned as the sheriff did. Under the black hat brim sunken eyes stared with fury and something akin to horror.

"Who is this man?" the sheriff demanded. He looked startled. Jerry understood. Lacerated, torn, dirty, he was a disreputable object.

"I'm Prince, the missing man," Jerry said to the sheriff.

Cristopher Craig's question was thick and labored, as if he found it difficult to articulate. "Where have you been?" he asked.

And the sheriff, a lean, tanned, open-faced man, said: "My gosh, mister, you look like a grizzly has clawed you!"

"I fell down the cliff," Jerry said. "It's taken me a long time to climb back up."

"Fell down the cliff, Jerry?" Sylvia faltered. "That—that would have killed you."

Jerry smiled at her, gestured wordlessly at his condition.

Cristopher Craig put in challengingly. "The last time I saw you, you were carrying a lantern. There is a fence along the cliff. You hadn't been drinking, had you?"

"I was thrown off," Jerry said. "Someone tried to murder me, too."

Cristopher Craig smiled. It was rather a ghastly smile. "I was right," he said to the sheriff. "A madman must be out there. Did you see what he looked like, Mr. Prince?"

"I didn't see his face."

Despite Cristopher Craig's self-control it was possible to see him relaxing with relief. "Too bad," he said sympathetically. "Tell us about it."

"He caught me around the throat from behind and shoved me over. I didn't have a chance to see him," Jerry said calmly. "But I did reach over my head and put a long scratch on his bald scalp. Queer you're wearing a hat in the house this evening, Mr. Craig."

CRISTOPHER CRAIG'S arm failed to block Jerry's hand as it snatched off the hat. There on the high-domed shiny skull three angry red furrows stood out plainly. Cristopher Craig flew into a rage. "What are you insinuating, damn you?"

"I think," Jerry said, "a microscope could analyze the scrapings under my fingernails and prove I made those marks."

Sylvia Breamer stepped to Jerry, flushed and excited.

"I'll help them," she said. "We came here knowing our lives were in danger."

Annette Craig's shrill laughter greeted that. "How absurd, Sylvia! You don't know what you're saying."

"Oh, yes I do!" Sylvia said bitterly. "We'll have it out in the open now. Since I was fourteen, John Craig has been the trustee of the money dad left me. I even had to live with you people. It wasn't long before I knew you were living off my money like—like vultures. Uncle John didn't have to make an accounting until I was twenty-five. How he fooled my poor father! Don't think I haven't known murder has been on your minds lately. So convenient if anything should happen to me. The money goes to him in that case. I've been traveling for two years just to keep away from you. And when Uncle John cut my money off and ordered me here to discuss business matters, I knew he must be getting desperate. This place in the mountains is suitable for any accident that might happen to me."

The face of rolypoly John Craig looked like dirty dough as he listened to Sylvia's torrent of words.

"My dear girl!" he protested.

"Don't call me that!" Sylvia stormed at him. "Your sanctimonious manner never fooled me! Poor dad didn't know what he was doing when he made you trustee with the provision that you would inherit if I died. When I came here with a husband, you and Annette had the shock of your lives."

"I won't listen to any more of this, Sylvia!" Annette Craig screamed. She was old, haggard now.

Sylvia said coldly: "I don't blame you. It's a sorry story. Fortunately dad made provision that, after I was twenty-one, no investments could be made with the estate without my written consent. You're trying to put the money in something now. Tonight Cristopher tried to make me sign papers. I refused and right away he tried to kill Jerry. I—I hope he gets what he deserves."

Cristopher Craig's face was bloodless but he still had self-control. "I suppose you're going to accuse me of killing my nephew and my brother's chauffeur?" he sneered.

"No," said Jerry. "I know who killed them."

Even the sheriff grew a trifle sarcastic at that. "You seem to know most everything that's happened," he said.

"Probably," Jerry agreed. "Early this evening I was knocked unconscious and carried off into the trees. I came out of it in less than an hour and told no one but Sylvia. I was robbed then of an envelope containing negotiable bonds. No fool would throw them away. That man entered the study just after that, broke into the desk, and killed Dwight Craig when he was discovered in there. He still has those bonds."

Hoarsely Cristopher Craig said: "You interest me, young man! Who broke into that desk?"

JERRY MOVED past the sheriff, speaking casually. "A pickpocket can always spot valuables in a crowd by yelling, 'thief,' and watching hands," he said. "It's human nature to check valuables on one's person. Kernan, you've been touching the front of your coat a lot this evening. What's in that inside pocket?"

From the other side of the table the hard-featured Mrs. Kernan shrilled: "Don't let him accuse you of anything, Harry!"

Mrs. Kernan had gotten around the table and was clawing at Jerry. He shook her off, knocked one of the young men aside, made a running dive and tackled Kernan's legs as the latter jerked open the glass doors.

Kernan dashed against one of the doors, shattering panes of glass; and from his outstretched hand an object slid across the porch floor and stopped just short of the edge.

"Get that envelope!" Jerry yelled to the sheriff who had followed them.

The sheriff picked up a familiar brown envelope, held it to the light and called to one of his deputies: "Hold that man, Kernan! This is addressed to Mr. Prince in New York. I guess he was telling the truth."

And Jerry thanked the moment when he had addressed the envelope to himself in case he had to drop it quickly in the mail. He looked back into the confusion which lad gripped everyone in the living room. Kernan's wife had disappeared.

"Come with me!" Jerry snapped to the sheriff.

He led the man at a dead run to Kernan's room. The door was locked. Through the keyhole Jerry saw a light inside. He stepped back, drove a shoulder against the door and burst in. Kernan's wife hastily closed a leather bag and faced them defiantly.

"Better look in it," Jerry suggested to the sheriff. "She's trying to hide something in there. I'd be surprised if it wasn't what came out of the desk drawer."

The sheriff found the papers, studied them with a puzzled air. "Something about an investment trust and gold mining shares," he said. "I reckon we can make some sense outta these later on, maybe."

Mrs. Kernan had backed against the edge of the bed, breathing heavily.

"I suppose you will!" she gulped. "But you'll get the Craig brothers, too. They got Harry into their crooked schemes, and when they were all involved too deeply to get out they promised to get the Breamer girl in with her money and clear everything up. But she wouldn't fall for it. Cristopher Craig had the proof of Harry's interest in that drawer. I don't blame Harry for trying to get it."

"Or my bonds," said Jerry.

"We could have used that money better than you," she said bitterly.

"And that," said Jerry to the sheriff, "is your case. If you don't mind, my—er—wife and I will leave with you tonight. The place seems to be a bit unhealthy for us."

"Don't blame you," the sheriff smiled. He scratched his tanned chin. "Funny thing about your name. I had a call the other day to look for a fellow by the name of Prince who was heading east. I'd almost think it was you if you weren't married. But this fellow was single and alone, and a well-known crook."

Jerry smiled. "That will give Sylvia one laugh for the evening anyway. Do I look like a—er—well-known crook?"

The sheriff grinned.

"I wouldn't know," he confessed. "You look more like a hospital case right now. But a well-known crook wouldn't be here at Mountain View married an' mixed up in this business, I reckon. I'll be glad to see that you get to Las Vegas after we get through around here tonight."

Jerry was chuckling as he turned to the door.

"I never knew before how much help a sheriff could be," he said.

www.ingramcontent.com/pod-product-compliance
Lightning Source LLC
Chambersburg PA
CBHW031333020726
47499CB00005B/1248